HEATHER ON FIRE

HEATHER ON FIRE

By
G. AND J. CUTHBERTSON
AUTHORS OF "BUNDLE AND GO"

THE MORAY PRESS
EDINBURGH & LONDON

FIRST PUBLISHED 1935

THE MORAY PRESS
126 PRINCES STREET, EDINBURGH
182 HIGH HOLBORN, LONDON, W.C.1

PUBLISHED BY GRANT & MURRAY LIMITED
126 PRINCES STREET, EDINBURGH

PRINTED IN SCOTLAND
BY THE RIVERSIDE PRESS LIMITED, EDINBURGH

BOUND BY
WILLIAM HUNTER & SONS, EDINBURGH

CONTENTS

CHAPTER I

The Coming of the Stranger

TO-DAY I have sat for hours doing nothing, only looking out over the dancing ripples of the bay, watching the swift cloud-shadows leap from island to island, or ride the waves between, treading out their sparkle.

This green strip of coast at Ardmair holds not only the sea in its arms but a bit of myself as well, and I am wondering how I ever brought myself to leave it, and, having left it, could bear to stay away so long as I did.

But I was headstrong and bitter, a young fool as I see myself now, and my going left pain behind me, and hurried me into grief and trouble, adventures in battle and siege. These I have resolved to write down. Whether the tale is worth telling you shall judge when you have heard it.

It was ten years ago to-day, in the last year of the last Stuart king, 1688, that I said good-bye to my boyhood, just such a day as this, the finest that September could give, with a fresh breeze blowing through the warmth of a summer sun and the smells of the earth almost as they were when the year was young.

I was fishing from the rocks lazily, dreaming a boy's dreams, with an eye at times for the big house on the slope of the hill to see if my father, Ardmair himself, was home from the back-end cattle mart at Muir of Ord.

A sturdy building this home of mine, plain and square, its walls many feet thick, built to withstand

9

the stress of wind and storm, as well as clan raid and
surprise attack.   It had to be so, since we lie south of
Assynt and there is no love lost between the McLeods
of Assynt and the Mackenzies. We Mackenzies have
always been King's men, and it was an Assynt McLeod
that betrayed the great Montrose to the Whigs.   Oh, I
know they say it was not so; but that does not matter,
for we know it to be so.   Did not the Marquis sit at his
board? But to my tale.

The shadow cast by the rowans before the door had
barely passed the lintel stone when I saw a man, riding
a horse with two white forelegs and a splash of white on
the rump—a kenspeckle beast, whose dam never browsed
on heather-tops—come over the hill from Loch Broom.
He posted heavily to the trot of the horse, with a military
seat, legs stiff and heels down, and drew rein, scanning
the crofts that fringe the bay, his glance travelling inland,
to rest lingeringly on the house of Ardmair.

I laid down my line, wondering what might be his
business.   If friendly, it was my duty to offer him
hospitality; if unfriendly, to see that he wasted no time
in going on his way. I clambered slowly over the rocks,
taking stock of him as I went. Whether Highland or
Lowland I could not tell from his dress. He wore a
dark, skirted riding-coat, jack-boots and three-cornered
hat, and there was just the suggestion of the gallant in
the lace at wrist and throat.

It happened that he paused opposite the door of the
first cottage in our croftship, where had been set down
a cogie of water new carried from the spring, and his
beast eagerly plunged muzzle, beginning to drink. There
was an angry shout from a woman, and the horse reared
as she struck at it. She was a big woman, " big Johan "
we called her, sturdy as a heifer and shapeless as a chaff

pallet, with a hare lip, a bitter look in her eyes, and the sharpest tongue between Gairloch and Coigach.

What she said I did not catch, but I heard him laugh carelessly. He had not sighted me, though I stood at the tail of his mount.

" You'll be travelling far? " she asked, as she sullenly allowed the bucket to be emptied, the while he searched his pocket for a coin.

" Beyond Assynt, little darling," he replied, tossing a coin on the ground.

" A dirty McLeod," she said, turning her back.

" Wrong, my jewel! Not a McLeod," came back the suave, sneering words.

" Worse than a McLeod you could not be, but better you are not," she flung at him fiercely over her shoulder. Then catching sight of me, " You turn your back on your betters," she added.

" So do you, my beautiful one."

He turned his head as he spoke, and shifting his seat stared down at me.

He was as dark as I am fair, and he had the heaviest eyebrows a man may see in a lifetime. They met over his nose like twin arches of a massive bridge, and underneath them was a pair of keen brown eyes that surveyed me with more curiosity than good manners, I thought.

" Will you be staying with us, or travelling, sir? " I asked courteously.

" Travelling, thank you. But tell me first, who lives in the big house? " He pointed with his whip.

" My father—Donald Mackenzie, tacksman of Ardmair."

" Hm! So you are a Mackenzie, are you? But of course you are all Mackenzies here. You took the land from the Macdonalds."

" Their fault to let it go," I returned shortly. " Are you wanting to see my father? He is from home, but we expect him hourly."

" Then I was misinformed," he said, of a sudden very alert. " No, I do not think I want to meet him just now, though he has often expressed a wish to meet me. But some other time, in my own country—a pleasure, a great pleasure."

He waved his hand airily.

" As a matter of fact I am going there now after a considerable absence. And I am on business not my own, but business that demands my presence, and discretion urges me to go. It was a whim that brought me north this way from Inverness. Curiosity, if you like to call it so. But discretion now vanquishes curiosity and so I will bid you good day, young Ardmair, though I would fain have stayed to talk with your father."

He saluted me mockingly.

" And good day to you, little one," he laughed, saluting ironically big Johan, who stood scowling in the doorway.

As he trotted off she hurled his coin after him, accompanying it with a malediction, " *Bas gun sagart ort !* " (Death without a priest to you.)

But he merely waved his hand jauntily above his head without troubling to look round.

I had a feeling that I ought to have detained him, but what use a *sgian* against a horseman armed with sword and pistols? And there were none but women and bairns about the doors. I went back to my fishing, speculating about him and his business.

I sat in a hollow between two big rocks, stirring only to draw in my line and bait it afresh. The sea was a shimmer of blue, so still that it mirrored the flying gull.

A pair of scarts, busy about the point at Rhu Cadail, where tideway rivers ran among the ripples, dived and dived again. A tern dropped like a stone within a yard of the shore.

A fine bit this of the north-west, for ours is a bay where the sea is wedded to the land, and, on the half-hoop of the ring that weds them, the crofts are the jewels that lie in a setting of gold when the oats stand ripe in the sun. Full between the encircling arms is our little Isle Martin, with its crown of heather about a lochan, and its fringe of a township. Far out in the Minch the Summer Islands, as beautiful as their name, might be the land where summer days are born.

One horn of the bay is terraced, sprouting bracken and ling. The other is sheer, the frowning face of Ben More Coigach, gashed and seared by tempests, stripped of herbage to the bare rock, seldom two days alike, rarely without a cloud on his brow; again, scowling blackly behind blowing veils of mist; to-day, a cliff of velvet—above, a tranquil sky.

It would be perhaps two hours later that I came up from the rocks, with the finest string of saithe I had had for many a day, and stopped at the tidiest croft on the rim of the bay to leave some of my catch. At the door two women were working at the quern, the one lifting the oats in handfuls, the other, with a light touch of her finger, keeping the upper stone spinning. The western sun was on their hair and I liked the picture they made bending towards the quern and singing in their sweet, low voices.

" A taste of my fine catch to you, Janet," I said to the older of the two, a Macdonald from the Long Isle married to Finlay Mackenzie, my father's right-hand man and very good friend. " And the little one is for you, Katherine," I told her daughter, offering the girl a fingerling I had kept specially for her.

She looked up at me saucily, saying: " Indeed, indeed you are over-kind. I could not think to take so much away from you. You will want to show that one to your father."

Katherine has a way with her, and I have known her since we were both little ones; only now I do not steal from her the gaily coloured pebbles found when the tide goes out, that some make into brooches. Instead I steal now and then a kiss, and a hard slap is what I get in return.

" Ardmair has been looking for you," she said, sitting back on her heels and suddenly remembering. " He was here asking for you."

" Then I must go. Think of me when you are eating the little fellow, Katherine. Give her nothing but the one, Janet."

I ran off laughing, kilt swinging, string of fish slapping against my bare knees, shouting a greeting to each croft as I passed, little thinking that never again would I run that road round the bay so lightheartedly.

Though I had the stature of a man I was but a boy at heart, with no care in the world, and had I known that I was not only hastening to the house of Ardmair, but going breakneck into a man's troubles and sorrow, faith! then, I would not have travelled the way so hard.

While I had sat dreaming of foreign wars and planning the future, the future was already planned for me. By rights I should have been back at the College in Aberdeen continuing my studies, but several times, at the recollection of why I was not bending back over books, instead of playing with hook and line, I had rolled over and over, laughing till the echoes cast back my laughter.

Even yet, though I do not condone, I cannot forbear to smile at that old folly.

After finishing at a grammar school in Inverness—and a very good school it was—my cousin, Tearlach Mackenzie, and I had gone to the College by the Don. Not of our own will, in truth, did we go, but because we were sent. With bare credit to ourselves we had completed one full year, and some weeks of a new session, when the College closed its doors to us on account of Tearlach's pistol.

It would be half-way through one dreary Latin period that it happened. We had yawned our way through the construing of some dull prose and were about to begin the translation of a new book of Virgil when Tearlach had a look at his pistol under his book. A very good Doune pistol it was, with a flint-lock, that had but recently come into his hands, and fine he knew I envied him the possession of it. I watched him for a little, then I glanced at my Virgil, and as soon as I saw the opening lines, the Devil, that looks after idle hands, set mine to a mischief.

"*Arma virumque cano*—I sing of arms and men," droned the good old man on the rostrum, when I slyly reached out and pulled the trigger. There was a flash, followed by a report that threw back in the narrow room mighty reverberations, and a lad from Huntly, seated on the benches before me, leapt all of a sudden into the air, roaring like a maddened bull and clutching his breeches with both hands. He had taken no hurt whatever, for there was no ball in the pistol, only powder, which had but seared the cloth, though to hear him you would have thought he had gotten a mortal wound.

When our class-fellows learned the reason of the uproar they added to it with great roars of laughter, and what with the smoke and the noise, and the smell of powder, there was an end put to the Latin period. The Dean thereupon summoned Tearlach and me to his room and told us, with many ungentle words, that the College of Aberdeen would welcome our absence in the future more than it would our presence.

And that is how Tearlach and I took our impenitent, boisterous way home in the middle of term and gave up all hope of ever writing *Magister Artium* after our names. Some regret we had at leaving, for we parted from many good friends, and never again could we take part in the wild tulzies of students against apprentices, where we cracked crowns merrily and had much ado to keep our own from being cracked.

I had to break the news first to my grandfather, a sick old man in Inverness, and I was sorry to disappoint him so sorely. He shook his head sadly—he was a good scholar—and said: " I have wished many a time you could have loved book-learning like myself. But no matter! It is done now and it cannot be helped. A pity, Alastair! A pity! "

" Ach, sir, it was just a foolish ploy," I said contritely. " I like the books well enough."

" Aye, but never the right books. Never the ones you were ordered to study. When you read it is for pleasure alone, and so, Alastair boy, you will never be a scholar. I wish there was more of the Ross blood showing in you."

" There is nothing wrong with the Mackenzie blood, sir," I said, somewhat nettled.

" Nothing whatever," he returned gently. Then after a pause: " Well, on your way, boy! And may the blessing of God go with you."

My parents' forgiveness was not long withheld, though

they too were sorely disappointed, and deemed it something of a disgrace that I had been rusticated.

But to return to that September afternoon.

It was when I reached home that I had my first word of the foray. I found my father newly returned and pacing the floor.

" Come, Alastair, I have been seeking you," he began at once impatiently. " Big Johan told your mother you had speech with a horseman who passed this way some hours since. Describe him to me."

Would anyone believe it? I had forgotten about the stranger. My success with the line and my passage with Katherine had put him to the back of my mind. That will serve to show how careless I was in those far-off days.

When I had described him to the best of my power, my father exchanged a long look with my mother. " No doubt about him. Just as I thought," he said at length, nodding his head slowly. " What did he say to you? "

I repeated our conversation, at pains to forget no word of it.

" He dared! " my father broke out stormily, when I had finished. " He dared come to my door! And he would without doubt have forced his way across my threshold if he had not feared I might have caught him there. *Dhe*, but he shall pay for his curiosity. And the pleasure of seeing me in his own country—he shall have it sooner than he bargains for. Aye will he! "

He strode to the door. " Finlay! Here! Murdoch! " he shouted, and we heard confused, excited jabber outside.

Re-entering, he said curtly to me, with a gleam in his eyes: " We leave at dark for the Reay country."

My heart leapt at the thought. Excitement, adventure

B

lay ahead, a journey to strange places and the chance to strike in my father's quarrel. I would not have been Gael if I had not thrilled at the chance to share in it all.

But my mother's face went very pale at his words. She is a fine-looking woman, my mother, a Ross from Fearn, blue-eyed and very fair, very unlike my father's people, who are all dark-eyed and dun-haired.

She took a step towards my father and laid a hand on his arm, her eyes as well as her voice pleading:

" Think again, Donald, before you do this. At least take counsel with your pillow, will you not? It is an old wrong now. Would it not be better forgotten? I am afraid! You might as well try to bore a stone with your finger as get the better of yon one."

He put his free hand over hers, holding it tight and saying: " Have you ever known me provoke a quarrel, Flora? This one was not of my making. The man who would put his finger in my eye, I would put my knee on his chest. The visit to-day piled insult on the old injury. Leave this to me. It must be settled. Better now than later."

" At least you need not take Alastair with you," she urged anxiously. " Have you considered——"

" I have considered everything. I would willingly leave Alastair at home, but if I did so, what, think you, would the men say of him? Never a one would follow him. They would call him unfit to hold Ardmair when his time comes for that. You would not have the boy branded as a coward? See to your sword, Alastair."

I climbed to my room and came down with dirk and broadsword.

" I would not stay behind," I declared stoutly, lunging at an unseen foe and parrying his blows. " What think you of my strokes, father? "

" Good, but not good enough. You learned too easily, Alastair, as you learn everything, and you are careless. You rely too much on that trick with the dirk."

" It has worked every time I tried it," I said a little crestfallen, dropping the point of my sword.

" Aye, but it may not work the next time. Stay with your mother while I see Finlay."

At nightfall we stood ready to march, myself filled with a rising excitement. My mother looked very troubled, but said little. In the doorway, as I glanced at the sky and hearkened to the suck of the outgoing tide, she whispered to me: " Come back to me safe, Alastair, and come back the same lad who is going away."

" Have no fear, mother," I answered her laughingly, with an arm about her shoulders. " I will come back to you the same as I am now."

And that is just what I did not do.

CHAPTER II

The Foray

FROM the start that foray was an ill-starred venture. I lingered with Tearlach, waiting for Ian Mackenzie and his brother from Isle Martin, and as we stood on the shingle a pair of ravens flew darksomely north over our heads, making for the cliffs at the back of Rhu Coigach. Never a croak came from these birds of ill omen, yet I knew it boded no good for us.

And as if that in itself were not enough, young Ian, jumping from the boat, flourished his sword and slashed open the cheek of his brother, Rory. Rory was left behind.

" Now what would you make of that, Tearlach? " I said. " Here is Mackenzie blood first shed in this quarrel."

" Tach! " said he. " We are left with seven now, and that's the lucky number. I'm seeing the good luck last on top of the bad."

And so we lifted foot blithely enough through Strath Kanaird, though the silence enjoined by my father put a rein to our high spirits. At another time our way would have been to the lilt of a Gaelic marching tune, but here we were slipping ghost-like by the clachans, with not even a footfall to set the dogs barking.

Besides Finlay and Murdoch, the bouman from Glasach, there was Roderick from Achall, and that same Ian of the too-ready sword.

Only my father and myself knew that it was through

Assynt and into the Reay country we were going, a far more perilous jaunt than stepping over into Glenbhain lifting a few beasts and scurrying south with them. This raid had some connection with the passing of the stranger; of that I was sure, but in what way I could not guess. Long before day broke we had stolen past the clachans of Knockan and Ledmore, and at dawn were sheltered in the caves high above a burn, with the bald crags of Assynt Ben looming grey in the morning light.

It was there, while we broke fast, Finlay questioned my father on the purpose of the journey, for by now we were in the heart of Assynt.

" How far do we go? " he asked.

For a full minute my father sat thinking before he answered, as if weighing his words.

" This is no foray into McLeod country," he said finally. " This afternoon a man passed my door, a man I thought never to hear of again. I thought him killed in Germany. You know him, Finlay. I bear him an old grudge. It goes back nearly twenty years now. But you who know the story know whether I can sit still, when he dares come to my door."

" Himself? " asked Finlay, surprised. " Yon one, himself? "

" Aye, himself! 'Tis to Reay we go, to settle yon old score, that few but yourself know the truth of. I am thinking it must be settled now. If you are of a different opinion, Finlay, you can turn back."

" There will be no turning back," said Finlay gruffly.

" Good, then! It is three days north we go and my quarrel with but the one man. There will be no lifting, and when I settle with him we return as quickly as feet can take us out of Mackay country. To go further would but get me into trouble with both Reay and Seaforth."

That we younger ones were disappointed I will not deny.

Wondering what the old quarrel was—twenty years back my father had said, so it could have nothing to do with me—I lay watching a stag on the hillside over the corrie. He walked slowly along the ridge just under the skyline and clapped in a hollow deep grown with ling, nothing showing but head and antlers. So still he lay there, it was with difficulty my eyes picked him out again, once I had looked away. His head and neck blended with the frosted brown of the ling, and but for the twitching of his ears against the flies, he was invisible.

I was dozing off when he suddenly leapt to his feet, cast a hurried glance over his near shoulder, and took into the corrie at a lumbering trot. Coming opposite a crack where an *eas* spouted, he fairly flew, sending the stones in showers from his hooves, as he crossed a stretch of scree. Plainly he had got the wind of someone and the scent was coming stronger down the gully than elsewhere. But the ways of the winds among the corries are strange, dodging round buttresses, slinking down the gullies, blowing all ways at once and often baffling one of the reward of a long crawl.

However of it, I looked to the head of the gully and watched intently. For one brief moment the sun glinted on a gun-barrel. That was all I saw, but enough. Never taking my eyes off the spot, I gave my father a dig with my foot. He was beside me in an instant.

" Keep well in the shadow," I whispered. " There is someone on the ridge over."

I glanced at the stag. He was well up on the rim of the corrie, out of scent of the hidden one, and, puzzled, was throwing his muzzle in the air, snuffing the wind. If the stag were the watcher's quarry he had but to slip down the gully and stalk from below. But never a shake of the bracken told of a presence.

" We are discovered and watched," I said.

" Sure enough," my father grunted. " Some of the McLeods from Ledmore must have heard us pass. The Black One himself will not outwit these McLeods. It's bundle and go for us now. Finlay! Murdoch! " He pushed at them with his foot. " Rouse the others. It's the road out of Assynt for us immediate. We are watched."

Further concealment was of no use, and, indeed, longer of dallying there a danger to us, for without a doubt there had been more watchers, and by now one of them might be over into Glenbhain scouring for reinforcements.

" It's a pity we did not go openly through Assynt," Murdoch grumbled, as we prepared to start.

" What! " my father stormed. " Ask permission of McLeods and pay road cess to them on our returning? Never, man! Ye'd arrive back at Ardmair as your mother gave birth to you."

And so we crossed Assynt Ben in daylight. That lightning traverse of Assynt still lingers fast in my mind, corrie after corrie, ridge after ridge, sweat drenching our faces and trickling into eyes already dim with the weariness of our climbing up, only to dip and climb again.

That back-land of the McLeods of Assynt! Faith, they are welcome to it for me, for nothing is yonder but mile after mile of bare limestone rock, which glints white in the noonday sun, searing the eyes with the glare.

And its burn beds, a desolation of boulder on boulder, under which the water tinkles and trickles far below. There may be fish in its waters, but I doubt that, though I have heard some say that strange fish, lank, like eels, inhabit its watery caverns, fish without sight or fin.

Streams full width at birth gush from hillside hollows, the water ice-cold at all seasons, so that one wonders it still runs. A land dead to man or beast, no life there save perhaps the eagle and raven, and to them only a sanctuary for the rearing of their young.

Over Assynt, and a flat brimming with lochs as thick as stars in the night met us. It was with a relief to all we came on Loch Shin and the drove roads from Reay to the Muir of Ord.

After three nights of travel, on the morning of the fourth day, we came on the shores of an arm of the sea, at that dead hour of the morning when dogs curl tighter and nuzzle noses deeper between paws.

We slid down the hillside to the shore, passing a number of sleeping crofts, and, finding a horseshoe of the shore where the sand had piled in great billows, searched along its western heel and came on a cave big enough to barrack a regiment. On our entry a number of rock-pigeons flew out, the claps of their wings carrying like pistol shots far back into the hollows.

" Our journeying is over," said my father. " When night falls I make a call on a man at a house a mile west from here. All I ask of you is to see that my visit is not interrupted. I will deal with him myself and alone."

We stole down on the house close after the duskening, when the ridge of the *moyne* across, still cut clear, like a razor's edge, the western sky, and scarts, late at their fishing in the tidal waters, went winging their way out towards their home cliffs on Isle Ron.

A stillness hung about the house itself, that cried loud in the night to my ears, " Caution." Over by the west gable, where the byre abutted, came the lilt of a milking croon, " *Sil a bho, sil an bhaine* " (Pour, O cow, pour forth thy milk), blending with the soft swish of the milk into the cogie. But no light was over there, and only the one room lit in all that big house.

The door stood open. But where in the Highlands was not the open door, except in the burgh lands of Inverness, where a man would tirl at a pin before the goodwife opened, since Keppoch and his Macdonalds were too near for comfort?

My father and I crept up to the window and peered in. There he sat on a high-backed, rush-woven chair staring moodily at a fire of peats, the man I had spoken with four days ago at Ardmair.

" Hold the passage, Alastair," and my father was two steps in the room, drawn sword ready in hand.

" Good evening, Ardmair," said Mackay, swinging his arm lazily round the back of his chair, but not rising. " The expected guest is always welcome. A great pleasure indeed, but may I point out to you the incivility of your entry. Pardon my remaining seated. My manners match your methods."

Faith, but yon one had the sneering tongue, and was a cool one to boot. I could not but admire his bearing.

" Pray be seated," he went on, " while I call for wine."

" Not I," said my father. " Rise, or I will spit you where you sit. We have an old score to settle, William Mackay, and I have travelled fast and waited long to settle it. I have men here at my back to see fair play this time, and that is more than you are accustomed to give."

" Yes," he drawled. " A weary trail that over Assynt. But why the secrecy? "

" Rise and draw," gritted my father, the veins of his neck swelling with rage, and rapping his sword-point on the floor.

Mackay rose coolly, placed the chair before him,

twitched aside a screen of tapestry, and three servants, fully armed, stepped behind him.

"I also, Ardmair, have men at hand to see fair play."

The clink of steel on stone came to my ears at the same moment, and looking over my shoulder into the lobby I dimly saw it filling with men.

"*Tulachard!*" I raised the gathering cry of our clan. "*Tulachard!*"

The fight was on.

Finlay was by me in an instant, but not before one of the Mackays was rolling on the floor. He had thrust at me. I parried with the dirk and cut him across the knees. In his fall he brought down the man behind and the pair of them were rolling in the dark, each trying his best to choke the breath from the other.

I left the passage to Finlay and turned to see my father engaged by Mackay, and for a minute witnessed as pretty a piece of sword-play as ever it has been my fortune to see. I had always known my father could fence, but never before had I seen such lightning wrist-work. 'Twas the long, heavy type of Dutch, cross-hilted, backed blade Mackay wielded, and though my father pressed him sorely, I would be loth to say he had him much at advantage. Parrying cleverly, Mackay was on the defensive all the time, such was the ferocity of the attack, until my father feinted with a cut from the right, which changed in a flash to a thrust for the throat of Mackay, who saved himself there, only by clever foot-work. His parry was late by seconds. My father feinted again, doubling in a back-hand cut for the neck, while the other's sword was still held high on first guard. The end was certain.

A pistol bellowed in the room. In the narrow space the roar rocked from wall to wall and set my ears drumming. My father fell back against me, his sword clattering on the flags.

" A curse on you, you meddler! " snarled Mackay, and turning felled his retainer to the floor. Why, I could not guess, for that pistol-shot saved Mackay's life, and he was a poor sworder who could not see that.

A blind rage filled me. I pushed my father behind me, and, with " *Tulachard !* " ringing out again, went straight for Mackay. My assault through the smoke-laden room took him so unawares, his sword did not come up on guard. I struck him square in the midriff. The point dunted on chain armour, and my wrist doubled with the jar. He went over through the tapestry into the space beyond, clear out of sight. A stroke beat down my sword, but my dirk went under the arm that drove it.

" Outside, Alastair," cried my father, and I ran for the outer door, to find Murdoch and the others holding off twice their number in an angle of the wall. Finlay and I broke on their rear and they scattered like lambs at the spaining.

" Up the hill," I shouted, " and into the open! These walls are a death-trap." And we took through a field of stooks, and halted only when the heather was under foot.

" What of the arm? " I asked.

" Broken, I fear, Alastair. Finlay, can you do something for it? "

" Better get away from the crofts," I advised.

My father turned and shook his fist menacingly at the house below.

" You bungled the business, Alastair. No need for you to mix in it so soon."

" Need there was," I said vehemently. " We were rats in a trap, as well you saw for yourself. Was I to stand still and get half-an-ell of Mackay dirk in my back?

The business was none of my bungling, and in my opinion you yourself would have been cold clay down yonder, for you had not vanquished Mackay. The man wore a steel corslet under the doublet."

" And you think I did not expect that? " my father said bitterly.

" You did! " I cried astonished.

" Yes, boy. I know him, and meant to get him in the throat."

" Anyway, what honour was left us I think I saved," I said defensively. " Better a good retreat than a poor stand, and the sooner we are on our way the better. There are three Mackays dead and wounded down yonder, and our own Tearlach is missing."

" What! " said my father. " Is our Tearlach behind? "

" He is; Ian has gone back to seek him."

" A black business! What am I to say to Mary? "

" If Ian does not learn about him I will go back myself when I have seen you safely on the road. Come," I urged, leading off.

My father seemed stunned. He had lost no little blood and the arm must have been very painful. Also the shock of finding his plans for the humbling of his enemy all miscarried had racked his pride. I took his arm and we made swiftly uphill, him leaning the heavier on me every step.

A blooded crew! No one of us but had marks to show for the tulzie yonder. How I came by a cut below the knee I know not, but my left brogue was squelching blood. Finlay had one eye closed, by a ding from a basket-hilt, which he told me knocked him ten paces along the lobby; but, however serious our predicament was, I could not keep back the laugh at him. Murdoch's saffron shirt was McMillan tartan, more red than yellow in it. And Tearlach missing! The good luck there, had not been on top of the bad for him. Still, I reckoned, we left as many marks behind us, and a good thing for us too, for there would be the less inclination for them to take up the chase on us.

At a croft south of the Crask, Finlay begged an egg and some meal, and setting my father's arm in splints plastered it with the compost, which would firm like stone and hold the bone in place.

The man of the house gave them willingly enough, with meal to spare and a drink of buttermilk—but what else could he? Five desperate men were apt to take what might not be given, and none in a mood for soft words. His wife stood behind him in the doorway, and a litter of bairns, startled from their sleep, keeked from behind her skirts, eyeing the battered wrecks heaving home for harbourage.

And now let me tell the further mischances of that raid and its ending for me.

Pride can urge men to greater follies than most other failings. Our pride was deeply cut. Here we were returning home with nothing to show but cuts and bruises. Also what galled my father sore was the loss of his broadsword. The blade of that weapon had been in our family for more generations than I wot of. It was said to have been wielded by Mackenzies at Flodden and Langside. Many a time must the grip of bog oak have been renewed, the blade thinner through many grindings, but still as as true and straight as a shaft of winter sunlight. A loss not to be spoken of.

We had cast west after crossing the Crask, making for the coast road south by Lochinver, when Finlay, on our second evening out, suggested the lifting of a few bestial " to ride home like gentlemen," as he put it.

Such was our temper we briskly agreed, and my father was in no wise loth. For himself, I think he hoped we might put trouble on the McLeods, through whose lands we must drive the *creach*, for he was hot to revenge himself on those who undoubtedly had warned Mackay of our coming.

" So be it," he said, when Finlay moved the matter. " Let the lifting be close on their border and they will have to reckon with the Mackays for giving passage to the drove."

Both Finlay and my father had in their younger days taken part in cattle raids, chiefly into Lochaber, and I knew that a raid into Macdonald country was never without risk of shot and steel. Watchful dogs! There were never bestial better guarded than the cows that came to Keppoch's folds, and those that lifted there lifted often their own. If the McFarlane or the Gregarach could beat Keppoch's Macdonalds at the lifting, as I have heard say, then gleg lads they be.

But this lifting of ours had neither spice nor valour in it, for these douce folk suspected nothing. Their fires were smoored and all were safely bedded ere we ventured among the crofts, lifted the bars from a night-fold and quietly drove off a *creach*.

" Had we the pipes with us and a score more in our tail," boasted Finlay, as we ran behind the drove, " I'd blast the road through Badagyle with ' *Tulachard*,' and defy all the McLeods ever foaled."

The beasts went forward in a jostling mass, those outside trying to edge a way into the centre of the drove, as is the way with cattle beasts huddled on the run. But that lasted not long. Gradually the leaders got their places and the drove strung out in a long line.

It was at the crossing of the Kirkaig we were stopped.

A single shot rang out in front, and the track ahead filled dark with clansmen.

"Bunch the drove and through them!" my father cried, and urged his garron on the cattle.

We yelled and went onward with a rush, the beasts bellowing, plunging forward from the stab of the dirks. Among the rocks of the ravine our pistol-shots rolled, the flashes one moment lighting, more vivid than day, the bunch of snorting, maddened beasts, playing on horns and eyes, or picking out a frenzied figure clinging to the rocks to avoid the stampede; the next, a darkness plunging on us as black as the pit itself.

At last we were through the ford. The drove was galloping hard up the brae when a gun flashed above me. A great clod of heathery peat, as big as a cow, lighted on my head, smothering me and knocking me helpless to my knees.

Before I recovered, a body followed the peat from the cliff. Two hands on my neck, a knee in my back, and my face was ground in the moss. Before you would turn round I was bound and blindfolded, jerked to my feet, hurried down the hill and through the ford we had passed. On the far bank I was heaved on a garron, and quickly taken north between two captors.

I questioned them, hoping to discover from their accent whether they were McLeods or Mackays, for the McLeods, though long of Assynt, have the Gaelic of the Isles, while the Mackay Gaelic is no Gaelic whatever to our thinking. But never a grunt out of them! I thought to surprise them into speech and sorely reviled their clan, ancestry and chief, but these lads had been well drilled. On another occasion, for a fifth of what I said, they would have holed me with dirks. I fell silent.

After a weary day of travel we halted at a cottage

somewhere farther north. I knew it was north we went, for the wind still blew on my left cheek, the soft, balmy west wind, full of the tang of the sea, over which it had wafted a thousand miles or more. And at that house I heard but one sentence in the English, enough to tell me the speaker.

He wore spurred boots, for I heard the clink as he dismounted. He walked to the door, while one went to hold his horse, and I had the feeling as he stood there that he was scanning me. Then he turned. " It's the young cub we've caught. Good! " And he gave a low chuckle.

'Twas the voice of William Mackay.

Deprived of sight, I had used hearing to good purpose, listening to every sound around me, the even twitter of the birds, the soft lowing of cows calling to be milked, the run of the burns we crossed, so that I knew the direction and time much better than my captors would guess. I knew for certain I was back in the Reay country, close on the Pentland Firth, for the last river we forded ran north, and I caught the smell of sea-wrack. And some time late on the second day I was dismounted, led up a steep, marched through a courtyard, unshackled, and thrust into a dungeon.

I drew the bandage off my eyes, but so stiff were my arms that movement came to them only with pain. I groped for a pallet and fell more into a swoon than sleep.

CHAPTER III

A Prisoner in Reay Country

IT is a queer thing to waken suddenly in the dark inside strange walls.

I woke with a start, my hands moist, my heart going like a piper's foot, my breath coming fast, and it was a full minute before I knew I was fresh from a nightmare. Slowly the horror of it left me, but even then I could not account for the windless dark of the place, the hard pallet.

I reached out a hand cautiously and found a stone wall. On the other side were the cold cobbles of the floor. It came back to me with a rush—I was a prisoner.

The knowledge did not disturb me much. If I did not manage to escape—and he is a strange man who in confinement does not plan and plan to escape—I knew that soon there would ring through the night the cry of " *Tulachard!* " and my father would have me out. He was no man to leave his only son long in enemy hands, and a word to Seaforth would bring him all the help he needed. The Mackenzies are a strong clan. From sea to sea, Ross-shire is theirs, and though they might have no quarrel with the Mackays, my father's quarrel would soon be theirs, when they found it just.

I had no wish to explore my prison, for I had often heard the story of a man who, in the night-time, finding himself a prisoner, rose up and felt his way about his cell. At the second step his foot found space, and it was only with a strong effort he kept himself from

plunging downwards. Morning showed him a gaping
hole in the floor, with a stream flowing far below. Had
he vanished by way of the hole, his captors would have
said of him that he had " escaped." I smiled wryly in
the dark at the gentle word for murder, and thought it
wiser to lie still than venture on such a journey.

There was a mighty scurrying of rats behind the
walls, and to quieten them I took off a brogue and
hurled it into a corner, where they seemed most diligent
about their business. At once all was still, and then I
heard a sound that made me pleased as a hungry bairn
with its lips at a cogie of new milk—the first soft stirring
of the tide followed by the slow swish-swish of the outgoing waves. It was like the voice of a friend calling,
for at Ardmair we live beside waters. A laughing burn
hurries by our gable-end to join the sea that sings at
our front door, and empty is the night for me without
their music. Swish-swish went the waves outside my
prison, the very sound of the ebb on a still night in the
bay at home, where it aye seemed to me like the swing
of a giant scythe through the ranks of the standing corn.

I would not be badly off I thought, even though four
walls shut me in, if I could have the sea for company.
I would be able to tell the look of it, as it changed its
tune, for ever since I was a bairn I have been able to
make clear pictures in my mind, at will, of those things
I am denied at the time and yet hunger to see.

It goes back to a day when I was a restless mischief-
loving brat, that must ever be in the forbidden place,
doing the forbidden thing, and one result of this was
that broken bones, got from a slide down a cliff face,
tied me to a bed I hated as a sea-maw hates a cage.
My mother was at the end of her wits to still my peevish
demands to be outside again.

" It is his own fault he is lying where he is now,"
my father returned sternly, " and he had better learn to
be happy indoors when he is not able to be out, for we
cannot mend leg bones for him in a day or even a week.
Let him go in his mind where his feet will not take him."

And so began the game of making pictures. My
mother would stand at the high narrow window, and I
would shut my eyes and tell her what she saw, from the
rim of the Minch to the hens about the door, and the
swallows about the eaves, she helping me when I forgot.
And we would travel the road to Garve or Dingwall,
on the wings of our fancy, telling all that we looked on
and all that happened on the way. It passed the time
finely, and often since I have been glad I learned the
trick of it.

I learned, too, the moods of the sea and the burns.
All the music we have is taken from the wind and the
waters, and the first piper made nothing new when he
made his first tune.

The burn that plunges down a brae face or swirls
about a boulder foot, that laughs among the pebbles or
lingers among the ferns, taught us our strathspeys and
reels, and the croons for the cradle-rocking. For drought
and spate it has a different key. Come rain, and it
grumbles deep in its throat; come sun, and it tinkles
high and merry.

The rise and fall of the sea are in the piobaireachd.
The moan and sigh of the tide, the drone of the long
wave that booms in a rocky cavern—we hear in them
the coronach, the wailing of lament. When a fresh wind
blows, and whips the white horses till they run galloping
between the skerries and the headlands, we get the notes
of the quicksteps, the lively rants of the clans.

And when the wind shrieks wildly up the strath and

a sullen sky frowns down on an angry Minch, so that
the great green rollers swing into the bay in menacing
ranks, to fall with a toppling crash on the shingle, or
hurl themselves in fountains of spray at the steep black
rocks, then is the defiant scream of the battle march in
them, with all the thunder of a thousand drones.

Maybe I should have been lying there thinking of the
trouble into which I had fallen, and concerning myself
about what lay before me. Maybe I should. But, by
some queer trick of the brain, the music of the waves had
me back on a bit of well-known shelving shore. And
anyway, what cannot be bettered need not be worsened
by worrying. I drew my plaid closer about me, rolled
over on my side and dozed off into a pleasant sleep.

When I roused again, it was full day on the window
set high in the wall, but my gloomy chamber got small
share of sunlight, for so small was the window that my
head in my bonnet would have come near filling it.
Some sound had disturbed me, and, listening, I heard
stealthy movements outside, subdued voices and laughter
with difficulty controlled.

"Some folk are merry this morning," I thought,
"and I wish I were one of them. But what have I got
to be merry about? I have a wound or two in need of
washing, and I have the hunger of a lamb at the tail of
a ranging ewe."

I was lying in an angle of the room, my head on my
outstretched arm, watching the shaft of sunlight that
came through the narrow opening. Suddenly a head
appeared, the head of a girl with rippling dark hair.
She had no chance of seeing anything at all, for, after
bobbing about strangely for a moment, she sank from
sight with the speed of a diving scart.

I heard more smothered laughter and a choked kind

of voice protesting: " I could not, Barbara. Indeed I
could not. Not a moment longer. But get up and we
will try again."

The thought rushed through my mind that, before
they tried again, I might have time to move and roll the
pallet I lay on, so that as Mistress Barbara looked in
she might find me standing on it looking out. I would
dearly have liked to do so, but I was not sure that I
could be quick enough. Again, my face was caked with
earth and blood that had trickled from a scalp wound, and
I was unwilling that any maid should be startled at the
sight of me. I half buried my face in my arm and lay still.

Soon she appeared again, seemingly with a steadier
support this time, for she framed her face with her
hands against the sun, and peered into the gloom of
my cell. I heard a little gasp of dismay, and then the
window-frame was empty.

" Do you know," came a voice, with fear and agitation
in it, " I believe he is dead. His hair is matted with
blood, and he is lying quite still. Now, father said he
was to be well seen to. He was to have every attention.
We must not leave him like that. Come along. Hurry!
We must do something."

" Thank you, Barbara," I said, as retreating footsteps
hurried away. " Now I may be seeing a platter with
a bit of food on it, and I would give my left hand for a
drink of water. "

Being left-handed, my left hand is the better of the two.

Presently the bolts were shot and a serving-woman
appeared with an armed gillie in attendance. She carried
nothing but a basin of water and bandages of linen, and
at the sight a groan of disappointment broke from me.
The man took up his position just inside the door, and
gloomed at me, but the woman set down the basin with

a look of concern, and stroked the hair back from my eyes. Never will I forget her surprise, when I shook off her hand, plunged my face into her basin, and drank greedily. She had thought me dead or dying when she entered, and here I was lapping up her laving water like a calf at a bucket of milk. Out of breath, I lay back and smiled at her. " I could drink Loch Shin dry, given time," I told her.

Tight-lipped and annoyed, she set about her task. She was quick at it and skilful, and soon had my wounds, none of which were deep, cleansed. The only one that stood in need of a bandage was the one below the knee, and indeed it might have gone on well enough without. But try as I would to draw her into talk, I could not get her to give me a word, nor a kind look. Usually I find women ready enough to talk to me, but not this one. It seemed a pity, for I believe her face could have been pleasant enough, but she had it set in a sour line.

Curiously, it was the man at the door who unbent to me. He asked if there was anything I wanted. I could have anything I needed, within reason.

" Something to eat," I said promptly. " A stool to sit on and permission to walk out of doors."

He went out, locking and bolting the door, and in a very short time was back with a generous helping of food and drink.

" I am not to be starved I see," said I. " Now can you do as well about my other wants? "

He went off again, and the stool arrived, not a very high one, but sufficient to raise me enough to see out of the window, which was what I specially wanted it for.

" You will be allowed outside once a day to walk," he said, " if you give me your word that you will not try to escape."

" Then I will stay indoors," I cried, " for I would be a fool to promise not to try to get away if a chance offered."

" So you will not give me your parole? "

" I will not," I said decidedly. " I warn you I shall escape if I can, though "—I looked round and shook my head—" I see small chance of it here and now."

He stood looking down at me gravely.

" Whatever brought you to the Kyle to make war? " he asked. " It is long since Seaforth carried war so far north."

" Seaforth had nothing to do with it. This was just a little bit of a family foray against one man of your clan."

" It was the rashest of journeys."

" Not so rash at all. Had it not been for a treacherous dog of Assynt, who cried to you our coming, we would have been home by now with a brave tale to tell."

" Well, you are in safe keeping here and your hot blood will have time to cool. We mean you no harm, but you will not take the home road for a while."

" That is not my way of it, but time will show which one of us is right. Seaforth may put a new tune to your piping. I hope you would not break the peace with Seaforth all for the sake of cooling my hot blood in your dungeon."

" I fear you are blowing at a cold peat, if you are counting on Seaforth's interference. He is too much taken up with keeping a finger on the reins of government to have either the time or the mind to get tangled with the short threads of small quarrels. It is a pity, lad, that you came at all. I have a son who is married to a Mackenzie, and I have a kindly feeling to your people."

He turned towards the door, but swung round again, before he had taken a step.

" I will tell you what I will do. I will let you walk once a day, but do not think that will make it any easier for you to get away, for you will walk only at high tide."

I had known early in our talk that this man was not the gillie I at first thought him to be. He spoke as one well aware of his own importance, but I was surprised that he had the authority to make rules for me.

" Have you the power to do that? " I asked, not concealing my astonishment.

" Yes, I think I can say I have that power. As long as I obey my orders to guard you well, I can choose my own way to do it, till my master comes home."

" So the black-browed one is from home? " I said. " There is small sorrow to me in that."

He scowled and fingered his dirk.

" No one will speak ill of William Mackay in my hearing," he said angrily.

" Then we had best not talk of him at all," said I lightly, " for I am sorry I cannot speak well of him."

" A better master there is not in the north, nor a better soldier, saving perhaps his kinsman, Hugh Mackay of Scourie. Both of them are talked of far beyond the shores of Scotland, and it is not for you to judge a man you do not know, and have never seen."

His voice was choleric, and his eyes now looked on me with a hostile stare, very different from his former kindly glances. Here was my tongue, which I might have bridled, had run away with me, knocking on the head a friendliness I ought to have done my best to encourage.

" I saw him a few days since, on his way north," I said mildly.

His anger faded and gave way to surprise.

" In the west? " he asked. " No; you could not! He

left again for the south this morning, but you did not
see him on the west coast."

I'll let William Mackay rest, I thought. I knew I had
seen him and had spoken to him, but I could perceive
nothing but loss for me in disputing this with my jailer,
who seemed disposed to be friendly again.

It must have been about three o'clock in the afternoon when he came to let me out for my airing. He
led me along a narrow gloomy passage, which seemed
to give access to my cell alone. A gillie stood at my
shoulder while my jailer himself turned the key in the
lock, and swung open a door which was studded thick
with nails, and was of an unusual strength.

I will admit my heart sank a little on seeing it, for
even the stoutest of Lochaber axes could make but
small headway against it. Then my spirits rose again
as I reasoned that there are other ways to make a rescue
than by battering doors in.

Once outside I was amazed at what I saw. It was no
ordinary house I was held in, but the castle of a baron
bailie, and a sturdy castle it was too. It stood at the tip
of a narrow tongue of land, in a position as strong as
any I know. Cliffs sheer on the west and north, more
gently sloping on the east, descended two hundred feet
to the sea, which surrounded it on three sides. On the
landward side, enclosing a grassy courtyard, ran a high
wall with strong gateway, in front of which a man stood,
his hand resting on his axe.

" A hard cage to climb out of," I thought. " But
what is this about high tide? There must be a way, if I
can find it, when the tide is out."

The arm of the sea that skirted the eastern slope
reached into the land for some distance beyond the wall,
which, as well as enclosing the castle on the straight

above, straggled down the brae face to the tide. There, if anywhere, seemed to be a way of escape.

I walked to the northern edge of the cliff and looked down. Sheer, sheer, and no sign of a foothold. Though a boat were waiting for me below, I could never hope to win to it. They had me here securely enough, but there must be a way out. And if low tide held the secret my father would learn it. The castle was not strongly manned if I guessed aright, and I would not have long to wait. A dark night, a surprise attack, and I would be heading for home.

My thoughts raced ahead while I stood there gazing up the Kyle, my arms crossed on my chest, a way I have sometimes when considering.

I heard the murmur of voices somewhere at hand, and a quick turn of the head showed me two girls, the dark-haired one I had already seen and one with red hair, each with an arm about the other's waist. They were coming slowly round a corner of the building, laughing and talking together, not thinking there was anyone near. When they caught sight of me they halted, and certainly they had no notion how the sound of their voices carried to me on the wind, else they had not spoken so loud.

" Look, Barbara, there's your prisoner," one girl said excitedly.

(" That must be Red Head speaking," thought I, looking straight before me.)

" What makes you call him my prisoner? He is father's prisoner."

(" That must be Barbara, the lady of the early-morning window survey," I said to myself.)

" Well, you saw him before. Why did you not tell me he was young? Young and bonny? "

("Bonny!" I repeated, disgusted. What young man wants to be called bonny? If Red Head had not been a stranger she would have taken back that word.)

"How could I tell he was young? I told you what I saw, and I thought he was dead. Callum says Anna got such a fright when he drank the water for his wounds."

They both laughed, and Red Head continued: "I like fair hair. Don't you, Barbara?"

(I began to feel I should not be listening there to them, but though I was like to laugh I stayed still.)

"Yes, I do; but not in a man. I would not trust a man with fair hair."

("Would you not, Mistress Barbara?" I thought, a bit nettled. "And maybe dark-haired maids might not be the kind to trust to either.")

"Well, I would."

(That was Red Head again. I decided that I liked the red one.)

"Do you know what he minds me of?" she went on. "The fair-haired men who came sailing over the seas to harry our shores, as we have been told. I cannot mind their name just now."

"Vikings, you mean? Yes, you are right," said Dark Hair slowly, as if considering. "He should be standing in the bow of a boat, ready to spring ashore, wings on his helmet, and the raven flag flying above him."

("What would she be at next?" I wondered. I wish she might have seen me standing in the bow, as I often did, ready to spring ashore and land the fish slopping about between the thwarts of our coble, on my head no helmet, but my old blue bonnet that—my grief!—I would never see again, it having been knocked off when the clod struck me.)

" Yes, and see his broad shoulders and powerful arms.
He must be strong, that one."

("You are right there, Fiery Locks," I told her silently.)

" Strong surely! But it would not surprise me if he
were cruel. The Vikings were a cruel breed."

(That was Barbara again. "What ailed this girl at me?"
I asked myself testily. No one before had ever thought
me cruel.)

" What say you he is thinking of? "

(That was Barbara wondering.)

" I would say he is thinking that the Kyle is a bonny
place, far better than he has ever seen on the shores of
Ross."

" And you would be wrong, Red Head," I said
quickly, before I had time to think, and this time I said
it out loud.

I looked at them, and they stood staring at me, dumb
with astonishment, the red tide flowing up over their
faces.

" Oh, insolent! " cried the red one at last, stamping
her foot.

" No," said Dark Hair, meeting my eyes steadily, her
face now pale when the flush had passed. " No; we
had no right to be talking about him as we did. It is we
who are in the wrong."

We stood gazing at each other, all three, till I flung
up my head and laughed. I could not help it.

Red Head smiled.

" But what were you think ingabout? " she asked
saucily. " Will you not tell us? "

" Willingly," I replied solemnly. " I was thinking I
could not trust a maid with dark hair. It would not
surprise me if she were cruel."

At that they turned and ran.

CHAPTER IV

A Blue-Bonnet sings

I

FOLK get used to things, as the drowning man said when he was going down for the third time.

I got used to the four close walls, so that soon I knew every mark on them, as well as every cobble of the floor. From the window I could see little—in the daytime, a huddle of crofts on the brae, fronting the western sky, some wandering kine feeding, and here and there a ragged pony tethered and cropping the grass about the doors; in the light of the moon, the young folk wandering the shore, digging for sand-eels or spearing for flounders. But between them and me swept the waves that I could never hope to win to.

It was hard for me to lie there idle, with nothing to do but watch for the early morning sun shaft, or the night shadow on the wall. Out of doors were the singing waters that I would fain have been beside. I rejoiced at the sound of them, but I wearied for human voices and the homely sounds of daily toil; I who had never been far from talk and laughter, and all day heard the home folk singing at their work. If they sang here at the milking or the spinning, the churning or the grinding, the walls were too thick for me to hear. Listening in the dark to the rats, my mind would be back at the nights filled with the pipes and the dance, the song and the jest, and I would be glad that I had such a good store of the old brave tales to think on, and gave thanks for that trick of making pictures.

I listened eagerly for each coming of my jailer, whose name I learned was Callum, but I lived for that hour each day when his turn of the key gave me leave to walk in the good outside air. No matter what the weather, I escaped joyfully into the out-of-doors. But Autumn that year was kind, and there were not many days on which I found her inhospitable.

The hour at which I walked varied, but there was rarely a day when I did not see the daughters of the house. At first they were shy, the flush rising to their faces as I passed, but the red-haired one—Nancy they called her—had a gleam in her eye and would throw me a laughing glance over her shoulder.

While at the castle I used to walk the cliff edge backwards and forwards in the sight of the sentry, till I had worn a track in the grass bare as a badger's run. But one day I stretched myself in a grassy hollow, out of a boisterous wind and in the eye of the sun, and there the girls found me. It was, it seemed, a favourite place with them, since it was sheltered from three winds—a lown place they call it in the Lowlands. They stopped short when they saw me, then walked away. But back they came again later. I smiled a greeting, and how it happened I cannot rightly mind, whether I invited them to share it with me, or they invited themselves, but anyway, after a little, there we all were, and talking together. At least Nancy did most of the talking, for yon Red Head had a tongue that went like a hill burn, though I will not deny mine could keep it good company.

She had brown eyes that, at a guess, I would say had gleamed for many a lad before me, and that threw little provoking glances sideways or through her lashes—a taking lass with a ready laugh and a bright colour that came and went very easily in her cheeks. I liked her at the first meeting, and I would have been slow if I had not seen that she liked me.

Few men would have looked twice at her sister when she was by, but I found myself looking often at Barbara, for never before had I met a young woman seemingly so little anxious to talk with me. She was stiff and silent, and I would have thought her without a smile or a laugh had I not known she could be as merry as the other. It was plain she did not like me. Ever in her mind seemed to be the thought that I was her father's prisoner. For an hour a day I wanted to forget that, but it was hard to do beside this cold daughter of the clan Mackay. I felt her eyes often on me, but whether her glance was hostile or only observant I could not judge, for when I looked at her she was no longer looking at me. When at last she spoke she said her father was in the south, that her mother was always confined to bed, and that the duty was laid on her of seeing that Callum satisfied my wants.

" My father left particular orders that you were to be well treated. Have you everything you need? " she asked.

" Everything I need, except my freedom," I replied, looking straight into her eyes.

She bit her lip, and her look fell away from mine.

" We cannot let you have that," she said, flushing and tugging at some blades of grass. " You put yourself in the wrong, and you must pay for it. Is there anything else we can give you? "

" Well, I wanted company, but I have got that now. It is a lonely life, a prisoner's, and I would be very grateful if I could have the same company often."

I wondered if I was over-bold, but my boldness was rewarded, for many a day afterwards, under the eyes of Callum, we walked the cliff edge, or sat and talked in that green bowl looking down on the sea. I wonder now

what we found to say, but we were young, and youth is
the time when folk can talk plenty whether or not they
have much to say. I know I told them of Aberdeen and
the narrow rooms of the College, where we sat packed
like puffins in a burrow.

And they told me of their schooling in Edinburgh,
that big town where the hours fly so fast no one can ever
hope to keep pace with them, whereas here in the quiet
places they halt long enough for a man to put into them
what he wills. I spoke often of my long friendship with
Tearlach, and made them laugh at some of the wild
ploys we had shared.

" I wish I knew what has befallen the lad," I said one
day. " There is one brave heart that will be missing me
if he ever won back over the hills."

" We could find out for you, perhaps," Barbara
ventured.

She could be kind at times, it seemed. I turned to her
eagerly.

" I wish you could. My sorrow! What a night was
that! My father wounded. Tearlach wounded and we
missing him in the dark and the rush of the fight. And
my father's sword lost! He would as soon have lost a
limb. It has gone from father to son for longer than I
can tell, and now it may be rusting in a corner, or carried
in no friendly hand."

" You should have left your sword in the sheath," said
Nancy. " You could have come to visit us without steel
in your hands surely."

" It was not you we came to visit, or we had done as
you say," I replied gallantly.

" We did not ask you to come."

" No, but you have pressed me to stay."

" You are very welcome," she returned, smiling at me

saucily. "But tell us, whom then did you come to see?"

"Oh, just one man my father had an old score against."

Here Barbara broke in hotly: "And you came among friendly folk for the sake of an old grudge against one man? You had better stayed at home."

"You do not know what he had done. Neither do I, but I am sure he should have got his deserts yon night."

"You do not know? That makes it worse. I have often heard the Mackenzies are a quarrelsome clan, though they have not dared come against us often."

"I am a prisoner in your home, Mistress Barbara," I said stiffly, "but that does not give you the right to pronounce on my father's wrongs, nor to cry down my clan. The Mackays have not always the right of it."

"And have the Mackenzies?"

"Not always, but as often as their neighbours. And I would like you to know that my father is the last man to force a quarrel without good reason."

"And my father is not the man to force a quarrel at all. The blame for your being here most surely does not lie with him."

A loyal daughter this! And she certainly had spirit.

"And must you both be quarrelling, who have no real quarrel at all?" asked Nancy impatiently.

"There is no need," I said, cooling down, "so long as the Mackenzies are let alone."

But Barbara sat silent and withdrawn, and took no further part in the talk. I thought she would have nothing more to say to me ever, but I was wrong. For what reason I do not know, but as the weeks went by, gradually her manner to me grew warmer.

There was a day when she told me Tearlach was safe. I had surprised her alone in the little hollow, for Nancy

D

happened to be in attendance on her mother. At the
time I would rather we had not met, for there we sat
without a word to say, either of us, and the silence grew
and grew until it was a burden. I cursed myself for a
stupid fool, for I have a ready enough tongue, but somehow I had lost it. I watched Callum pacing above us and
tried to think of an excuse to go and speak to him.

At last she broke the uneasy silence with the news
about my cousin. He had reached home.

" And I ordered a message to be left with your mother
that you are safe and well," she said quietly.

" Well, now," my loosed tongue cried at that, " are
you not the kind one! I have thought many a time she
would be wearying for news of me."

And there we were quiet again, me clearing my throat
to speak, but finding no words.

" You miss Nancy, don't you? " she asked after a bit.

" I do that," I said hastily. " She is the lively one,
never at a loss for talk."

That was true, but I had blundered into saying an
ungracious thing. The silence fell again like a heavy
hand. Faith, this girl was not easy to talk with. There
was plenty in my mind, but all I could do was to sit there
gulping, chewing the tip of a rush and growing hot.

" Are you wearying to be home? " she began again.

Certainly I was leaving her to make all the fresh starts.

" Wearying! " I drew in my breath. " Need you ask
it? I cannot be happy so long as I am a prisoner, or a
hostage, or whatever I am. I could not be better treated,
but I am wearying for my own folk and the things I am
used to do. I have a dog, now, that I am missing sorely.
We are never separate and he lies by my bed at night.
Sometimes in there "—I nodded my head towards the
castle—" when I am half sleeping, I reach out my hand

to find his head, and I start awake every time I am cheated."

" What is his name? "

" *Dileas*—Faithful his name and faithful he is. I wonder what he is doing without me. Can you tell me how long I am to be held here, or what your father means to do with me? "

" He did not say. It all happened so quickly and he had to go back to Edinburgh. But I think a message was sent to your father."

" You should not have been left with so heavy a charge."

" What do you mean? I am not finding it too heavy."

" If I am not set free soon, there will be blood spilled here. It may be little, or it may be much, but all of it will be innocent. Have you thought of that? "

She looked startled.

" What are you saying? Do you mean that you think your folk will come here in force for you? "

" I am sure of it. Can you see them tamely sitting yonder with folded hands? "

" Oh, this must not happen. My father should have thought of this. Surely he thought of it! What can we do? I am not afraid, but my mother must not be alarmed. She is very far from well."

" Would it alarm her to see yon braes in a blaze? The houses smoking, and your harvests in a charred heap? For that is what you will be seeing."

She caught her breath.

" I hope not. Oh! I hope not. What must I do? "

" I could escape," I suggested.

" You must not try," she returned sharply. " You would be shot if you were seen trying to get away."

" Show me where to try," I said, glancing round, " and
I am very willing to risk the shooting."

" Oh, this is dreadful," she said, as if to herself. " I
must hear what Callum thinks."

" I have warned Callum. The first day I was here.
And he did no more than smile."

" Yes, yes, of course. He will be for holding the castle
and he would like that fine. He would be in command
again, and is not that his dream! He is an old soldier is
Callum, and fought in the Civil War."

" Did he so? Aye, we fought on the same side in those
days, for you were for the Stuarts then."

Nancy joined us as I was speaking, and the talk drifted
away to other things.

I had been confident enough when I prophesied to
Callum the coming of the Mackenzies with fire and sword,
but, indeed, I had often wondered since what was delay-
ing them. They had had plenty of time to gather men
from Seaforth and march north. I did not believe a word
of Callum's story that Seaforth was too busy to help me,
for Callum did not know the loyalty of our clan. Of
course, if the chief were in Edinburgh that would explain
partly the delay. They might await his return. Or my
father might be waiting again for the dark of the moon.
So I argued with myself, finding excuses, but in my heart
was a little hurt feeling, because they were not bothering
themselves with overmuch haste.

Lying alone in my cell I had heard the honking of wild
geese, high overhead, on their southward flight. The
year was nearing its end. Since I had come there two
moons had waned and another was near the waning, and
I was still laid by the heels. My friends would come, I
did not doubt, but I wished they were not so tardy
about it.

II

There came an afternoon I often look back on, one of the finest of that fine autumn. The sky was an azure canopy, the sea an azure floor, with the light waves dancing gaily upon it, scattering the sparkles they had broken from the sunbeams. Little ripples were playing on the shore, running up the golden fringe of sand, to fall back, laughing, in a curtsy of foamy frills. Golden was the tangle, the colour and the smell of it joyous to me, fresh from my cold grey walls. Porpoises rolled lazily in a sportive school and a seal's head rose silently close to the cliff.

The girls joined me, bringing their sewing, and so mild was the day that they laid aside their plaids. There was no air stirring in the hollow, yet suddenly some dead leaves rustled and swirled in that strange way they will sometimes do on the stillest day. The girls looked up from their work astonished.

" An eddy wind," I cried, throwing my brogue at it. " The fairies are travelling."

" My aunt in Edinburgh and her minister told us there are no fairies, and it is wrong to believe in them," said Nancy, watching me retrieve my brogue.

" That is all they know about it," I said. " I could tell them better. There was a man in Isle Martin who lay down to sleep on the hillside, and when he wakened he was on an island ten miles away. Then he was carried back in an eddy wind and a great fear was on him that he would be dropped in the sea. Who but the fairies could have carried him? My father heard the story from the man's son. If I were not afraid that they would drop me in the wrong place, I would say that I wish I were travelling now in an eddy wind."

" What ails you at Kyle-ron? " Nancy demanded. " Is
it not bonny enough here to-day to make you wish to
stay? "

" Bonny indeed it is, but not bonny enough for that."

" It cannot be better anywhere than here," she
declared petulantly.

" I wish I could show you Ardmair, Mistress Nancy,
as it was the day I last saw it," I said, shutting my eyes
to call it back to mind. " For no place in the world could
I have the same fondness."

I opened my eyes and found Barbara watching me.

" I do not doubt you that it is a fine place," she said,
turning her head to look up the Kyle. " But you would
feel the same way about this if you were Barbara Mackay.
And had you been born on the bleakest moor or the
cruellest coast, you would still have praised it as the finest
place, for you would be seeing it with more than your
eyes. The place that is dearest to us may seem dull
indeed to the stranger. Where home is, the heart is."

Her eyes were full of dreams as she turned her head
again. How had I never observed her eyes before, eyes
with a fine, steady glow, where her sister's were but
flickering lights? She had never given me much chance
to see them, with this queer game we played of each
glancing away when the other was caught looking. But
for the first time I knew their colour: they shared the
blue of the summer sea with the grey of a summer mist.

A little saddle of freckles sat astride her nose, and
when she smiled she had a trick, that I found very diverting, of crinkling this saddle. I began to think Mistress
Nancy's laugh came too easily. A man can have too
much of a good thing, like the kitten when it fell into
the bowl of cream.

I was sorrier than usual when Callum signalled me.

Never for a moment did that old watch-dog let me out of his sight. Dirk and claymore he carried, musket and targe, and there he would pace with that slow strut of his that said: " I think the world of Callum Mackay."

I rose to go, throwing a handful of thistledown at Nancy. Barbara rose also, walked with me a step or two, till we were out of ear-shot, stood still, then, putting a hand on my arm, said breathlessly: " Be ready to go to-morrow morning. It will be low tide an hour before dawn."

That was all. She turned away at once, and left me wondering if I had dreamed her words. I looked back, but she gave no sign, and I walked in a daze to Callum, who marched me indoors again and turned the key.

I was so excited that I could not think, and it is hard to tell how I felt. I walked up and down, up and down, laughing low to myself, wanting to sing out loud. I was half afraid to let myself sleep.

I was awake long before I need have been, holding myself in, hearkening to every sound.

Barbara was coming for me, Barbara of the slow smile and the steady eyes. She would not fail me. I could not have been so sure of Nancy, but Barbara—— She had been very friendly of late. She liked me better now. She had said, " Be ready," and here I was, ready.

The key turned in the lock quietly, not with the great click and rattle that Callum made. I stood up and groped towards the door. I felt her hair brush against my face as she leaned towards me, whispering, " Be silent."

I needed no guide along the flagged passage I had trod often enough to know by heart, and never had I gone along it so fast and yet so noiseless. Barbara had difficulty with the bolts and bars of the heavy outer door, and I could hear her breath come quick. Myself, I held my

breath till we were outside in the cool dark and the big
door was locked behind us. Locked! And we were on
the outside.

" Wait here a moment," she said in my ear, and I
guessed what she was meaning to do. She had gone to
lock the main entrance door as well. A clever young
woman, Barbara! And then she was back, with her hand
in mine, hurrying me across the soft turf of the courtyard
to the outer gate. I hoped the lad with the axe was not
waiting for us. He was not, and I thought at the time
that Callum kept careless ward at night. We seemed
long undoing the bars again, but at last the big gate
rolled back and we were outside. I was free.

I drew a long breath and looked about me. It was
a dead hour. There was a hazy sky with a little bit of a
moon waiting up late for the sun that was slow to rise.
It was not yet light enough for me to see clearly more
than a stone's-throw away, but every minute was bringing
the light nearer. It was very still. Only the gentle lap of
the waves broke the silence. Barbara stooped and groped
among some rushes at my side. Still stooping, she held
up to me something I had thought never to see again—
my father's sword.

" Where did you get it? " I asked, taking it eagerly
from her hands, fondling it, and finally buckling it on.

" I sent a man to get it for me. It was picked up where
your father dropped it."

" I think I can see his face when I let him have it.
Indeed I do not know whether he will be more pleased
to have it or his son Alastair back again."

" Come away from here," she said quickly, giving me
her fingers again, and guiding me between some low-
growing bushes. Where the high ground fell away we
found a track that took slanting down the slope, and

here we could not walk abreast. I had taken good care
of that small hand that lay soft in mine, and I was loth
to let it go.

When we reached level ground I found the secret of
the road into the castle. When the tide was out, only
the channel of a river cut us off from the far shore, and
across this channel there was built a raised causeway of
stones.

I took her hand again as we crossed the ford, for the
stones were slippery with a slimy weed. The salty smell
of the tangle was heavy in the air and a sigh of heart-
break was in the tide. It was lighter now and the face
of the world was strangely grey and sad. Grey sea and
a grey sky, grey thistle-heads about our knees and a
dewy mist, grey along the grass—that was what I saw
when I stood to take my leave of Barbara Mackay. Her
hand still lay in mine, for I could not let it go, and I
think she had forgotten it was there.

" You will get into trouble for this," I said, with
compunction.

" I know that well," she admitted, " but I am doing
it to save our crofts and let the poor folk have peace,
for nearly all our men are with my cousin Mackay's
true corps of Scots in Dutch service."

She was watching the tide come into the river mouth,
wave on rising wave, and I could not take my eyes from
her. I should have been blithe to go, and instead I was
lingering, finding that even freedom was a loss since it
was to take me away from this girl of Kyle-ron.

From Inverness to the bounds of Coigach many a kiss
have I snatched from a maid, getting a cuff or a kiss in
return, not one of them meaning anything at all. Indeed,
my mother has been sorely distressed at times by just
that habit of mine, thinking that I am the kind that

loves for a day and rides away. But she was wrong, for the trouble with me was that I liked all the girls so well that I had never found one I liked better. And now here was the one. I had felt sometimes that I had won her favour at last, and I was in desperate fear of losing it. Yet, now I had to take the risk, for I knew that I would never be happy if I went away with only a hand-shake. But it was to be no easy kiss this; and time was passing and the tide was rising.

" It is time you were going," she told me, her head still turned away.

" I know it," I said miserably. " This is the hour I have been living for, and now that it is here, I could wish it away again. I do not want to go."

That brought her head round and her eyes searched my face wonderingly. She was very pale and her eyes were more grey than blue. Whether it was her fingers that spoke to me, or her eyes, or both, I am not sure, but they told me she had the same regret as myself and that made me bold.

" Barbara," I said—just the one word, but I put a lot into it.

I threw an arm about her and then I did it. I bungled the first kiss, for she suddenly bent her head to hide the colour that was flaming in her cheeks. But I made a good job of the second, and a better job of the third.

The light was creeping higher across the sky. The east was brightening. How had I ever thought the morning grey? It was silver! The sea was silver and the dewy grass was a silver sea. The thistle floss was silver, mingling with the bracken gold.

" It was worth while being a prisoner at Kyle-ron," I said happily, " and now I can go away contented. And how, think you, you will like Ardmair, Mistress Barbara?

And a plaid of the Mackenzie tartan? Och, you will like it at once, *mo chridhe*, dear one of my heart, when you see the fine folk that step about in it—my mother and my father and Tearlach and all of them. Do you know, I have not been thinking about them so much of late, for it has been your face that has been coming between me and my sleep."

Suddenly from a branch at our heads came an outburst of song that made us glance up startled.

" Where is he? " asked Barbara, peering among the branches.

" He is above your head—a blue-bonnet. When nearly all the birds are silent, he is the one will sing for you. Is he not the noisy lad, for the small size of him? "

" He is no bigger than my brooch, but his happiness is so big he cannot hold it."

We laughed at him, for we were happy too.

" What is he saying, do you think, Alastair? "

That was the first time she had called me Alastair, and I had never liked my name so well.

" Do you not know? He is repeating our old saying, ' Dark is the berry but ripe; dark is my lassie but bonny.' "

" What nonsense you talk! I have no looks at all. Nancy is the bonny one. And blue-bonnets know nothing at all about lassies."

" This one does. Hear to him! He is saying, ' *Mo chridhe, mo chridhe, mo chridhe*,' over and over."

" Is he then? Well, I am thinking he should not cry it to the winds. But you, who can read the birds' song so readily, do you not think it sounds more like scolding?"

" So it does now," I said glibly. " He is scolding me for leaving you behind. Barbara, what would hinder you to come? Come away with me, this morning, at once."

Her eyes were downcast. She shook her head sadly.

" It would not be right for me to go just now, and you know it. And oh! Alastair, we have been forgetting that we are enemies, you and I. My father will never let me go to you."

Faith, I had indeed been forgetting the hostility between Ardmair and Kyle-ron. I felt as if a cold wind had suddenly blown between us.

But I was not the one to wait for any man's permission to take what should be mine, and " the young cub," as he had called me, would show William Mackay that he had claws.

" I will take you without asking him," I answered boldly. " I will come back for you and steal you away."

" Fear is on me, Alastair, that I will never see you again."

There was a break in her voice and tears were in her eyes now.

" I will come back for you, *mo chridhe*, as soon as may be. As sure as the sun is rising, I will come for you or send for you. You can be very sure you will see me again."

I laughed at her fears and raised her chin with my free hand.

" Do you not trust a man with fair hair? "

" Och, that! " she said, laughing back at me. " I knew you were listening yon day. I saw you turn your head. No! Nancy did not know, but I did."

" You knew, little enemy? Then you will pay for that saying."

And she paid till she took back her words.

" Am I cruel, as you said? "

" Och yes, you are! No, then, I should not have said it. You are not."

" And what made you dislike me? "

" I never did dislike you. I liked you from the first moment I saw you standing yonder. But what was the need to let you know that? "

There was a hint of Nancy in the look she gave me under her eyelashes.

" But we quarrelled at times," I said, astonished, " like seamaws after the same herring."

" Well, then, is it not the fine thing to have got all our quarrelling by? "

Rubbing her cheek against my shoulder, she added: " Oh, Alastair, would it not be the beautiful thing now if you were just coming instead of going? "

Suddenly her look changed to alarm.

" The tide! Look at the tide. I will never get back."

I picked her up and carried her through the ford, she meanwhile giving me directions for my journey.

" Make for Loch Shin and the Mackenzie country. Go by the Crask, and run now. How foolish we have been."

" Not a bit of it," I said, setting her on her feet. " How wise we were to delay our parting to the last possible minute. Hear to that blue-bonnet. ' Give her one more kiss,' says he, and so I will, *Beannachd leat mo ghraidh* (Farewell, my darling)."

I pushed back through the ford, where the tide was now running strong, and I had to struggle against it. I turned again and again to wave. The last look I got of Barbara, she was standing just as I left her.

CHAPTER V

Farewell to Ardmair

IN those days I could run, few better, but that morning I ran as if Death himself were after me and his breath on my neck. I had spent some time at the ford. I was glad I had spent it to such profit, but I had to win it back. In case some should come after me from the castle, I had to stretch the miles between them and me, and that would be better done before it was full day.

After stepping the tussocks through bog and rushes, I made for the ridge, bearing well away from the crofts. Though as yet there seemed to be no life stirring about them, this was not the time I would feel most at my ease to meet anyone. The Mackenzie tartan would not be too welcome among the Mackays since the foray, and the news of it would have spread far by this time, for in the north whisper a story in Dornoch and it will be in Skye ahead of you, however fast you travel.

I knew Ben Clibreck, and if I steered for him I would be about right for Lairg. At first, scattered clumps of dwarf trees offered a chance of concealment, but once I had skirted the foot of Loyal, five-headed giant and noblest of all the bens of the north, I was in a country with no cover whatever. I slowed to a trot and thus travelled a vast moor, torn in two by a rough track that lost itself in the sky ahead—weary, weary miles, where I seemed to stand still or travel backwards, so like was one bit of road to the other.

Early I passed a band of Egyptians about to break

camp. They were in a large hollow on the side of the track, and some bairns, shaggy as collie dogs and almost stark naked, ran out and stood in my way offering horn spoons for sale. The men, a murderous-looking crew, eyed me appraisingly, and the women, busy about the scraping of pots, held out skinny hands, the colour of earth, and, in a lingo I could make nothing of, appeared to offer me a fortune in exchange for silver. But I knew my fortune, or thought I did, and I cried a laughing greeting to them, saying I was in haste and would see them some other time. The weight of my father's sword was a welcome burden to me till I was well past their camping-ground.

I came on but one clachan of any size that day. It was sheltered by trees, stood near a loch and had a change-house from which a fine pillar of smoke was rising, making me think of a good meal cooking. But I skirted the clachan without stopping. The needy must keep moving and so must he that travels in hostile country. I was needy enough, for I had not a doit. I had, however, a few handfuls of meal given by Barbara. Some of this I mixed in the heel of my brogue with water from a burn, and on again I went, ready for any-thing. By sunset I was no longer able to make the same speed, but " Lairg before nightfall " I kept saying to myself, and Lairg before nightfall I found.

Oh, the beauty of that road dropping to Loch Shin! I was glad to see ling and bracken again after the miles of deer-grass and rushes, though bracken and ling alike were dead. But there was the island in the loch, the real one a crown upon the one shadowed in the water, and the lights of the houses told me I was again among my own people.

Next morning, having borrowed a horse, I set out to

ride through Strath Oykell. A fine strath this, well
wooded and well watered, and I rode quietly, not pushing my beast, and stopped at a ford of Oykell, the very
ford crossed by the Great Marquis in his last desperate
journey. There I spent the night, returning the garron
to Lairg and setting out early next morning on foot by
a wild and lonely path through the mountains, going by
Loch Damh. I was the gay lad when I saw the sun gleam
on the Rhidorrach Water, for then I was almost within
sight of home. Whistling a lively port, and dreaming
brightly of the future, I stepped briskly down Glen Achall,
every pool of the river, every tree and boulder, known
to Tearlach and myself. When I had last passed this
way the leaves of the rowan-trees were green and the
berries were hanging red. Now berries were scattered
and branches were bare. Bracken gold was tarnished
and spent, bowed in draggled heaps. The heather rang
its rusty bells in a dirge for its vanished purple, and
cannoch flags flew tattered and stained. I stopped my
whistling and shivered, as a foreboding of trouble
gripped me.

Less than an hour later I came down the hillside
upon Ardmair House. I heard the sound of churning,
and looking through the window saw my mother at the
making of butter, but sadly, with no gay lilt to hasten
its coming. As my shadow fell across the pane she
looked up, put her hand to her mouth and stepped back,
staring at me out of eyes big with dread. I ran indoors
and threw my arms about her.

" Now, God be praised for this! " she cried brokenly.
" Alastair, is it yourself? I thought——"

" I know fine what you thought," said I. " I read it
in your eyes."

" I thought I saw a fore-vision come to tell me of

your death," she said, trembling, tightening her grip on me. " God be praised it is not so! "

" No vision, mother, but a hungry man," said I, sitting in at the table. " Nothing but a little drammach at dawn have I had this day."

" But, Alastair, how are you here? " she asked, hurrying to lay food before me.

" That tale can wait till I have eaten," I answered.

She hung about me while I ate, as mothers will, attending to my needs, asking if I were well, if I had been well cared for, and a dozen other questions.

" My father does not seem to have been in a hurry to have me home," I said, between mouthfuls.

I spoke carelessly, but in my heart was that gnawing little pain of disappointment.

" What do you mean? " she demanded.

" Only that I thought he would have tried to rescue me long ago. But it seems I was not worth rescuing."

" Alastair," she said sternly, " do not let me hear you talk like that. Surely you know your father better. He has been very ill, so ill that even yet he is lying upstairs, never out of bed."

" But we set his arm on the way home," I said defensively, for that piece of news rebuked me for my distrust.

" Yes, but the wound would not heal," she explained. " Poison must have got to it, for the arm swelled and put him in such a fever that he would not know me. We did everything for him we could think and he only tossed and cried out the more. It was only after big Johan cut his nails and, saying a spell, buried them away, that the Devil let him have peace. She says if the wound had been in his hand instead of in his arm, the Devil would have had more power and your father would have

E

died. But I doubt," she finished sadly, "that he will never swing sword again."

I unbuckled slowly the sword I had carried home so gladly, and looked long at it, as it lay on the table. So I had narrowly missed not seeing my father again! And how would I have felt towards the Mackays if the worst had happened?

But my hurt was not yet healed.

"Tearlach?" I questioned. "I have a cousin I would have gone to rescue from the pit itself, had he needed me. But he would not stir a foot for me, seemingly," I ended bitterly.

"Alastair, be still! It was all we could do to keep Tearlach from going after the message came."

"That I was well? You mean that message?"

"No! The message from William Mackay—that if your father lifted a hand to rescue his son, there would be no son to rescue. You were to be killed if a Mackenzie crossed his march while he was away. His sentries had their orders, and they would obey him. Meanwhile, he promised you would come to no harm. Tearlach went to Brahan to speak with Seaforth, but Seaforth was in Edinburgh. We were waiting till he returned before we could act. What more could Tearlach do?"

"Nothing! I see it all now. I understand why the castle was feebly manned, why Callum was careless of posting a sentry at the gate at night. Elsewhere there were sentries, and it does not need a garrison to guard one unarmed man. Och, it will be a big disappointment to William Mackay when he finds his guest wearied of his entertainment and took the road."

I laughed, and rose to my feet.

"Can I see my father now?"

"I will find out if he is sleeping still." My mother

turned at the door and came back. " But you have not told me, son, how you came here."

" I came on my ten toes, mother, except for a bit of Strath Oykell that I travelled on four legs."

" Alastair, you must always be joking. You provoke me. Tell me, did you escape? "

" Well, you see, mother, William Mackay has a daughter. In fact, he has two, but one of them does not matter just now. The other one, Barbara, matters a great deal. Yonder is a girl, now, whose like is not in all Albyn. She it was helped me to escape."

" That was kind of her," my mother said primly, " only the wish is strong in me that my son would not talk so warmly of every young woman he meets."

" And do I? When, then, have you heard me praise one more than another? Before they were all alike, but now I have found the one girl—what is the matter? "

" What are you saying, Alastair? What are you saying? You are not telling me that the one girl is the daughter of William Mackay? "

She sat down heavily, and on the hand that gripped the edge of the table the knuckles showed white. Her eyes burned in a face gone suddenly deathly pale.

" That is what I am telling you. I know her father is my father's enemy, but——"

" The daughter of William Mackay! Oh, my son, my son! "

" Mother, if you saw her, if you could only speak with her——"

She moved her lips, but no words came. She sat rigid, clutching the table edge with stiff fingers, staring at me out of those burning eyes. I could not recognize this distraught woman as the mother who had never failed me before.

" I know you think evil of her father, but a black ewe may have a white lamb, and William Mackay has a daughter whom you would be proud to call your daughter. I am going to bring her to you——"

" Stop ! " Her voice shook, with anger I thought. " You shall not marry the daughter of William Mackay."

My head went up.

" I will do just that. I have promised to go for her, and a Mackenzie does not break his word."

" You shall not marry this girl. Oh, Alastair, Alastair, was there no girl in all Ross-shire you could have chosen? Any one I would have welcomed that you brought to me. Katherine——"

" Katherine is like a sister to me. I want but the one girl and her name is Barbara Mackay."

Suddenly my mother gave way. She put arms on the table, and laid her head on her arms, and I knew that she was weeping. But I was not sorry for her, only proud and sore. I walked to the window and stood looking out at the bay, but not seeing it.

After a long, dragging silence she lifted her head and said quietly: " Alastair, come here and sit down. You do not know the reason of your father's hatred of William Mackay. Well, you shall hear the story, and judge for yourself between him and us, and decide what you must do."

She went upstairs to tell my father I had returned, and, I suppose, to acquaint him with the pitiful mistake I had made of loving in the wrong place.

" They should have told me before," I said, kicking the peats on the hearth savagely, " if they had anything to tell."

Of the final interview with my father I do not care to think. I am not proud of the way I acted, for I grieved him deeply by my obstinacy and self-will. He was greatly changed. Sickness had laid a heavy hand on him, and I found him hollow-cheeked and wan, weakened so that he could scarce lift a frail hand to greet me.

It was with the ghost of his former robust voice that he said: " It is indeed you, Alastair. Thankful am I to see you safe home, boy, for I have blamed myself hourly for taking you with me on the foray. Your mother said no good would come of it, and she was right. It was ill-timed and ill-planned. A score that had waited so long to be settled might well have waited a little longer. I should have schemed for a sure reckoning rather than a quick one, and I might have known a warning would go ahead of us through the McLeods, after our seeing the watcher in the corrie.

" You need not blame yourself, father. They did me no harm."

" Aye, they did you harm if it is as your mother says and you have set your heart on one of yon evil brood."

" Father, whatever you have against the man, I will not allow you to speak against Barbara."

He laughed feebly.

" Why do you laugh? " I demanded.

" It is not mirth that makes me laugh, but the strangeness of the thing that it is my son who champions the daughter of yon viper. Be very sure of one thing, Alastair: he will never consent to give her to you."

" I shall not ask him," I said defiantly. " I shall bring her here in spite of him."

" You will not bring her here."

" That will I."

" You shall not bring her here. There can be no home found in Ardmair for that young woman. It is time you heard what your mother has to say."

He looked to my mother, who was standing at his hand.

" Tell him!" he commanded, and closed his eyes, exhausted.

And she told me a story that changed the look of the world for me and sent me out from home with a black rage against my father's enemy, a resolve that some day I would meet him, and that after the meeting only one of us would remain alive—a story that showed me I had better try to put Barbara out of my thoughts.

When she had finished I stood staring at nothing, hearing only a girl's voice, with a sob in it, say: " Fear is on me, Alastair, that I shall never see you again," and my own braggart answer.

Dhe ! What a liar she would think me.

I saw my dreams scattered like mist before a driving wind, and in that moment I decided to leave home and seek service abroad.

Vainly my father pleaded with me to wait till he was better, saying that he needed my help more than ever, that no one could so well market his salmon and his herring in Inverness, that Finlay had plenty to do with the cattle to look after; but I listened to him with my eyes fixed on a crack in the wall above his head and refused to give way.

" Wait only till I am stronger, and go then if you still want to," he urged me.

" You must manage without me," I returned roughly. " I am going now."

" Then go, if you must, and God go with you, Alastair," he said sadly. " Take the Mackenzie sword. I will not be needing it again. Musket and dirk I still may use, but the bone of my arm was badly set, and the play of the sword will be barred to me in the days to come."

My mother turned from the window, tears in her voice as well as on her lashes, and laid a pleading hand on my arm:

" Alastair, if you go, you take the light from this house. You must know that. Can you not bide; at least till your father is on his feet again? "

" No, I cannot," I cried impatiently. " How can I settle to the old quiet ways after this? I must keep doing something different—fighting, marching, seeing different lands. It is no use speaking," I finished dourly.

There was a long silence, in which I felt their eyes on me, and so kept mine following the crack up to the ceiling, not wanting to meet their gaze.

Then: " When will you be wishing to start? " my mother asked quietly.

" At once," I returned shortly. " Without any further loss of time. The sooner I am on my way the better."

She shook her head and led the way downstairs, while my father repeated his farewell: " God go with you, Alastair."

" God be with you," I said low, and stumbled down the stair after my mother.

It did not take long to make my few preparations. I went to saddle a garron, and, hard task, to say good-bye to my dog. I could tell him what I could not tell my parents and let him see what I tried to hide from them. He listened with an understanding look, and if his neck was wet when I left the stable I must say in my defence that I was only seventeen, which is not a great age after all, though then I thought myself very much of a man, and was ashamed of my weakness.

I did not linger over my farewell to my mother, for she had a look on her face I feared I had written there, and I did not want to read it often. With a last kiss from the saddle I was off, trotting quickly past the crofts and hoping with all my heart that none would stop me to ask questions. Some I pretended not to see, and when Katherine came to her door, and cried how pleased they were to see me back, I waved my bonnet silently and rode by. I left her shading her eyes with her hand and looking after me puzzled. I was minding yon bright day I had tossed her the little fish, the day William Mackay had ridden through Ardmair, leaving trouble behind him.

I took over the hill to Rhu, on the shore of Loch Broom, for I had to see Tearlach. He ran out of the house like an overjoyed puppy and nearly bore me to the ground with his boisterous welcome. I answered his questions as patiently as I could, and then abruptly asked him if he would come with me, as we had often planned, to fight in the foreign wars. He was plainly taken aback and stammered excuses, going red in his efforts to explain his refusal.

" I see, I see, Tearlach. It was only talk. You never meant to come."

" I swear I did, Alastair. I would come now, if—if only—— You see, there is someone who might not be willing for me to go," he blurted finally.

A light dawned on me.

" A girl, Tearlach!" I said, astonished. " But I might have known. You would be the one to stay with the women rather than march with the men."

That was not a fair saying and I knew it, but, then, I was not caring whether I spoke the truth or not.

He glared at me for a moment, then asked quietly: " Can you tell me what has happened to my Cousin Alastair? Maybe you will know him."

" Whatever in the world do you mean?" I demanded.

" I had a cousin, as blithe and kind a lad as there was in Ross-shire. He went away and there has come to me now a stranger, bitter and scowling, and I am wondering where he has buried the lad I knew."

My eyes fell and I busied myself adjusting a stirrup rope.

" Who is the girl, Tearlach, who would keep you from me? " I asked, not looking at him.

" Katherine."

I stared at him, dumbfounded. Merry little Katherine, with the saucy tongue and the hard heart, in love with Tearlach! I could not believe it. I had been conceited enough to think she had a fondness for myself.

" I am sure I wish you both well," I said, not able to take my eyes off him, trying to see him as a douce married man, and finding in him something different from the old Tearlach.

" I am thinking it is a woman who has helped at the killing of my cousin," he said, on his side observing me as closely.

" Why should you think that? " I demanded. " Your tongue is running away with you."

" You are running away from a woman, if I know the signs, and I believe you are wise. You know the saying, ' The stone which my foot meets not, hurts me not.' "

" Wisdom at second-hand," I said scornfully. " It is new for Tearlach to give advice, like an old man. Well, since you will not come with me, I must go alone. Good-bye, Tearlach. Keep close about the house, for practice."

I gave a laugh, not my old easy laugh, but one with a drop of venom in it, I envying him his happiness. I mounted, wheeled the garron and jogged off, but halted at a shout. Tearlach was panting after me, and when alongside thrust into my hand his fine Doune pistol that I had admired so much in our young, daft days in Aberdeen. I did not know how to thank him, and he had no words to say as he gifted it. We clasped hands, a strong, warm grip that hurt, and yet it lightened the bitterness that lay at my heart.

I followed the Alltyre burn, in whose pools I had guddled, along with that same Tearlach, many a plump little trout, and was following the ridge on the other side when I heard a whine.

"Dileas!" I turned in my saddle to find he had followed me, my deer-hound I had since when he was a puppy. I sat looking down at him, not knowing what to do. Here, at least, was one friend who wanted to come with me.

"You cannot come. Home, boy."

I waved an arm towards Ardmair. He sat on his hunkers and looked me steadfastly in the eyes, but never a move he made to turn about—unusual, for at all times he obeyed my lightest word.

"Go back, Dileas. Home!"

I turned quickly and put my horse through the ford. Half-way up the next long rise I looked back, and there he was at the heels of the garron. This time I threatened him, stormed at him, and ordered him back roughly, but he paid no heed. I thought then of leaving him somewhere. But I could not turn back with him to Tearlach, for would not that have been an unlucky start for a journey, and we were already on the outskirts of the Macdonalds of Loch Broom, whose lands, since near a hundred years, Seaforth held. They bore no love to the Mackenzies. But, indeed, for whom had the Macdonalds any love? Once the greatest clan in the Highlands, under the Lord of the Isles, now broken into factious remnants, children of Ishmael, their hand was against every man and every man's hand against them. No! The Macdonalds could not be trusted even with a dog belonging to a Mackenzie.

" Come then, if you must," I said with a grin, " and share what fortune brings."

He frisked round the garron with a leap and a bark, and then was off, trotting ten paces ahead.

By the time I had walked the garron up the long hill that gives the first sight of the head of Loch Broom it was late in the afternoon. In sullen grandeur the day was dying, and from the west he was making his last bequests. On the massive grey head of Ben Dearg he set a fiery crown, and scattered crimson streamers across the eastern sky. On a twin peak of the great An Tealach he flung a beam as bright as noonday and filled the mighty corrie below with shadow of deepest blue. He drew a cloak of velvet about the shoulders of the Braes. The far hills of Harris he called from the clouds and gave them form and boldness. The summer Isles he dowered with mystery and set them black in a molten sea. Then lower and lower over the rim of the world he slipped, his flaring, reddened eye peering to the last at the land he was leaving. And at his passing the waters of the Minch were dyed as with waves of blood. The day was dead.

The day was dead, and what a day it had been. Begun so happily in Strath Oykell, how drearily had it gone. No more whistling of ports; no longer ardent haste. Could it be possible that eager lad, so pleased with the world, was the same with myself now? Oh, that we could always end a day with as light a heart as we begin it! Oh, that the castles we build in the air did not crash in ruins while yet we are piling stone on stone!

The day was dead. Soon the year would be dead. And dead was my old glad life.

Heavy clouds, the very colour of smoke, were massing behind me. Saddle Mountain was putting on a stormy nightcap, and he is the one who tells us our weather. I did not like the look of the sky; it had been too red in the east. I flicked the garron with the rein and pushed on.

CHAPTER VI

Across the Dirrie More

I

I MADE good speed up the shores of Loch Broom past Ardcharnich, where a keen evening wind began to rustle the dead leaves on the hazels, and sour-faced, resentful Macdonalds gloomed at me under their bonnets.

A pair of whooper swans winged south over my head, whistling loudly, beating the air with their powerful pinions. A sure sign of wild weather that!

Storm clouds were piling up behind me, but the last wash of daylight still trickled among the pine trunks as I breasted Braemore, high above Corriehalloch, that deep gorge, where the rocky walls, clothed with dripping ferns, fall sheer for over two hundred paces to the ribbon of river below, and the sides so close a desperate man might undertake to leap across. A buzzard sat, omen-like, on a storm-riven pine, and the thunder of the Measach Falls came to me above the rush of wind through the tossing pine roof overhead.

As I came out on the Dirrie More, the great waste which stretches to the shores of Loch Garve, the wind leaped at me, and with it came stinging snowflakes, driven as a wedge between the ranges of An Tealach and Ben Dearg, sweeping among the rushes by the track, twanging them like harp strings, hissing among the heather tops and swirling in a mad dance in the hollows.

But the force of the blast was at my back and drove me onwards pleasantly enough until the snow began to pack in

drifts. Night came riding apace on the heels of the storm,
and I began to think it were madness to attempt the track
to Altguish that night, and had thought of returning to
the shelter of the pines above Braemore when a whimpering cry came from the lee of a boulder by the track.

" God save me! " I cried, the hair rising on my neck,
and the legs of me hanging limp as strands of dulse. But
the beast under me gave never a snort nor made a quiver,
and thinks I, if that was the cry of a urisk, then it is a
queer night for him to be out in, for the fairy-folk, as I
have always heard, appear mostly in the light of the moon
or in the calm of the midsummer evening.

I looked at Dileas and he stood sniffing forward, but
with no sign of fear, and on the whimper coming again
he trotted round the boulder. Then I knew that sound
for no urisk note, but the cry of a child.

I was off the garron in an instant, and peering in the
half-light behind the boulder found a woman with an
infant hugged to her breast, but scantily wrapped in her
plaid. I whipped off the blankets we use for saddle, and
made shift to cover them, but the woman was stiff already
with the chill, and would soon be off in her last sleep,
unless heat were got to her soon.

Then I remembered how a traveller, hopelessly lost
in a blizzard one night on that same Dirrie More, had
disembowelled his horse, crawled inside the carcass and
passed the hours of the storm in safety. The same might
save the lives of these two helpless folks. But I could
not bring myself to take that course.

I wheeled the garron and urged him swiftly into the
teeth of the gale on the home track. But my reckless
hurry was like to be the undoing of me. The garron's
shoes balled up with snow, and coming to a hard, wind-
swept bit of the moor, he slid the length of it, like a

sledge, legs splayed out, finally coming down with a crash. I shot over his head and burrowed in a drift. The beast was on his feet before me, but when I went to mount—my sorrow, he was dead lame! Without loss of time, leaving him to follow slowly, I set out to walk the road for help.

Dileas put his nose to the track and led the way back. It was not difficult to know the general direction to travel, for the wind whooped straight in from Loch Broom, but without Dileas I would have wandered wide, for the gale buffeted me till I travelled like a horse with the staggers, and not until I tried the trick of running forward during the lulls did I make sure progress. The roar of the wind in the pines above the gorge was a welcome sound to me, and when I came under their shelter my ear-drums rang with the stillness of the wood, that had the quiet of a kirk compared with the howling bedlam beyond. Not that the wood was really silent, for the loftier branches boomed and creaked and a shower of dead cones tumbled about my ears.

A light shone in one of the houses and without waiting I pulled up the latch and entered with a flurry of snow-flakes.

The room was loud with the sound of the chanter. 'Twas a night of *ceilidh* and the piper was holding the floor, while two lassies were stepping it right smartly in a dance to his playing. I stood for a moment to get my breath before the piper noticed me. The wind fled from his drones and they clattered on his elbow, the while his mouth and eyes opened wider and wider.

" God preserve us! 'Tis the wraith of murdered John of Cnocdhu! " shrieked one of the dancers, flinging her apron over her head.

For a minute the room was in an uproar. I wondered

at the reason of it, but it was not until later I learned that my face was streamed with blood from a cut on my brow. Certainly I must have appeared a fearsome visitant, shrouded in snow, blood spattered, with Dileas behind me draped in white, his two eyes gleaming in the light of the cruisie.

"*Beannachd Dhia air an tigh*" (The blessing of God on the house), I said. "There's a woman and a bairn on the Dirrie More."

A stillness fell on the company and I repeated my words.

"Who is she?" quavered a crone, sitting on a stool over against the wall, again making the sign of the cross.

"I do not know, but if help does not reach her soon she and the little one will perish."

"What tartan is she of?" asked the piper, now scowling at me for having had him at advantage.

"Tartan! I did not see. What matter?"

"She'll be Duncan Roy's wife from Ardcharnich," cried a maid sitting next the crone. "She would be over to her sister at Dundonell and storm-taken on her way home. Quick, Padruig, gather the lads. Move, man, or the women will take the road before you."

Padruig dropped the pipes in her lap, and took past me for the door.

I beat the caked snow from my trews and plaid.

"Sit you," said the *cailleach*, turning a peat-creel over by her side. "Ishbel, a drink to the stranger, and water for the washing."

A coggin of hot ale, with honey in it, was put in my hand, and I had scarce finished when the piper was back with five Macdonalds, lanky hounds of the hills, not an ounce of spare flesh among them, ill rakers to meet at the wrong end of a dirk or broadsword.

"Where is she?" questioned the leader, a man outstandingly tall.

"In the lee of the big stone on the west side of the track beyond Corriehalloch, wrapped in my blankets."

"Length of good life to you," wished the *cailleach*. "Was that not the good deed!"

I rose to go with them, but the leader pressed me down on the stool. "No need. No need. We know the spot. Cuchullin's stone, we name it."

"You will not find it to-night. It is raging like the furies out there, and the stone will be buried." Then a thought came to me. "My dog! He will find her."

"Well thought on! Will he travel with us?"

"With you, but not of you." And, pointing to the door: "Find her, Dileas," I ordered.

The tall one bent to lay a hand on him.

"Stop!" I cried, not a moment too soon. "Do not lay a hand on him, or he'll slash the fingers off you. He is a one-man dog, and only my mother and I dare touch him."

"All the better dog for that," was the reply.

"Go, Dileas," I again commanded, and Dileas stalked stiffly through the company for the door.

The *cailleach* peered in my face. "You'll be Alastair Mackenzie, the left-handed, of Ardmair."

"The same, good mother; but you have not seen me before."

"Sheila Macdonald sees much without seeing and hears much without hearing. You're a skilly lad with the pipes. Is it not so? Give us a spring."

"Not yet. It may be a lament the night will be hearing and a keening in the house of Duncan Roy."

"Och, ye croaker! It is not a night in the snow will

F

kill a Macdonald. Roy's wife will be about the milking before a week is out. I know her hour is not yet."

A platter of deer's flesh was brought me and before I had finished there was a whine outside and Dileas burst in, shaking the snow from his coat. The women flocked to the door and waited the slower-moving party pressing in from the night.

" All well," sang out the leader. " As warm as an egg in the nest, and the little one full of life."

He left the company and placed his hand in mine: " Macdonalds never forget. Some day Seumas Macdonald will repay."

" Faith," he continued, handing me my saddle-bags, " but that dog of yours is the queer one. He was not for leaving after we put Roy's wife to the blankets, and kept whining and digging in the snow over east of the way, until we came and found your gear. And then it was myself alone he would let carry it. Stay with us, and we will have a day on the hill with him. There is a great stag in the corries of An Tealach none of our dogs can turn to bay. I'll warrant he will do it, for he has a big heart."

" No," I said, " that is what he will not do. He will not face a hind, far less a stag. The hunting spirit of him was broken, from being loosed when little more than a puppy at a grown stag, and the life near crushed out of him against a burn bank. He is deer-shy, but will face anything else that walks or runs."

" My sorrow, but that is bad telling. The man was a fool that broke him."

" Not so! The man was my father," I said shortly.

The Macdonald saw my annoyance, and turning to the company covered the awkward moment.

" Are ye not the laggards? " he roared. " Here we

have a guest with us this night, who has done a great service to the Macdonalds, and you stand idly by listening to women's gossip. The pipes, Padruig! The pipes, man! Give us a spring and let the lilt lift the roof."

" Not I," returned Padruig, " the lad is a piper of note, and my thumb is staved through a slip coming down Braemore. Let him play."

He fondled his left thumb meaningly.

I smiled to myself, for when will you not hear the like of that story when strange pipers forgather?

" Shame on you, Padruig! Is it a Macdonald crying retreat before contest? Up with the drones, man, and give us, *Macdonald put the Brae on them*. No Macdonalds need be ashamed of that air, though 'twere played by a ranting caird." The crone raked him with her taunt.

So Padruig swung up the drones, and they roared braggart defiance on the new air but recently composed by Keppoch's pipers to celebrate their victory over the Macintosh clan at Mulroy.

This lad had the piper's gift, the quick lift and ripple on the chanter holes, fingers dancing soft and sure. I knew I was no match for him at the light music, especially with a strange right-handed stand of pipes.

So it was a pibroch I put to the chanter, the lament of Patrick Og, and the playing of it suited my mood.

" Faith, lad, you're into it, you can play the big music," broke in a man at my elbow. " Who learned you the art of it? I could not be staying longer away from here and you playing."

" Is he not the churl now? " said a lass, with dancing mischief on her tongue. " Three pretty women here and never a mention of them. Play again, sirs, 'twas only the pipes Ian came to hear."

" Och, sure and it was not," drolled Ian. " But are

the pipes not just like the lassies? Neglect them and they like it ill. The best place for each is the crook of the arm."

"Fairly spoken," laughed the lass. "Has he not the honeyed tongue?" and she gave him a mock curtsy.

So with song, dance and story the evening passed quickly, and I found myself taken to the hearts of these folk.

Just before the *ceilidh* ended, a man appeared at the doorway.

"Is't Duncan Roy?" cried a woman. "How is the good wife now and the little one?"

"Fine! Fine!" said Duncan.

"The little one would be thinking it was another dip in the burn he was getting to harden him," chaffed Seumas. "He will be a thrusting lad yet. But here is the one you seek."

He brought Duncan forward to me, and the grip he took of my hand spoke more than words.

"When do you journey?" he asked.

"Morning."

"So soon? My house is yours, for as long as you care to stay."

"I thank you," I said, "but I leave in the morning."

"Very well," said he, "the finest garron in the glen will be at the door here for you."

I was given a bed on the floor by the side of the smoored fire, but sleep was long in coming. Dileas, stretched at my feet, slumbered peacefully, except for an occasional twitch and quickening of the breath. Was he, like me, dreaming of good days that would return no more?

I lay watching the dull glow, the thin curl of smoke from the gathering peat, the shadows playing on the

walls, the light flickering on the glistening, smoke-
blackened cabars, the feathers of soot that hung from
every sapling branch and heather twig of the thatch.

In the ben of the house, a roosting hen, waking
suddenly, flapped angry wings and complained drowsily
about her perch. A cow stirred restlessly, rustling her
bedding of dried bracken, scraping her horns against the
boards of her stall.

At the far end of the big room, huddled under blankets,
lay the still forms of my host and some of those who
had been of the merry company. Sound sleepers all! I
had tormenting thoughts to keep me awake, while I lay
there at the hearth of these Macdonalds, the bitterest
enemies of my clan.

Into such strange places does fortune, blindfolding us
at the start, lead us by paths not of our choosing, by
chance encounters we have no power to avoid.

II

Morning broke bright and clear. The storm battalions
had drummed their way up the glen, leaving calm
behind. The snow that had invested the night with
terror now robed the day with beauty. So blue the sky,
so white the world, it seemed that all the billowy clouds
had sailed to earth to form that silent tideless sea. The
dark pines above Braemore had changed their sombre
plumes for the gay feathers of a cavalier. Loch Drum
wore the fetters of a light frost. The Glascarnoch, grey
and swollen, chafed its way between piled drifts. About
the tree roots ran the tracks of questing fox and marten,
the dainty prints of small birds. Pools of black shadow
lay about the foot of boulders, heavily crusted with snow
to leeward, lightly dusted to windward. But the long

expanse of the Dirrie More was overlaid with a dazzling whiteness that blinded. And in all the stillness of the shrouded world only a pair of hoodies moved, raking the mountain slopes relentlessly for food. They would see to it that the storm, which had brought death to the weak, would bring life to them.

At Altguish I rested for an hour before taking the road for Garve. Already the drifts were lessening, for the storm driving from the north-west had spent its rage on the high tops round Ben Dearg. At other times the track we followed would be by the Glascarnoch, but now the moorlands were soft, so it was the hill road by Lochan Breac I had to take, which meets the main drove road by Strathcarron and Loch Luichart, the road of the Islesmen and the wild McRaes from beyond *Bealach-nam-bo*.

So as evening fell I came down on the township by Loch Garve. Standing as it does, a day's journey from Inverness, there is hardly a night in the year but travellers to or from the west and north-west will be found at its doors, and even news from abroad may be had here a few days out of Holland and France. At the back-end too, when the cattle droves are coming to the Muir of Ord markets, a thrang place it is, with a score of drover lads crowding the change-house, making the night winds beat with the sound of piping and song. Or if you would seek a quarrel, that is the place and then the time to find it, for never a drover lad but carries a ready dirk to meet a careless word.

Often enough the Ardmair cattle rested there, and almost from my toddling days I travelled with the droves. More nights than I can mind I have spent in jovial company among the cattle folk. The harvest being gathered and the summer toil ended, it was our last jaunt from home before the coming of the long winter nights.

Now I was never the one to steer shy of the women-folk, and a *ceilidh* with the lassies around is very fine in its way, but its way is different from the ways of men when they forgather for a roistering night in a roadside tavern. There is a careless abandon in menfolk at these times, that speeds the happy hours. Tearlach, who at a home *ceilidh* will sit glowering in the corner, with but a cheep in his thrapple, then roars in a lusty chorus, or steps up readily enough with a song of his own. Never a pressing is needed for Finlay to tune up the Jews'-trump or for Murdoch to thrash a rant out of the landlord's old fiddle, and if the quality of entertainment is sometimes poor, then, faith, it makes up for it in quantity.

But no sound of merriment came from its doors that evening as I led the garron round the back and tied it under a lean-to. One traveller alone occupied the room, and he never lifted his head to look at me when the landlord laid before me oatcakes, butter and a whang of green ewe-cheese, and put a tankard at my elbow.

" A bad day for travel," the landlord said, inviting himself to a seat beside me, and calling for another beaker.

" It is so," I said, " but easier here than farther west. The storm blew itself out before it reached here."

" You are travelling east then? "

Now I knew well enough my host was curious to know the reason of my journeying, but such is the courtesy of our people that never the blunt, direct question as to business will be thrown at one. Had I desired to keep my affairs private, then a change of talk would have ended all further prying, and the rebuff would have been taken in good part. And that I think is all to our credit, for yonder in the burgh lands of the south they have a way with them of asking a man's business in no uncertain fashion, and if not getting satisfaction for their idle curiosity will have the stranger haled before a magistrate to answer anent his doings. Verily a man has little freedom in the towns, where the stranger is looked on with suspicion. So I answered him readily enough.

"Abroad!" he repeated, with surprise. "Holland or France?"

"The foreign wars I was thinking of."

"A dollar Mackay? Surely never!"

"Perhaps so, with a change of name, for no Mackenzie could serve with the Dutch Scots, but maybe French service will suit my wants."

"Now is it not fine to be wandering and see the world?" he said. "Yet they tell me the soldier sees little of the lands he travels in, and the happiest sight of all to him is at the bend of the road in the glen when he gets his first glimpse of home. There is only one ending to all roads—home. But why seek foreign wars? If rumour be true we may be seeing war at home. Dutch William has landed, they tell me, and Mackay of Scourie with his regiment is in England."

Mackay and his Scots Brigade! Then William Mackay of that corps would be now in England.

"Scots wars never last long enough to keep a soldier of fortune in brogue money," I said aloud.

"No; not long!" he admitted. "But hot enough while they last, and one battle is plenty for some, for they never see another. My father went out with Montrose, and his bones are lying raven-picked somewhere in Campbell country. That's a side to war the young blade never thinks on."

" There will be no war," broke in the stranger, who had been listening to our talk. " King James has not a friend left at Court. Even his own family has deserted him, and the army has gone over to Prince William."

" But the Scots," protested the landlord. " They will not submit quietly to a foreigner usurping the throne of the Stuarts."

" The Whigs will see to that," said the other quietly. " The whole of the west county is in favour of it, and helped to plan that move."

" The Highlanders will not have it," I affirmed, with a show of heat.

He looked at me quizzically.

" Highlanders? The strongest clan, the Campbells, will be with Prince William, and for the others, they are too busy quarrelling among themselves ever to form a united front."

He put a sneer in his speech, which I disliked heartily.

" What warrant have you for that? " I asked.

" Common hearsay. I know little of the clans."

" Do not be so sure of it then," I countered. " If Seaforth or Lochiel takes the field, the others will come out."

" The Macdonalds would not serve under either," he stated.

And that being true enough I fell silent, for I would not admit he was right.

He smiled in a superior way, and I began to wonder what the man's business was in these parts. Was there already a move among the clans to gather, and if so, under what leader? I put the question to our host.

" None that I have heard of," he answered, " but given the leader, I agree with you, the clans will rise for King James."

"And what will that avail?" asked the stranger. "Neither the Highlandmen nor the Irish can ever hope to win against Prince William's forces. No! There will be no war," he ended decidedly.

"You seem to be very sure of it," our host said.

"Perhaps I am." He smiled in a knowing fashion, and suddenly changed the conversation to talk on commerce, the price of cattle, timber and salmon, of which he showed such knowledge as led me to think him some merchant man from Inverness or the south. But later, when I went out to see to the garron, our host followed me.

"What think you of him, there?" he asked, jerking a thumb towards the room.

"A merchant?"

"More than that if my guess is right. He is out to spy the land, but that lad is not brisk enough with the beaker to let his tongue loose. I doubt if we would ever learn his business. We'd best to bed."

Next morning saw me early on the road by Loch Garveside, through the pass of Rogie, by Muir of Ord, to Inverness, and it was full dark before I clattered over the new bridge and put up at an inn in Bridge Street.

I had but to arrange for the returning of the garron to Duncan Roy before turning in to spend my last night in Scotland. To-morrow, unless chance ruled otherwise, it would be farewell to the land of my fathers, for . . . perhaps for ever.

CHAPTER VII

I sail for Foreign Ports

COME morning I walked down the river-front to inquire after ship abroad.

Out in the firth, now sparkling in the sun, lay near a score of small but stately coasters, trim set in rig and spar, bowing and bobbing to each other like dames in a dance, as the jabble of the tide and a light west wind set them at variance, them not knowing bow from stern, and sailor-men hauling on anchor ropes, until they, the minxes, should settle to the pull of the tide.

Over their hulls the green sweep of the Black Isle, as we call it—though yon is no isle at all, where only the soil is black, and that with a rich fertility—lay basking in the sun, while the spars, clear cut against the northern sky, raked the head of Wyvis Ben.

I spoke to a tarpaulin who sat on a mooring stump, sucking a long-stemmed pipe, reeking like a morning fire.

" I want ship abroad."

He took the pipe from his mouth and looked me up and down.

" Abroad?   Carolinas or the Indies, now, ye'd be seeking? The world's a wide place, young man, and ye would better limit your choice a bit."

" Well, France I was thinking of."

" Plenty to choose from," and he waved his pipe towards the ships, now riding like a flock of gulls, head to tide. " But ye're at the wrong port for France. It's not everyone sails out of Ness abroad.   The Port o'

Leith now! Ye might get passage there, but not from
Inverness. These ships trade mostly coast-ways. But
the *Cromarty Lass* there, loading at the quay, goes out
on the next tide. Ask of her master, a Munro out of
hungry Dornoch. If it's passage ye want, and have
enough of the ready, Murdo Munro's not the man to
refuse."

" Will he land me in France? "

" He'll land you in Jerusalem, if ye make it worth his
while," he said, with a chuckle.

" You know him? "

" I'm his mate, bo'sun and navigator all in one.
Come along and speak to him."

He rose and rolled down the quay, where the *Cromarty
Lass* lay swinging lightly to the tide, every landward roll
of her a creak of basket fenders.

The master stood at a hatch, directing a number of
seamen loading casks in her after-hold. His hair was in
a pig-tail and hung down on a greasy saffron shirt, open
to the waist, showing a sinewy sea-tanned chest, with
the edges of bulging shoulder muscles peeping under the
roll of the weave. A belt, loosely pulled, barely held up
the trousers, which rested in a pair of long sea-boots,
so there was no telling what the man was like below,
but I judged the trousers housed little but muscle and
bone. A pair of ear-rings dangled, and his lean face had
the ready opening of a laugh on it.

" Murdo," hailed his mate, " here's a young cock
from the glens wants passage to fortune."

" If he kens that same road, Davie, he's welcome to
navigate this sloop till fish come on land. I've been
looking for his like thirty years now. Come aboard."

I walked down the gangway and joined him.

" So," says he, looking at me, " where are ye for? "

" France."

He cast a quick look at Davie.

" We're for The Hague," he said, " but it's only a matter of a hundred and fifty knots down the coast to Le Havre. But if it was worth my while the business might be managed."

" How much would you say it was worth? " I asked.

" Say seven pounds, and a trick at the helm in calm weather—I'm short-handed this trip—and I'd consider it. Not another in the trade would look at ye for less than twenty."

" Three," I said, " for both of us," pointing to Dileas.

He burst into a jovial laugh. " Davie, heard ye ever the like? Ho-la! By the deep! Add the clan, and ask of me a guinea for taking you. No, no. Seven it is, and that's the McKillops' invitation. Take it or leave it."

I swung on my heel.

" Ship oar, man! " he bawled. " That is no way of making a bargain. Isn't he the dour Hielan' stot, Davie? " he said, in an aside.

" Well, four," I said, " and that's final."

He looked at me with a twinkle in his eye.

" Done," says he, " and Murdo with it. Four be it. Ye'd bargain the breeks off a Hindu, man, and that's what I never saw them wear. Where learned ye the trick o't? If Murdo but had it he'd be a rich man this day."

He spat on his palm and held out his hand. " A pound to seal it now."

I gripped and sealed the bargain.

" But, mind you, a pull at the ropes if needed, and a turn at the tiller by day."

" Fair enough," I said. " Foul or fair, I'll do my turn."

" Ye ken sailing? "

" Small boats, lug-sailed cobles. I have crossed the Minch in my father's boat."

" Heaven help us! Hear to him, Davie! The Minch in an open boat! Those Islesmen for the handling of small boats! I would not cross the Minch in an open boat for all the gold in India's temples, and, let me tell you, the roofs are flagged with the same."

" I am not an Isleman," I said. " I am a Mackenzie from the west coast, and often enough we cross in open boats. How other could we do it? "

" Avast, man. Ye make deep-sea sailors look like laddies paddling on a duck-pond. Get your gear and come aboard."

" When do you sail? "

" At flood, and we go out in the dark at that."

" Plenty time," Davie added, looking over the side.

I went to the inn, paid the reckoning and walked back to the harbour, where I passed the time pleasantly, for wherever ships and boats are I find interest enough for the longest summer day.

The *Cromarty Lass* now tugged at her moorings, hatches down, ready to warp out. Seen without the clutter of cargo about her decks she looked a small bit boat for the open sea. Single-masted, cutter-rigged, narrow in the beam, manifestly built for speed, she sat the water like a gull, neat in the trim, a trifle up by the bow, meeting every plash of the tide like a restive horse, and singing a happy glug-glug under her bows, as if longing for the ocean deeps.

" Well," sang out Murdo, head and shoulders out of a hatch, " what think ye of her? "

" I was admiring her trim. A fine boat."

" She's that and more. My little sloop can show her stern foam to the best of them. Give her a steady wind

with a bite of devil in it, and none can touch her. Just
wait you till we clear Whiteness and ye'll feel her
lift."

I jumped on deck and, handing Murdo my satchel,
slid below. A mixture of many smells assailed my nostrils.
Each boat has a distinctive smell of her own, and it would
puzzle one to guess the ingredients that go to its making.
The mouldy whiff of bilge, which has something both of
sea and land in it, whelms all. But swilling around in
forecastle and cabin are odours uncountable, a rumour
of tar and of damp cordage, a sniff of the galley, whiles a
cling of bygone fish, the salt tang of bleaching sea-wrack
drifting in at portholes, all making a queer compost of
smells, that clings to her like peat-reek to the tartan.

" Choose whichever bunk ye fancy," said Davie, pointing to two empty bunks in the small cabin. " Murdo
and I bunk here, the lads forward."

" The dog? " I questioned.

" He canna come in here," said Davie. " I mistrust
his looks, and I'm no' for the breeks chewed off me. I've
but the one pair."

" Well," I said, " I would better be on deck. I'll rig
up a shelter there."

" As ye will," agreed Murdo; " but mind ye, if we hit
wild weather, ye'll drench."

I searched around and found a place aft under the
boat-chocks, which would suit me well. With the help
of one of the sailor-men I had a cosy shelter of canvas
rigged.

" That'll gang ' pouf ' overboard, like an auld wife's
plaid, at the first blast o' real wind," said Davie.

" I'll chance it," I said.

" Och, ye're a match for Murdo there. He's aye
chancing things."

" Time they were here, Davie," said Murdo, coming
to our side and scanning the shore.

" Fully that! Another half-hour and we grate and
miss this tide."

Scarcely had he spoken when a string of ponies trotted
through the mirk, each with a couple of small casks on
his back.

" Quickly, lads! In with them," ordered Murdo.

I jumped ashore with the others and seized a keg.
Faith, but it was heavy! Gunpowder without a doubt,
and French kegs at that! What could Murdo be loading
that cargo for, and the sloop returning whence it came?
In less time than it would take to whistle a tune all were
on deck.

" Ye can row? " cried Murdo to me.

" Surely."

" Bundle then. Here, Jimmy! Into the boat with him
and warp her out."

I ran to the bow and slid down into the boat after
Jimmy. The thud of feet jumping aboard told me we
were cast off. A rope sang through the air. Jimmy quickly
tied it to the rowing-boat and we pulled into the tide,
until the rope sang to its tightening and her bow came
out across the stream. A few pulls more and the *Cromarty
Lass* was down on us. We cast off, sprang to the stern
and pulled ourselves aboard. Up went jib and mainsail.
She staggered, bucked the tide with a couple of resound-
ing smacks, then slid into the stream like a hot knife i to
butter, skimming a way between two anchored ships
with little more than the paint to spare.

" Davie, ye deevil," roared Murdo, " ye'll have my
sloop foundered one of these trips! Ye cut it over-fine
there."

Davie laughed and swung the tiller over a point.

" As sure as death," said Murdo to me, as we walked towards the bow, " Davie there's got a sixth sense. He can smell the land and take a boat out of a firth in blank darkness. I ken not how he does it, but, believe me, he'd navigate a boat through the neck of a bottle. Just watch him take a bearing on Craigton Point, and swing round Longman. It's deep, twenty fathom opposite Kessock, but shoals away on the east side of the firth, which calls for kittle steering. Yet Davie will swing her close on Longman, and then over for Munlochy Bay and the old run of the river on the west side."

" It is dark enough to see even now," I said.

" Davie doesna see. He feels her under him. An extra puff of wind when we come past Munlochy, and again at Avoch, just tells Davie where he is, like a blind fiddler tapping his way hame wi' a stick. Wait ye till we come up the firth and see him take her round Chanory. It's deep again at the Fairies' Gap, with little to spare, and if ye swing a ship there a point overmuch, and lose the wind in your sails, the roost will run her on the banks of Ardersier before ye can blink an eyelid."

Murdo left me, to see to the stowing of the last of the kegs.

" A bit cargo stuff I promised to land at the Port o' Leith for a friend," he said, referring to them. " Just an obligement! Pickings, man! Poor pickings! But a man like myself cannot afford to miss a chance of making a little here and there."

" As ye took me," I said, with a grin.

" My fair-haired buckie, it's deevil the plack I'll make off you. That hound o' yours will eat the galley out before we round Fife Ness. Murdo's seen better days than troking out of Ness with a stinking cargo of kippered salmon and saut-herring, and for that stuff in the kegs, my mind durstna dwell on it. What an unholy lift we'd get if it exploded."

"Where did you sail before?" I asked. "In India?"

"That same, lad! The best time I ever had. The East India Company had not been long trading there and I shipped out of London Port for Surat. The officers of the Company were then thinking of buying Calcutta for a trading post, and we next sailed there. I was mate on her. What a boat, man! All belly for cargo and a bitch to roll in a beam wind. Faith, I left her quick."

He chuckled reminiscently and spat over the side.

"The officers had done their business and were below with the captain at the bottle. We were coming down the Hooghly, a rip-roaring snorter right on her beam, and her rolling and bucking like a barrel, the tiller-haft under my arm butting like a billy-goat. One of these native boats, crammed to the gun'le with pilgrims—I'll warrant threescore in her—was tacking up and ran right across our bow. Heaven my judge, I couldna fail it. I cut her clean in two, and when I looked back over the stern, there they were, black heids bobbing in the water, close and thick as Hielan' sheep in a fank. In my scare I forgot the tiller, and the next thing I kenned was me sprawling on the deck, and the blunt nose of her bunged to the portholes on a sandbank.

"'Ye're in for it now, Murdo,' says I, as I picked myself up. At that the captain came tearing up with a cutlass in his hand.

"'Murdo,' says I again, 'it's time to leave her,' and I popped over the side. And that's how I lost my chance of making a fortune in the foreign trade."

"And how did you get home?" I asked.

"Oh, I worked my passage on a Portugee. Deevil the

word I kenned o' their lingo, but before we reached Lisbon I could swear wi' the best o' them."

" It must be fine to have travelled and seen the world," I sighed.

" Och, aye; but the best sight I see on a trip is my mother's cottage in Dornoch. I'll be up in a crack," he added, and left me to go below.

I had taken an instant liking to this man. What a diversion he was, his speech far different from the manner of my telling, full of strange oaths and smatterings of many tongues, the reddings of a score of ports, with a story to every one, and nothing he loved better than the telling of them.

Night crept up on the heels of day, a night prodigal of stars. From horizon to horizon they sparkled, these treasures of darkness, till it seemed the sky rained stars down into the sea. I felt I had only to climb the mast to touch them, so close had the heavens come to earth.

I went forward and stood long watching the bow-wave curl in foam to the figurehead, a glow in it as if lighted from the depths.

The bow-wave—there is magic in it! At any time the rise and fall of it can hold me enthralled. " I am taking you," it calls to me, " you know not where. The land of adventure lies just ahead."

" How is she? " asked Murdo, after we had cleared Whiteness.

" A bit pull on the main," said Davie, " and she'll steer herself. She's a bit inclined to come up into the wind. Ease the jib a trifle."

Jimmy and another hand hauled on the ropes, until Davie was satisfied.

" Now she's balanced. Isn't she a sailer? " said

Murdo, with pride. " If this wind holds we'll be in the Forth in three days."

Hold it did, and no need to whistle for a wind. On the third day we rounded Fife Ness and slipped into the Forth. We had one tack close-hauled for the north shore, and after, a quick run to Leith Roads, where Davie swung her deftly into the wind. Her canvas flapped and slapped noisily, the while Murdo scanned the shore, After a time of waiting, whiles tacking to take up lee-way, Davie again swuug her into the wind and took up the Forth.

" The man I was expecting to meet is not forward," said Murdo, " and that's a misfortune, for damn me if I want to sleep with that cargo a night longer."

" Meaning the powder ? " I said.

" That same. The sooner it's out of my hands and in the Castle of Edinburgh the better. I'd rather it blew up the Dutchmen it's meant for than douce sailor-men like Davie and me. Let's go up a bit and I'll make inquiries ashore."

The firth here narrows considerably and it was a joy to witness Davie bring her up, sails aback and on to the other tack, for here the tides run treacherous round an island, and little room to wear a ship. But being fore-and-aft rigged the *Cromarty Lass* could sail close, and Davie manœuvred her through in two tacks, and dropped anchor in a bay beyond the Queen's Ferry.

Through an alley in the woods we could make out the top of a square fortalice peeping above a rise of meadow-land. All that could be seen from the deck were the stepped gables, the heavily flagged roof, and one small window high on the east side.

"Run up the signal," said Murdo, "and see if Midhope replies."

Davie ran a short pennant to the mast-head. A cloth

fluttered twice from the small window in reply, and immediately Murdo ordered out the boat. We all had to bear a hand at the lowering of it.

" How long will you be gone ashore? " I asked, keen for the prospect of feeling land under my feet.

" Maybe an hour! Maybe less! "

" A stretch to my legs is what I would like."

" A what? " laughed Murdo. " It's a stretch to your neck ye might get on this ploy. We might meet with gentlemen there not overpleased to see Davie and me ashore. But come and chance it. Ye can run, and that slicer o' yours might come in handy. Davie and I are no' just what ye might say skilly at the steel-slashing."

All this while he was buckling on a whinger of sorts.

I jumped into the boat and, holding out my arms, caught Dileas as he sprang.

" I'll but walk the shore till your returning," I said.

" Best not," said Murdo. " Come up in the woods a bit."

For about a musket-shot we trod a path through the trees, when suddenly a whistle shrilled, and Murdo, wheeling, shouted " Run! " and was off for the boat, Davie at his heels, at a surprising pace for sailor-men. Dileas was off the path, and I burst into a thicket to search for him, when three soldiers flashed by at a run. My retreat was cut off.

Keeping to the wood I ran parallel with them, until coming to the fringe of bushes above the tideway. There were Murdo and Davie piling into the boat with never a back look, and rowing like devils possessed for the cutter, while the three pursuers kneeled on the beach and fired, with no result, for never a slackening came on their strokes.

" Up anchor! Up foresail! " I heard Murdo roar

while the boat was still three fathoms off. Before the
soldiers had muskets again loaded the *Cromarty Lass* was
headed down the firth, the boat trailing in a spume at
her stern.

A growl from Dileas and I turned, to see a pudgy
lieutenant bearing down on me, blowing like a broken-
winded horse, his three-cornered hat awry over one ear.
His drawn sword was in his hand, and with what little
breath he had he squealed an oath and drove on me. He
could have been dirked like a haggis, but I saw no reason
for coming to blows with him. Whatever his quarrel with
Murdo and Davie, it was none of mine. I stepped round
a tree trunk, and his foot catching a root he shot over
the shingle bank and landed among the sanded sea-wrack
below. A quick glance showed me the *Cromarty Lass*
far beyond hail. I turned and ran.

" The farther from these gentry the better, Dileas,"
I panted. " They are over-handy with the grey lead for
our fancy. It seems we have been keeping bad company
lately, you and I."

Dileas barked and bounded ahead, glad to feel firm
earth under him, and indeed myself was glad to feel the
same, although my four days on the cutter had not been
spent without profit or pleasure. I added to my knowledge of seamanship and the handling of small craft. The
company of Murdo, too, helped to blunt the edge of my
depression.

Holding to the braes above the shore, so as to keep the
firth in view, and skirting the burgh of the Ferry, Dileas
and I ran at a steady pace for close on three miles. At
times I glimpsed the *Cromarty Lass*, but she showed no
sign of slackening canvas or drawing in to the shore, and
indeed was steadily outstripping me. I lost sight of her
entirely when she slipped behind an island, and there I

found my further progress barred by an estuary. Swim or row, there was no else for it, with a full tide flowing.

I hailed a fisherman across the water for passage, but he pointed upstream, shaking his head.

" There's a brig not a mile up," he shouted.

I looked through the trees, glimpsed the span of a bridge and made up the water.

Here I came on a road running east and west, and, taking east, in less than an hour had my first sight of Edinburgh, and since I had given up all hope of ever again seeing my trews and satchel, which were by now far beyond Leith Roads, I saw no reason why I should not make a closer acquaintance with the town, of which I had heard much.

CHAPTER VIII

I Make Friends in Edinburgh

I

THE short December afternoon was nearing its end as I approached the city of Edinburgh. I was making for the Kirk Brae as I had been directed, intending to enter by the West Port, when Dileas altered my plans.

A hare broke cover at his feet, and on the instant he was off like the wind along the highway known as the Lang Dykes. I whistled and whistled again, but Dileas paid no heed. It was not like him to be disobedient, and half laughing, half annoyed, I walked on, knowing there was another port I might use, farther east. Dileas was enjoying the chase, for it was long since he had been so well matched, and as I stood at the dyke-side to watch the pair my annoyance faded. They were now off the road and going hard among the whins and rushes of the moor that lay to the north. Neither was gaining, and, indeed, it looked as if they might both end in the sea. Some moor-fowl, startled from a heather bank, rose, protesting harshly, and the hare swerved. Then they were over the brae face and lost to my sight.

I met a few country women who had been to the town, plodding homeward with bundles under their plaids. They eyed me distrustfully and hurried by, giving me my first taste of the dislike many Lowlanders have for the Gael. Indeed, it was more than dislike; some of them seemed to be in mortal terror of me. When they had passed I was the only one on all the empty road. Of Dileas there was no sign at all.

At the end of the Nor' Loch I sat to wait for him, my mind and eyes busy with the scene before me. For many miles back I had seen the Castle, a proud fortress high-perched on a crag, rising above a soft, encircling haze. Now I studied it closely. Impregnable, I thought it.

The sun had dipped, so that nothing of him was seen save where he had slashed a low-hung cloud with a thin sword of gold; but the sky was mellow with his after-glow. Against it loomed the battlements, black as a starless sky, towers reared on dark deeds and mystery, walls built up of perils and regrets. A flag stirred faintly on its staff. A solitary light travelled slowly round the ramparts and vanished. Dark and sombre houses, close-piled on the ridge, reached for the clouds with their high-peaked gables. Here and there a window flamed, as candles were lighted within. Gardens, melancholy in the dim, winter dusk, hung dizzily over the loch. A strange and wonderful town this, where beat the heart of Scot-land! A town like a cliff face, that threw the wavering flickers of her tallow candles, as well as the shadow of her great Rock, into the still waters that filled the valley at her feet. Often had her Castle been assaulted by foes; more than once had its towers crumpled under cannon fire. Yet here it stood proudly aloft, as though it never had known siege and reduction. And I who, yon day in Strath Oykell, had ridden the road, building my frail castles in the air, saw with wondering eyes a real castle in the air, of solid and substantial stone, that, in spite of time and the worst that men could do against it, stood.

This town stirred me and called to me in a way there is no accounting for. Perhaps it was because of the old, sad tales I had heard at grammar school, for the names of her great ones, long dead, were hammering at the doors of memory. Perhaps it was the gloaming hour that laid a spell on me. I know not. But I do know that, while I sat there, her every stone whereon her story is written in blood and flame seemed to cry to me that here was my place, and not in foreign wars, as I had planned.

" A man might live there," I thought, " and perhaps learn to be happy again."

A wind began to whisper among the rushes and gently ripple the water. The afterglow had faded and I felt the chill of falling night. The haze, grown grey as mist, clung closer about the Rock and the sloping gardens. I overcame my reluctance to rise and stood to my feet. It might be that I would find a place here. There were whispers of a falling crown, bold talk of what men might do. When I had heard them vaguely in the north, I did not believe them. Still, I might be needed here. If so, I would be glad to stay.

I remembered Dileas; he had been long gone. I whistled, and he fell in at heel unobtrusively, not oversure of his welcome, and I forbore to scold. Hitching my sword into place, and with a tug to my bonnet, I went forward, turned into the Leith Wynd and began to climb the steep. It was so narrow near the top that when I passed a woman toiling up ahead of me my hilt clinked against a wall. It was so dark that I would not have known my fellow-traveller to be a woman had I not heard the rustle of her petticoats. Doorways gaped to right and left, giving out sounds of footsteps and murmurings, and for the first time in my life panic had me by the throat. The tall houses smothered me, narrowing down the sky to a mere ribbon. There was no room to swing a broadsword; a dirk might not be sure enough to ward off a blow delivered quick from one of those yawning pits of gloom that led I knew not where. I would have turned and fled, but the sight of lights ahead encouraged me to go on, and at length the mouth of the wynd delivered me into a broad street. I stepped through the handsome two-storeyed port that is the main entrance to the town, the Netherbow Port, and found myself in the High Street.

Here I discovered I had but changed one evil for another, darkness for din. The hoarse cries of street vendors, the angry shouts of brawling men, the rush of feet over the causeway, the creak of sedan-chairs, the jangling of bells—the medley of noises smote harshly on ears trained to catch the smallest sounds of the open and but newly come from the quiet of the loch-side. The torches of the link-boys threw orange streamers of flame along the blue dusk, and the smoke from them blew in my face, setting me to coughing. Uncertain I stood, jostled by the hurrying, thrusting crowd. Close to my ear a man with a hiccough bawled: " Sour milk! Wha's for sour milk? " so suddenly that I started away from him in affright, and the rude fellow doubled up with merriment. Dileas whimpered, and the hair along his neck bristled, as fear of the unknown gripped him also. The street was very wide, a channel running at each side of it, in the middle a broad, well-paved causeway where the folk walked.

And there we stood, Dileas and I, on the crown of it, and drew much curious attention. I caught bright, interested glances from underneath plaids, and I observed wrathful, scowling looks. The sights and sounds of this strange, huddled community confused and bewildered me. A trio of drunken roisterers, linked and bawling a bawdy song, staggered against me, sending me plunging over a barefooted callant hopping on the causey-stones to warm himself. I felt the blood flaming in my face, but seeing that the three had already forgotten me, and were concerned only with keeping their feet, I picked up the sprawling bairn and did my best to comfort him. He made off at once, seeming more afraid of Dileas than of the men who had upset him.

My first concern was a bed for the night, and I wandered uncertainly up the long street, not knowing where to apply. My grief! How I wished for Tearlach at my elbow. I was lonelier in this crowded street than when travelling alone across the Dirrie More. In an angle of St Giles', where I was unobserved, I paused again, to watch the throng busy about the booths with their Saturday-evening marketing, the women clamorous and quarrelsome over the prices and driving sharp bargains. Lanterns were being lighted and hung by householders at the level of the first storey, this, as I learned later, being demanded of them by the magistrates, who themselves provided certain large and very handsome lanterns at the busiest points. All this seemed very fine to me, but it showed me night was drawing on, and I was no nearer finding a bed. Something brushed against my knees and I glanced down, to find a huge sow routing among the garbage in the corner. With all a Highlander's loathing of the pig I drew aside hastily, my lips curling with distaste. Dileas evidently shared this feeling, but he had a different way of showing aversion. With an agonized squeal the sow shot out into the stream of traffic, but it so happened that her mad career was quickly checked. The same three roisterers who had collided with me were now returning in search of further potations, and this time collided with the sow. Down they went on top of her, and grunts, squeals and frantic cursing came from the heaving, struggling heap of arms, legs and bodies. Soon an uproarious crowd ringed themselves about the

fallen, joining their jeers and laughter to swell the pande-
monium. I laughed as I had not laughed for many a day.

But under all the noise and bustle there was something
sinister, though I was not aware of it. Had I been a
townsman I would have known that some of the brawling
and shouting were more than ordinarily violent. I would
have sensed an excitement among the marketers, and
noted that as certain groups approached noisily, others
to avoid meeting them withdrew hurriedly into a close-
mouth. Danger—but I did not know it—though not yet
openly stalking the causey, was preparing to march once
again through the old town.

II

I was watching two chairs, which had swung down
from the Lawnmarket, stop on the other side of the street
to set down their passengers, when I saw a half-dozen
men close round them, brandishing staves. Then, high
above all other sounds, I heard a woman's scream. On
the instant, drawing my sword, I raced towards the
chairs. One was being toppled on its side, and I was just
in time to help a woman out of it. Thrusting her behind
me I pricked the fellow nearest me in the wrist. A howl
of rage and pain broke from him as his cudgel clattered
on the stones. A quick glance showed me a young man
at the other chair. His sword had jammed in the drawing,
but he was using his cane to good purpose, backing slowly
to a position beside me, one arm guarding the woman he
had rescued. Meantime I was laying about me with the
flat of my sword, holding my dirk menacingly in the
other hand. Out of the tail of my eye I saw I had found
an ally about my own age and build, who had already
cracked a crown with his cane.

"Your shoulder to mine, brave man," I said happily, glad to be finding something to do that put a stop to my aimless wandering.

"Make for the close on your left hand," whispered a voice behind me.

We edged along the wall, belabouring with enthusiasm the *scalags* before us, who were already tiring. The man facing me decided at this moment that he had had enough and made off quickly. The others soon fell back and lost themselves among the bystanders.

"Come inside quickly," said the woman I had helped. "Ye had best come inside and wait till we are sure these scoundrels are not likely to come back. They made a mistake, the muckle fools. They mistook us for folk they were waiting for."

She turned into the close and led the way up a dark turnpike stair. I waited for a last look, to make sure there was no threat of a rush on the doorway, then, twisting my fingers into Dileas's hair, I brought up the rear. Och, the horror of the close, stifling darkness! Never like this the dark of the woods or the shore at night, which was a friendly dark that maybe held the *daoine sith*, the little people, but I carried a charm against them. I had no charm against the folk that peopled this gloom, save maybe an inch or two of dirk, and I stumbled upwards, thinking it was like climbing up the gullet of a giant. At the first floor my hand, groping for guidance, met the stuff of a woman's dress. Then I heard a whisper that made my heart stand still, for it was Barbara's voice.

"Alastair!" she said eagerly, fairly hurling herself at me, and at once her head was down on my shoulder. Before I had time to think my arms closed tight about her. I heard her laugh happily before she raised her head.

"How are you here? Did you follow me?"

" Follow you? " I repeated stupidly.

" Yes. Did you not know I was here? But I see you did not. Then how do you come to be here? Well, never mind; I can hear that another time. Is it not the beautiful thing that we should be together again." She gave another excited, happy little laugh. " Do you know this? I would give all I have to see Nancy's face at this moment, if she could see us."

" Nancy's face? "

It seemed I could do nothing but repeat her words like a foolish echo. I could only hold her, rejoiced to have her in my arms again, and for one mad, tumultuous moment I felt: " What does anything matter but just the happiness of us two."

" Yes, Nancy's face. You will be wondering what she has to do with it. Well, I gave her our secret after she had promised to keep it, and she told on me. The minx! And my mother was so much afraid that you would come for me before my father came home, and her not able to do anything to stop you, that, in alarm, she packed me off at once to my grand-aunt. So here I am. And is it not wonderful, as well as diverting, that almost the first man I speak to in Edinburgh should be just yourself? Do you not see why I am laughing? Nancy cheated me and we have both cheated Nancy. I sent a message to you at Ardmair, but you will not have got it."

At the mention of Ardmair I stiffened and set her aside, for with a sick heart I minded how impossible it was that we two could ever be friends.

" Barbara, what ails ye, lassie? " an anxious voice called overhead.

" Nothing, auntie. I am coming. It is very dark," Barbara offered as explanation of our delay.

"What shall we say to my grand-aunt?" she whispered,

as we climbed three further flights of the long stair, she with a hold of my hand. " Ought we to tell her, or shall we pretend we are strangers? "

I grew hot and miserable at her words.

" How can I," I was thinking, " break it to her that just now I am only pretending we are friends? How am I to tell her I cannot see her again? "

" You are hurting my hand, Alastair," she said, with a little gasp. And, indeed, I was crushing it cruelly, not knowing what I was doing. " And you have not answered me."

" I will tell your grand-aunt the first chance I get," I said, with difficulty. " Leave the telling to me."

And with that we passed into the house.

" Barbara, you're not hurt, are you? No, I see you are not. My! That wee tulzie round the chairs has put a bit colour in your cheeks. And your eyes are like stars, lassie. It looks as though a wheen cudgels and swords were the medicine for you. And here's my braw defender. Take my warmest thanks, laddie. Come here to the fire."

Barbara's grand-aunt was seated in an arm-chair with a high, carved back, but she rose, gave me her hand to kiss, and sank in a graceful curtsy. Eh! but yon old lady was the surprising one. She was over seventy, she told me, but she was sprightly enough to make me think her little more than half that age. Her eyes twinkled like a girl's, and she could throw glances as inviting asNancy's at Kyle-ron. And she was bonny still, with her powdered borrowed hair and her curls and her fine satin dress, that she spread about her feet like a great half-moon when she sat. She had been a toast in her day, had yon one, and was not like to forget it. I expected to see in her agitation and fear, but found instead indignation at the rowdies and contempt for the cowardly chairmen.

" Your name, young man? " she demanded. " My name is Stewart—Mistress Alison Stewart."

" Alastair Mackenzie, at your service," I said, bowing.

" Where are you from? "

" Ardmair, in Ross."

" Another wild Hielander, like Barbara! This is my grand-niece from Strathnavern—a Mackay, Mr Mackenzie."

I bowed, and Barbara threw me an amused smile and dropped a demure curtsy.

Her aunt turned quickly to the young man who stood by her chair.

" Your name, my other braw defender? " she asked him.

" Jock Grant," he said, bowing to her and then to me, adding, with an engaging smile, " only of Edinburgh."

" Jock Grant," she repeated, observing him keenly and seeming very interested. " That name brings back a lot to me. What Grants are ye o'? "

" I'll tell ye that," he said jocularly, " when you have told me what Stewarts ye're o'."

" The lad's discreet! " she said, addressing the ceiling. " But you're right not to be too free with your tongue in this toun the now. Though it'll do you no harm to say whether you're from Glen Moriston or Strathspey, surely."

" Maybe not. But it might tell whether I am for King James or the Prince of Orange."

" Well, well," she said, " keep it to yourself then. I'll tell you, though, that I was an Erskine o' Gogar before I married a Stewart o' Doune, if that tells you anything. But I used to ken a Jock Grant, who lived in Hyndford's Close, and, indeed, you're the very spit o' him."

" My grandfather," he said, with interest, a grin

H

splitting his freckled face. " I believe he was a lad for
the lassies."

" What makes you think that? " she questioned,
looking up at him with a twinkle in her eyes.

" Something tells me. And something tells me he did
not marry with the one he started off with," he told her
boldly.

" You're right; he did not. But I likit him fine for a
while," she confessed. She was silent for a minute, then
she laughed, saying: " He had a havering tongue. We
must be friends, you and me."

She stamped on the floor to summon a serving-woman,
whom she ordered to bring claret for Jock Grant and
me, and cordial for herself and her niece.

" After our bit shake, Barbara," she said, sipping it,
" though we are no' at all shaken."

All this time I had sat staring at the fire, not seeing a
chance to break in on the light talk, and Mistress Stewart,
thinking she had been neglecting me, turned towards
me, saying: " Are ye biding with your friend? "

I did not understand her question, and the ready-
tongued Jock put in: " He was no friend of mine
till we met in the tulzie down by, but now that I've
seen how he handles yon muckle sword I'm thinking
he's the very man I would like for a friend in a tight
corner."

I gave him a friendly smile.

" Indeed, I would rather have you on my side than on
the other," I told him. " I am sure you are as good as I
am with the sword."

I had taken an instant liking to this freckled lad with
the cheerful grin, and would have gone on speaking to
him, but Mistress Stewart was not the one to be long
left out of the talking.

"Have you been long in the town?" she asked, determined to satisfy her curiosity.

"Not much more than an hour, I believe. I was thinking of seeking a bed when I heard your niece scream."

"It was you that screamed, auntie," Barbara said accusingly. "Wild Hielanders do not scream."

"I'm no' denying it was me that gave the skirl. And what for no'? How would folk have kent we needed help? I've seen the day I did not need to skirl to bring me a man. When I was your age I could not walk a stone's-throw—and my stone's-throw's no' very far—down the High Street without a man buzzing at my shoulder like a wasp at a cherry. These days are by wi', but as long as a skirl will bring me a man when I need him, believe ye me, I'll skirl. But, laddie," she continued soberly, "this is no time o' night to be seeking a bed, and the toun in such a hotter. Ye're likely to land in trouble, whichever side ye're on. Ye saw what happened to us. They mistook us for Papists. Papists! And Barbara's father's in the counsels o' the Prince of Orange, and she has I know not how many cousins and friends in his army."

"I will be on the other side," I said stiffly.

"That but adds to your danger, laddie, for King James's looks to be the losing side. Well, well, neither Mass nor Covenant will make me take sides again. I'll attend a Mass, sign a Covenant, or accept the Test, just as they say. It'll do me no harm, for I'll keep my own counsel and think my own thoughts. I have the warrant of Sir George Mackenzie, the King's Advocate, for that. 'You cannot be tried for what you think,' says he, 'so long as you conform outwardly.' Ye need not glower at me like that, Barbara. Oh, I know that is not your father's way; he would go to the wuddy for the Covenant. But I've grown old in the politics o' Edinburgh, and I've seen—what have I no' seen! The Marquis o' Montrose beheaded up by and Argyll crawin' crouse; and no' that long after, Argyll's head on the self-same spike o' the Tolbooth, his crawin' done; the Covenanters herded like kye in Greyfriars' Kirkyard. And now I'm like to see the Papists dree the same weird."

"I am no Papist, Mistress Stewart, so I have nothing to fear," said I.

"No? Well, I differ. I doubt ye're a ramstougerous lad that'll land in trouble if trouble's within a mile o' ye. Away back where ye came from if ye're wise, Alastair Mackenzie, for one thing I've heard about the wild Hielanders, to their credit, is that they dinna quarrel like cats in the name o' religion. Away back before the storm bursts here. The temper o' the toun this night minds me o' what it was like another Saturday night near fifty years ago. And the next day was ' Stoney Sunday,' when the apple-wife o' the Tron hurled her stool at an archbishop's head. And soon there was not a whole pane o' glass in St Giles' Kirk windows, with the stones flying thick and fast from side to side o' the street. Me take sides again? No fears! My head sits bonnier on my neck than ever it'll do on a Tolbooth spike. I would offer ye a bed if I had it to offer, in return for what ye did for me, but we're sma' boukit here. Jock Grant, take this lad, and dinna leave him till ye see him safe settled, or he'll maybe get a lang-hefted westland billy in his wame. Will ye do that?"

"I'll do that, Mistress Stewart."

"Well, then I want the pair of ye to come here the morn, and see an old woman safely to kirk and back, and have a bit dinner, such as it is on the Sabbath. I'll no' take a denial. I'll be needing a man's arm, I'm doubting."

"Would it not be wiser for you to stay at home, Mistress Stewart?" asked Jock Grant.

"Wiser? Maybe! But I'll not be kept from seeing what's going on," she said indignantly. "You're to come here for me. Now mind, it's a tryst."

She smiled, and shook her curls at the young townsman.

"It's a tryst," he repeated, answering her smile with a broader one and bowing.

"I am afraid I will not be able to come," I said stiffly, wishing myself out of that house.

"Nonsense. Ye'll come with Jock Grant. What's to hinder ye?"

"I think not. You will excuse me," I replied as stiffly as before.

Barbara looked at me, startled. Mistress Stewart rose and caught my sleeve, looking up at me.

"Young man, what ails ye at us? I can see as far into a man as another, and what I see is a nice bit laddie any mother might be proud of. And yet, there ye stand, acting as if ye were a thrawn deevil. If ye've taken an ill-will at us, what's it for? Ye did me a great service when ye saved me from being coupit in the gutter. Do me another service by coming here the morn. Or else," she finished belligerently, " tell me what ails ye."

And now, here was a strange thing. I saw Dileas leave my side and cross the room to Barbara, who had been speaking to him softly in the Gaelic. Before I had time to warn her not to touch him, he laid his head on her knee and gazed at her, laying his heart at her feet. Dileas offering friendship to a stranger! The thing had never happened before and it gave me a queer pang. A lump rose in my throat, and I stood looking at Mistress Stewart miserably unhappy, unable to speak.

" What ails ye? ' she demanded.

" Nothing. I will come," I said hoarsely.

And there I was, out in the night, with nothing explained, never having been able to cut across the current of talk that had flowed so strongly in Mistress Stewart's room.

III

At the close-mouth Jock Grant remarked: " We'll take the crown o' the causey; it'll be safer, for more reasons than one. I wish I kent what to do with you. Have you business in the town? "

" No, I am only passing through, and if you could find me a lodging for the night, it is very grateful I would be, and I would not trouble you any more."

" Aye, but that's the bit! Mistress Stewart was right when she said there was likely to be trouble in the town. It's hotching wi' westland Whigs spoiling for a fight, and you look just the kind o' lad that would ram his heid into a nest o' them." He lowered his voice. " I gather ye're for King James. You needn't fear to speak to me, for I'm against a Dutch king myself."

" The Mackenzies have always fought for the Stuarts," I replied, " and as I must sell my sword to live, it may be that King James would be glad of it."

My companion gave a yelp.

" Dod! I think ye're the lad I'm looking for," he said heartily. " I like the cut o' ye. You can handle a sword bonnily enough, and, man! I think we'll make a braw pair. Would you be for sharing my room this night, and we can get better acquainted? "

I gave a sigh of relief.

" Indeed I will be very pleased," I returned, over-joyed to have found a friend.

" Well, then, that's settled, and I'm glad to be able to keep an eye on you. My lodging is just past the next close. I bide wi' a widow, and her auld runt o' a good-mother, a nebsy, long, dry-neckit body, wi' a grudge against a' body, and me specially. But the good-daughter's a grand housewife and can make a dish o' kail would near gar a dead man sit up in his coffin to sup." He halted and looked doubtfully at Dileas. " But I forgot, there's the dog. I'm thinking he will not be very welcome."

" I will never be parted from him," I said decidedly.

" No, of course not," Jock agreed hastily. " Well, up with you, up these fore-stairs and we'll try our luck."

When the door was opened a flickering light showed a comely, red-cheeked woman of middle age, who stared at me in amazement.

" I've brought you another lodger, Mistress Binnie," said Jock easily. " He's a great friend of mine, and I'd like you to make him welcome."

" If he's a friend o' yours, Mister Grant, he'll be very welcome, if he will share your bed."

" What's that ye're saying? " called a sharp voice, and an old woman, leaning on a stick, hirpled into the lobby. She had a long, sharp nose, and a bony hand clutched a shawl about her shoulders.

" Let's take a look at this friend." She swept a hostile glance over me. " A Hielander! I ha'e nae broo o' Hielanders. Where did ye fa' in wi' him? We're no' takin' in a' and sundry."

Catching sight of Dileas, who had prudently kept well in the rear, she said shrilly: " Keep that brute outside. I'll not have him in here."

" Is the dog yours? " asked the younger Mistress Binnie. " Would you want to bring him indoors? "

" There is nowhere else for him to go. He goes everywhere with me," I explained quietly.

" Well, ye can go down the stairs again," the sharp old tongue broke in, " and take special care to see that he goes wi' ye this time."

" I could not part from my dog, Mistress Binnie," I said, addressing the younger woman. " He would not stay with a stranger. I will be sorry not to taste the fine kail I have heard of," I added, smiling, " but it cannot be helped."

Making up her mind in a hurry she stood aside, opening the door wider.

" Come ben," she said pleasantly.

" Ye're gyte, woman, clean gyte," the old woman flung out scornfully, and, muttering to herself, made her way painfully back to her chair in the kitchen.

" Eh, my, but you hold the cartes," said Jock, looking at me enviously when we were alone together. " One look at your yellow hair, and no more than one smile from you, and the women are ready to rise and run."

" I am not wanting them to rise and run for me," I returned gloomily.

" What's that? " He stared at me unbelievingly. " Then you're a queer buckie, and things are ill divided. One look at me and all that the lassies see is that my ears stick out like jug handles. And what's wrong with sandy hair? "

" Nothing whatever."

" Nothing whatever, you say. Well, I wish you would tell that to the lassies. They just dinna seem to like mine."

" What does it matter what they like, so long as men like you? " I offered as comfort.

"But you see, man, I'm fond o' them, and I'd like them to be fond o' me."

We talked of many things that first night, and even after we lay down we found much to say to each other. After a time there came a hammering on the door with a stick.

"Will ye stop that yattering and let a body sleep in peace!" came a querulous demand.

"Never heed the old limmer," said Jock, in an undertone.

"The auld limmer heard ye the noo," the voice came again triumphantly, as its owner retreated with full honours.

I laughed in the darkness, finding it a pleasant thing to hear Jock's chuckles and to picture his wide, amused grin.

Lanterns were extinguished at ten o'clock and the noises outside gradually died away, until the only sound was the echoing tread of the Watch going the rounds.

A queer day this one, that had brought so many happenings at the end of it. For long I tossed uneasily, bitter thoughts crowding back, and it was not till the small hours that I fell asleep.

CHAPTER IX

The Storm bursts

I

THE High Street, as I saw it on the quiet Sabbath morning, looked peaceful enough. It lay dark and silent, lighted only by a moon that had risen some time during the night, and was still wanly doing duty till the sun should rise. Rime lay pale on roofs and window-ledges, and my breath made a cold, grey cloud before my face. Pigs, exploring runnels with their snouts, seemed alone to be stirring. Tales of trouble brewing in the town appeared highly fantastic, and that thought I put into words to Jock as soon as the sandy head stirred on the pillow.

" Aye, it doesn't look like it the now," he said, sitting up, yawning and stretching his arms. " No more does Athole brose look like barley, yet the one's the brew o' the other. Are ye aware that the Prince of Orange is as good as on the throne o' England? And the magistrates here—a peely-wally lot—that three years back sent a loyal address to King James larded with praise and flattery, have turned face about and are sending the same address, a wee bit altered, to the Dutchman. The Duke o' Perth's shaking in his shoes, and I'll wager you he'll resign the chancellorship."

" Why should he? He can turn with the others."

" Not so easy for him. A while back he turned Roman Catholic, and there's a terrible strong feeling against Catholics in this toun. Covenanters from the west country have been crowding in, ever since the news of the Dutchman's landing came. They're armed and they're bitter, small blame to them, and the Catholics are fearing trouble, for anything may happen."

"I cannot understand that," I cried. "In the north some of us are so far from a church that we welcome the priest when he passes through, and some of our folk even go to confess to him. We are all friends."

"Well, dinna try that on here, and say nothing o' it to the auld wife ben there. You'll be an Episcopalian?"

"Yes."

"See that ye keep your tongue on that as well, or we'll be in the street, bag and baggage. By the by, where's your baggage?"

"On a boat somewhere in the firth, and I do not expect I will ever see it again. But it does not matter. To-morrow I can get what I will be needing."

"Ye're hardly needing a razor, but seeing we're to take a couple o' womenfolk to the kirk this morning I'll lend ye mine."

"I wish we had not promised to go," I said gloomily. "I would fain stay away."

"Man, man, what ails ye? I wish I had your chances," he grumbled. "Look at last night! The old woman took a fancy to me because my grandfather was seemingly a jo o' hers, but the young one—while I'm gazing at her, my eyes begging for a look—here she's gazing at you as if she could eat ye up. Deil take it, she never even saw me! And all the time, what are you doing? Glowering at the fire, with a brow on ye as dark's a thunder-cloud, as though there was not a petticoat within miles. I tell you, if a lassie looked at me like yon I would not be long in picking her up and putting her in my pooch."

There are times when it is given to us to see ourselves

through another's eyes, and it may be a very humbling
sight. That Sabbath morning I saw myself as I appeared
to Barbara Mackay, and I made a sorry figure. Her eyes
were not seeing clear, it is true, but the fault for that
did not lie with her.

Arrived at Mistress Stewart's, that lady pounced on
me to carry the stools, while Jock lent her an arm. Barbara
I hardly knew in her fine town dress. Her petticoat,
under the tucked-up skirt, was of rich flowered stuff, the
kerchief covering her shoulders of the finest linen and
lace. Only the steady eyes and the dark hair were the
same, when her silk-lined plaid fell back and showed
them. But beside Mistress Stewart she did not seem
grandly dressed at all. The old lady's petticoat was of
bright satin, overloaded with ribbons, lace and festoons,
and it and her skirt trailed backwards on the ground.
Her hood showed a boungrace, with bands of finest
foreign lace, and she wore a sapphire bodkin in her hair.

It was Greyfriars' Kirk we attended, and it was as well
we had brought our seats with us, for there was an un-
seemly scramble for those in the kirk, the folk hurling
bitter recriminations, and even exchanging blows, while
they struggled for possession. The congregation was
larger than ordinary that day, for it was swollen by
numbers of strangers in the town. Surprised, and hardly
able to keep from laughing, I watched two *cailleachs*, old
crones, who quarrelled venomously, each grabbing a
stool by turns from the other's grasp, the victor ending
by pounding with her prize on the discomfited one's
back. At Aberdeen we sat in pews decorously, and this
seemed to me strange doings for a kirk in the capital.

Mistress Stewart complained of the cold, the chill
from the old grey stones creeping into her limbs, numb-
ing them. Three women who were on the stool of

repentance shivered in their sackcloth, and blew on their fingers for warmth. I did not find Greyfriars' cold, comparing it with the little kirk of Loch Broom, as I saw it the winter before, ruinous, like so many kirks in the north, without a door, almost wholly without thatch, the snowflakes drifting in and settling on the plaids of the still worshippers, and melting in puddles about their feet. Leaning my shoulders against a pillar, my eyes fixed on the dim, vaulted roof, and hearing little of the long, long sermon, I allowed my thoughts to wander. They ranged far beyond Loch Broom, to the home on the cliff face of the girl at my side. I saw her steal glances at me, and once she seized the fringes of my plaid and crushed them fiercely in her palm, but I pretended not to notice. Had she but known it, I was parting from her again, in spirit, at the ford.

As soon as we were through the doorway she put her hand on my sleeve and drew me into the kirkyard, walking towards the empty part that is called the Covenanters' Prison—away from the knots of folk, gossiping or exchanging news.

" Alastair," she said breathlessly, " there is something I must ask you. I have been very unhappy, because last night you were so strange. You must tell me the truth. You are not glad to see me in Edinburgh."

I walked beside her for a moment, saying nothing, my eyes on the ground.

" I will tell you the truth; I am not glad to see you here," I said at last.

She drew in her breath sharply.

" Was I not sure of it! "

" I cannot be coming to Mistress Stewart's house and you sent there to be out of my way. It would not be honourable," I said, not knowing what else to say.

" Now I know that you are telling me lies," she said hotly. " That is not your real reason. Were you not coming for me secretly, and my father and mother not knowing? Tell me the truth."

I could not tell her I had vowed to kill her father. I could explain nothing without destroying her faith in him, and, since I could not marry her now, I had to leave her that.

" I cannot tell you anything more," I said.

She halted, her face gone very white, and stood leaning against the wall of a vault.

" I could win auntie over; I am sure of it. And we could be married here, you know, very easily."

She raised pleading eyes to me.

" But what is the use of talking of that," she went on despairingly, " now you have changed! "

" I have not changed."

" Och, have done! Why will you be saying that when every word and look tell me different? The word I spoke in jest at Kyle-ron was the true one. You were not to be trusted. There is someone else; I know it."

" There will never be anyone else," I said angrily. " You were the first I ever asked to marry and you will be the last."

She flashed a quick glance at me.

" Then tell me why you are different."

" I cannot tell you, but there is a reason. I wish to God," I groaned, " that there were not."

She was silent for a little, then she burst out wildly: " What reason could there be, if I had your love, as you said? There is nothing, nothing, that should keep us apart if you loved me. You said at the ford——"

The tears were on her cheeks now and she could not continue.

This was almost more than I could bear, but I managed

to say: " You would be better to forget what I said at the ford."

" Then you did not mean it! "

" I give you my word I meant it all."

And now her chin was up, her eyes scornful.

" The word of a Mackenzie—I would not give a doit for it! But it does not matter. I can be doing very well without you. I know now the kind you are. You wanted to escape back yonder, and so you made me sorry for you, to get me to help you. Then, to reward me, you pretended to love me."

" Stop! Barbara, you know that is not true."

She gave a pitiful little shake of her head and said low: " Och, would not love be a bonny thing if it would but last! But it does not. Oh, it does not; and I should have known. Look round you; we are in a kirkyard. My sorrow! That is just the place for us, for here lies the pride of Barbara Mackay, that I've but newly killed for you. And here lies my love for you, that has died in this hour. And here lies my faith in all men, and that is the cruellest thing you have done to me, for you have killed more than my faith in yourself. And my happiness is dead too, so we did well to come among the graves. You should be proud of yourself this day, Alastair Mackenzie. You have done a full day's work, and the day but half gone." Then she added, with a little gasping sob: " Och, I think my heart will be broken."

At that I reached out a hand blindly, and when I could speak I said: " You may not believe me, but that is just what mine is."

" Is it? Then I am sure I am very glad of it," she said fiercely, shaking off my hand, and walked on ahead of me.

And that is how we went back to Allan's Close, with never another word spoken.

II

Jock glanced curiously at me as I entered, and he must have seen something was amiss, for he loyally made talk to hide my distress. When we were ready to sit down to the meal prepared I said gravely: "Mistress Stewart, I should not have come here. I cannot accept your hospitality without telling you that I am the last man you should have invited to your house, seeing that your grand-niece was sent to you specially to be out of my way."

She was carving the cold, salted mutton, which was the usual Sabbath day's dish in winter, but stopped, with uplifted knife, and stared at me suspiciously. Then she flashed a quick glance at Barbara.

"Ye kept it dark," she said to her shortly.

Turning again to me she demanded: "Did you follow her here aince errand?"

"I did not know she was here till we met last night."

She looked from me to Barbara and back again, then she laughed till her shoulders shook and the tears ran.

"Oh," she gasped, "what would your mother say if she kent it was my skirl brought him to your side again? This is the finger of Providence, and I'm no' fit to strive against Providence."

She went off again into another peal of laughter.

"My dear lad, you've owre nice a conscience. If I had been you, I would never have let on. I like you a' the better for telling, but I'm just saying what a poor, weak sinner like me would have done in your place. Well, I've no quarrel with you; quite the opposite. I'm no' a Mackay, and I've never had much troke wi' the Mackays. I'll no' make their quarrels mine. Eh! but I would not have missed this ploy for a pooch o' siller.

Sit ye down, Alastair, my friend, and if so be that you want to come here to see Barbara, I'se no' hinder you."

"You might leave the asking to me, auntie," said Barbara, a bright spot burning on her cheeks. "I have not said I wanted to see him. And I do not."

Her grand-aunt gave her a sharp, searching stare.

"The more fool you, then," she snapped, "and the next time you come to visit your auntie I would not leave my manners ahint me, if I was you."

It was a great relief to me when that meal was ended and we could rise to make our farewells. Barbara, white and silent, turned away her face when I bowed to her, and my heart was heavy beyond telling, to leave her like that. Mistress Stewart walked to the door with her hand on my arm.

"There's something here I cannot get to the bottom of, but I want you both back as often as you like to come. I like a man about the house." She patted my sleeve. "Now mind, be sure and look in, in the by-going, and never heed that carnaptious lassie."

"And that is the ending of it," I said bitterly, under my breath, crying in my heart her name, "Barbara! Barbara!"

I found myself in the Lawnmarket, whither Jock had guided me, without my knowing how I came there. I was grateful for his silence. We continued up the Castle-hill, where there were many walking in the December sunshine, between sermons. Little knots of gentlefolk stood about, talking gravely, and many wore an anxious frown. In spite of Jock's lamentations that the lassies did not like him, his hand was often enough at his bonnet, as he replied to their smiling greetings.

"It's you that's the draw," he explained to me,

I

" They would never have seen me if you had not been by. I ken the limmers! "

We stood at the foot of the steps that led up to the great studded door of the Castle.

" Alastair," said Jock, " I have not told you, but I will be inside that door, I'm thinking, within a week. I have been doing a bit o' work for the Duke of Gordon, the Governor, one of the truest men in the King's service. I'm a soldier, or rather I was, till this stramash with the Prince of Orange. Maybe I should have told you before. But I'm wondering if, on the day I join the garrison, you'll come with me."

" I will not be knowing what to do," I said hesitatingly. " I would like to serve along with you, now that we are friends. I do not see that I could do better. There is one thing. You say that the Dutchman is as good as on the throne of England. Well, I am hoping that service under the King will give me the chance I am waiting for."

" What is that? "

" The chance to settle a long score against one of Dutch William's officers; he serves under Mackay of Scourie. I can wait, but that score must be settled at last. I cannot go footing it into England to meet him, but I am hoping he will come here to me."

" It is very likely, for Mackay of Scourie will be in command of the Dutchman's forces in Scotland. That is sure, if anything is."

" Well," I said, taking a long breath, " I will leave my mark on him, if I die for it."

" What's his name? Maybe I can help you."

I hesitated; then, with an edge on my voice, said: " One of the Aberach Mackays, a cousin of Scourie's."

Jock whistled, his eyes round with surprise.

" I think I begin to see daylight," he said thoughtfully.

" In what way? "

" Why you could not put that lassie at Mistress Stewart's in your pooch."

I said nothing in reply, and he stood fingering his lip, taking stock of me curiously.

" Upon my soul, Alastair," he said, as we turned away, " I would like fine if I could make a bit splash in auld Scotland's story, inside that gate."

And in truth Jock Grant made his bit splash as he hoped.

When we returned to our room we found that Mistress Binnie had been at the end of her wits, distressed by the plaintive whimpering of Dileas, whom we had left shut in. He had been at it all the time we were out, nearly scratching down the door. Here, at least, was one who would always miss me, and who still had faith in me!

We were sitting at our evening meal of sowens, talking quietly, when he raised his head from his paws to listen.

" What's that? " I questioned sharply.

A sound broke in on the stillness of the room, like the distant roar of a river in spate.

" What did I tell you? " demanded Jock, on his feet in the instant. " The storm's burst."

We buckled on our swords, made a grab for our bonnets, and took the fore-stairs at a scurrying run, and were pelting down the High Street, Dileas at our heels, in the time it took Mistress Binnie to reach the door we had slammed.

Like ants disturbed in their hills, the townsfolk were pouring from their closes and hurrying east. Again came the roar of an angry crowd, followed by clamorous cries. We found the street blocked from side to side at the

Netherbow Port, with a surging tumult of men and boys,
from whose throats came now that menacing bellow,
now furious demands for the port to be opened.

"A wise man the Provost," whispered Jock to me.
"He's locked the port early."

Everywhere men were seeking the key, but nowhere
could it be found. Sullen, enraged and muttering threats,
at last reluctantly because there seemed nothing else to
do, the crowd began to scatter to their homes.

"Do you think the trouble is over, Jock?" I
asked.

"I think it's over for this night," he said, relieved.
"There's still a lot o' soond, but soond breaks nae heids.
I'm glad to see this rabble skailing."

"Was it not the good thing the port was locked! How
did the Provost come to think of it?"

"He kens the temper of an Edinburgh mob. It was a
wise move, for most o' the Roman Catholic gentry live
in the Canongate, and I ken if I was one o' them I would
show the Canongate my heels this very night."

As we walked away half-a-score of men poured furtively
from a close on the south side of the street, over their
arms, and trailing on the ground, the silk and velvet of
women's gowns; under their oxters big, unwieldy
bundles.

"God help the poor devils!" Jock exclaimed.
"Plundering's begun! And it being the Sabbath, with
no lights in the streets, that ill work will prosper all the
more."

Hardly had the pillagers passed when on their heels a
woman came, a young woman seemingly, for she ran like
a hare, and without ever a pause or a back glance plunged
into the dark of a near-by court. Behind her lumbered
two burly fellows, who wavered for a moment, then,

guessing the road she had taken, plunged after her into the darkness. We were across the causey and on their tails without a word exchanged. We found a girl crouched in a corner, her plaid torn off and thrown on the flags, the stupor of terror holding her still.

With a leap I was at the throat of the man who had a hand on her, a man with a small head, round as a cannon-ball, and an ugly look on the face of him. He was taken by surprise, but butted savagely, catching me on the chin. Shaken, I loosened my hold and paused to win back my breath, and a kick which would have lamed me, if it had landed as he meant, glanced past my knee. Fury rushed through me in a boiling flood, and I flung him, caught off his balance, reeling wildly backwards. He fell heavily, his head striking the stones with the crack of a nut, and he lay still. I turned, to find Jock sitting astride the other *scalag*, dunting his head forcefully on the flags.

" That was no fight at all," I said.

" Just a pair o' burgh rats," he agreed contemptuously, rising to his feet.

I picked up the girl's plaid and put it round her shoulders. She shrank back from me, a haggard dread on her, and I smiled to reassure her, saying: " Now we will be taking you home."

" The port is shut; I cannot go home."

Fear seemed to have taken her voice from her, for she spoke scarcely above a whisper.

" Then, what friends have you? "

She shook her head.

" We could take you back to the house you have just left."

She shuddered and covered her eyes with her fingers.

" My uncle's. No! They burst open the door and

struck him down, old as he is, when he faced them. He
cried to me to run, and I got out through a window. A
band of them are there yet. They are leaving nothing,
nothing but just the bare walls."

She told it in the same frightened whisper, with little
gasps that were very pitiful.

Dhe ! This might have happened to Barbara last
night, I said to myself. I sweated at the thought.

Why, I asked fiercely, must folk come from the
country, where doors stand open all day to the winds
and the sunshine, and shut themselves into the dark of
these high-piled dens that smelt filthily, and where
scalags, like those at our feet, routed like swine? What
if this girl had been Barbara! I cursed silently as I
thought of her in the hands of beasts like these. And
yet the Lowlanders, many of them, think of us as
savages, but I never met clansmen greater savages than
these. A dirty fighter that one, too! A black death to
him!

Jock and I looked at each other, puzzled what to do.

" Mistress Binnie? " I questioned.

" Impossible! Never think of it. The auld wife would
raise Auld Hornie if we took a Catholic to her door,"
Jock said. " The only thing I see for it is taking her to
Mistress Stewart. She might take her in. We can try,
anyway."

" Now listen," he went on to the girl, " keep your
plaid over your face, and walk as if you were just
taking a daunder to look at the crowd, and the crowd's
that busy wi' their own affairs, they'll never notice
you."

But, indeed, the girl could not walk very well, and we
had both to help her. By the time we had reached
Mistress Stewart's she was leaning very heavily, and

seemed too exhausted to care where we were taking her. Arrived at the house, Jock made the necessary explanations, while I stood just inside the door, supporting the girl. She was very young, seen in the light of the room, a slender, frail little lass, conquered by her night of terror. Her head fell back on my shoulder, hair as fair as my own spraying over my sleeve. Her eyes were closed, and the long, dark lashes rested on cheeks so pale there scarcely seemed life in them. There was an angry scratch on her left temple.

Barbara's eyes were cold as she looked at her. It is strange how little sympathy a woman, usually kind and generous, will sometimes show to another in trouble!

" Is it safe for you to be taking her in, auntie? " she asked, standing far back from us.

" Safe? It's far from safe. But what would you have me do? Put the lassie in the street again this night? Who is she? I've seen her often about the town."

Jock did all the talking.

" One of the Lindsays. She lives beyond Duddingston and came to visit her uncle yesterday."

" Of course! I should have minded her. Well, then, you could take her to the Duke of Gordon's; he's a friend o' her uncle's. Blair's Close, on the Castlehill! "

" Too late. He has withdrawn with his servants into the Castle. The mob smashed his coach and stole his horses an hour syne."

" No! Did they though? Then things are worse than I thought. Of course I'll keep her here for the night, but come for her early the morn."

" We'll get her through the port as soon as it's open."

" Do that. I'll have her ready for you. Away wi' you both now. And if I was you I wouldna get taigled wi' more strange females for a whilie."

She signalled to Barbara to help her with the girl, and waved us vigorously from the room.

CHAPTER X

At Duddingston

I KICKED my heels impatiently at the stair-foot. I had decided that I would not see Barbara again. It was indeed a hard blow Fate had dealt me bringing me here, when I had fled from her and was doing my best to forget her. " Where a woman is, temptation will be," said the good Saint Columba. Well, inside the Castle I would be well away from temptation, so the sooner I was there the easier for me. This I was thinking as I waited for Jock to fetch down the girl we had fought for in the close the night before. She had not much spirit, I decided, as I recalled the scene. No, Barbara would not have been like that. A Highland girl would have fought, with the pin of her plaid if with nothing else, and the Mackays are all good fighters, give them their due. The morning air was very keen. I wished Jock would hurry. There was a thin sprinkling of snow, and again there was that pale moon that looked so weary in the early hours. Jock came at last, after what seemed to me a long delay. The girl had nothing to say; whether she was shy or still frightened, it was hard to tell.

Some women were drawing water at a fountain and looked at us speculatively. A couple of muckmen were cleaning out a close where there was to be a wedding. Booth-keepers were taking down their shutters and complaining to each other of the cold. The rioting was over and the rioters were still sleeping. Some broken staves and burnt-out torches, with here and there a chair-back or chair-leg, littered the causey. Jock pointed to a crucifix that lay near the gutter, and the girl drew closer her plaid. When we approached the Netherbow she said haltingly: " My uncle! Could we see if perhaps he is in the house? "

We found the door gaping wide, swinging on its hinges in the draught from a broken window. There was no sign of life inside, nothing but just the bare walls, as the girl had said, and a heap of smashed furniture, a forlorn shell of a house we were glad to get out of.

It seemed that a couple of horses and a Lindsay servant man had been left at the " White Horse," but on inquiring for him we found he had vanished, taking the horses with him.

" Nothing for you, then, but shanks' naigie," Jock told the girl. " But it's only a step to Duddingston; we'll be there in a crack."

Once outside the city wall we were in a lonely little glen, with only the ravens and the sheep for company. Along the foot of Salisbury Craigs, round the haunch of the Lion hill, the dawn-light haloing his head, by the still waters of Duddingston Loch, where wild-fowl were stirring, Jock guided us, till he delivered the girl safely at the door of a mansion that stood beyond the village.

" I'm glad she's safe," said Jock, as we turned hastily away, not wanting to wait for thanks. " Poor bit thing, she got a sair fright last night. Now, Alastair, I have two old aunties here, and it's time I was giving them a look-in. We'll get a bite too, and that'll not come amiss."

He pushed open the door of a house near the kirk, and walked into a room where a fire was burning brightly and a woman was brushing crumbs from the table into

her cupped palm. She straightened up and cried:
" Jock, what brings you here at this time o' day? But
I think I can guess, you rascal, and ye'se get none this
time."

" Now, Aunt Janet, I came to see you, but if you've
never a welcome for me or my friend here we'll e'en
take the road again."

" Sit down," she said shortly, " both of you." Then,
raising her voice, she called through the doorway of an
inner room: " Betsy, here's Jock."

" Back again! " exclaimed an answering voice. " He'll
be after more siller. What does the wastrel do with it,
I ask you? "

" I cannot tell, but if you have any sense you'll give
him none this time. He's got a friend with him."

" A friend! " came from the unseen speaker. " Is the
friend after siller too? "

Jock grinned happily, but I felt myself flush with
embarrassment.

" They're both a wee hard o' hearing," he whispered,
" and they forget other folk hear well enough."

" Come out, Aunt Betsy," he shouted, " and show a
little kindness to your poor nephew."

The two sisters stood framed in the doorway, tall, big-
boned women, with a strong resemblance to each other.
Betsy's was the older face and the kinder one; Janet's
the stronger and the better-featured. Betsy stooped a
little and her hair was dead and grey. Janet carried
herself like a trooper. She had one lock silvery white,
that lay like a feather among her still dark hair.

" The kindness I'm going to show you is to give you
some good advice," Betsy said severely, though her eyes
were soft as she looked at Jock.

" No use to me, Aunt Betsy," he said mournfully.

" It's queer, now, I never could find a use for advice.
I aye give it away, the same as lots do besides
me. But if you could spare me a kiss, and a bit
bannock, I'll take them and my cauld welcome away
with me."

He rose and kissed both his aunts resoundingly. Janet
held him at arm's-length, saying: " We'll not grudge
you the bit bannock, though isn't it just like you, Jock,
to come for a meal when it's over, and the next one a
long time ahead! "

He sniffed.

" Well, I smell hot bannocks, and they'll sit a lot
better inside a toom stomach than cold advice. And
while I'm eating I'll tell you the story of what brought
me here."

" I'm thinking it's your usual errand," his Aunt Janet
said, still suspicious, " only this time it's maybe siller
to give away."

She looked at me and I said quickly: " It is not for
me. I have plenty for all my wants just now."

" Then in that case," was the reply, " you're the right
friend for Jock, though, I'm warning you, he is maybe
not the right friend for you. You'd best keep your
sporran buttoned."

" I am not afraid of him," I said, sitting in happily to
a platter of bannocks and ewe-cheese.

" Now, Aunt Janet," said Jock huffily, " you must
agree I aye pay you back when I borrow. Don't I
now? "

" Yes," she admitted grudgingly, " you do. But with
the next breath you're borrowing again. I wish I saw
an end to both borrowing and paying back. But what
brought you? You have still to tell us."

Between mouthfuls, Jock told of the tumult in the

town, and at the tale his aunts raised their hands and looked very distressed.

" I hope, laddie, that you'll keep out of the fighting, and your friend too," his Aunt Betsy said anxiously. " Jock, you're a great worry to us. The one and only thing you can do is fight."

" Yes," her sister put in, " and if your father had not left you a competency, where would you be? You chose the soldiering, and now what are you? "

" I've tried to be a soldier," he protested, " and I think I made a damned good one."

" You are not even a soldier now," she said sharply.

" I've been disbanded, if you like, Aunt Janet, but I'm still an officer in the service of King James, and I'm thinking before long I'll be busy enough."

" Laddie, would you not go north and stay quietly with your uncle in Glen Urquhart? " his Aunt Betsy pleaded. " At least till this blows by."

" Aunt Betsy, I could not. I was bred in the town and I ken but ae trade. I'm sorry my aunties do not like me, seeing they're near the only relations I've got. Alastair, you and me will away, for we're no' wanted here."

He looked round for his bonnet, but instantly his aunts were urging him to stay for dinner.

" Well," he said, mollified, " maybe we will. We'll take a bit walk till it's ready."

We strolled towards the loch-side, past the kirk, where a woman who had been set to wearing the jougs stood rigid against the wall fronting the road. She glared savagely at us as we gave her a careless glance in passing.

" One man is going to eat his dinner in peace this

day," Jock said, laughing, " but she's no' cured. I can tell by her glower."

We climbed the slopes and sat on a large, flat boulder to look down on the loch. Many a time in the days that followed, when we rarely had a chance to be still or be alone, I looked back with pleasure on the quiet of that hour. The sun was bright, striking brilliants from the frosty ground and stringing a girdle of gems across the water. Coot and mallard sailed out from the rushes and paused lazily to float in the ripples. A pair of herons fished industriously on the far side for their dinner, flapping heavily to a new fishing-ground when done with the old. The Castle of Craigmillar brooded sadly over its ruined walls, but it still dominated the country for miles around. The little thatched cottages of Duddingston village slept happily in the sunshine, only the spirals of smoke telling of preparation for the midday meal.

" I did not know it was like this near the town," I said, looking round me with pleasure.

" Aye, it's bonny! Duddy's bonny," Jock said reflectively.

He lay back on the stone and tilted his bonnet to keep the sun-glare from his eyes. He went on softly, almost as if he were speaking to himself: " When I was sodgering in yon England, many a dark night in a bivouac what I was seeing was Duddingston Loch, sparkling in the sun as it is the day. And many a night, when I lay near stifled with heat on a barrack floor, I was pinin' for the blasts o' the Windy Ghoul. I could picture it a', the Whinny Knowe, and the whinchats' nests wi' the wee blue eggs, the Girnel Craig, and Samson's Ribs, that so often I've tried to climb as a laddie on my hands and toes and the knees o' my breeks."

So Jock, as well as myself, made pictures of places!

We were both quiet for a while, for I had a sudden hunger for the wash of western waves and the sight of great bens rising steeply from the sea.

" Dod, but we mustn't let a good dinner spoil," said Jock, making off suddenly down the hill at speed.

It was a good dinner that awaited us.

" Annie's gone out of her way this day for you, Jock," his Aunt Janet declared. " I'm sure she never takes this trouble for us, the limmer."

" I'll see Annie about this later," Jock chuckled, " to thank her. Annie's a bonny lassie."

" Bonny? She's just a purpose-like, brosie lassie and no more, and you'll let her be. You'll not go near her."

" As near as she'll let me, Aunt Janet. I got no nearer than the end of the dish-clout the last time."

" Then I hope you get the same again. You let her be."

" Where is she? "

" She's out with Adam Robb hunting the sow, that had to bolt just as the dinner was being dished. Adam's our man," she explained to me, " that mucks out the byre, and the sty, digs a bit, sleds the turf for the fire; indeed, turns his hand to anything."

" Will you look at these carp now? " said Aunt Betsy. " Adam brought them in for you. He minded you were fond of them."

" That was kind of him. Did he net them himself, think ye? "

" I know not, but he never bends his elbow to get fish for us." This was Aunt Janet speaking again. " Isn't it queer why he should bother about you, that never did a thing for him, and we, that have done many a kindness to him and his, get never a fin by way of thanks. They're a pair, Annie and him! "

" Come now, Aunt Janet; he's far owre auld for Annie. That would never do."

" You're wilfully misunderstanding me, but I'll say my say in spite of you. See to this bird—the best layer among my young hens. That's what Annie does for you when I tell her to kill a fowl. The laird will never see that one now."

" Well, it's her notion of a fatted calf, bless her! She was doing her best to welcome the prodigal."

" You've said the right word this time, anyway. But eat it up, seeing it'll never lay eggs more."

As we finished eating, Annie arrived, blown, but full of talk about the chase, a strapping lass with strong young arms that made light of heavy work. When she had eaten she set about carrying off the pewter to be cleaned.

" I'm coming through to ask after your health," said Jock, rising. Whereupon she flung him a saucy glance over her shoulder.

" And I'm coming with you to see you keep within bounds."

His Aunt Janet shook the crumbs from her lap and followed close on his heels.

Presently there came a screech in a lassie's voice, laughter and a shout from Jock.

" Hear to that laddie," Betsy Grant exclaimed, smiling happily. " He livens up his two old aunts every time he sets foot here. I like fine to have him about the house. It's dull, dull, when he goes."

She rose and closed the door stealthily, then drew in a chair close to me.

" My sister is younger than me," she said, low, " though maybe you would not think it. You'll have noticed how hard of hearing she is; it makes her a bit short in the temper. Oh, my me! but she's a fashious woman to do with. She's tidying for evermore; or else sanding and polishing. She would polish the stars if she could win to them, and sweep along the tidemark if so be we lived at the seashore. She would so.

" She's not fond of dogs—she'll not keep one—but," she said, rising, " I'm going to let that poor beast of yours in and see what I can find for him. Oh, the time it is since I saw a deer-hound! "

She set a platter on the floor.

" It is forty years since I left Glen Urquhart, laddie—time enough to change into a Lowlander—and the last I saw was at Shewglie. Jock's father persuaded us to come south when my father died and my older brother heired the house and married, and, would you believe it, we've never been back.

" My, but he has made a mess," she said, looking ruefully at the floor. " I'll smart for this when Janet gets a sight of it."

The minute the younger sister entered the room her eyes fell on Dileas, happily licking from the floor the food that his tongue had scattered. She gave Betsy a look that said more than words, and that lady hastily left the room in a confusion, saying she wanted to see what Jock was about.

As the door closed, Janet took the chair her sister had just left and said softly, with a swift glance at the door: " You may not think it, but my sister's gey ill to live with. She's deaf as a post, as you'll have noticed, and that makes her sharg at me when she does not hear. Believe me, whiles she would try the patience of a saint. I leave a room redd, and it's like a dog's den with five minutes of her. Send her to seek something in a drawer and she'll stir it till it's like fish guts and a body can find

K

nothing. You can aye tell where Betsy's been by the wool ravellings and crumbs and clippings. She could keep a grown woman working after her. Look at that floor now. It's your dog, so I'll not say much, but what was hindering her to feed him outside? I ask you!"

Smiling to myself at the two sides to the same story, I said how grieved I was at the bad manners of Dileas and asked to be forgiven for bringing him.

" My bark's worse than my bite," she said mildly in reply. " It was Betsy I was angered at, not you. I am very pleased to see you here with Jock. He's a nice bit laddie and he makes it cheery for two dull old women."

Jock came in to hear her say: " You seem a quiet lad. Try to keep him out of mischief."

He stood stock-still in the doorway.

" Him quiet!" he said indignantly. " And leading me into two fights in as many days. It's me that's looking after him; and I wish ye kent me better, Aunt Janet. But you're like a' the women, taken with his bonny face and yellow hair."

At that I lunged at him, and soon we were rolling on the floor in a wrestling bout, till the old ladies, screeching that their furniture would be broken, begged us to be done.

" That will serve to show you how quiet a lad he is," said Jock, taking my bonnet to dust his breeches. Whereupon I dusted my hands in his hair.

" Well, we're for off," said Jock. " It gets soon dark."

" Listen here," said his Aunt Janet, " before you go. I'm not sure you did right in bringing that Romanist lassie home. You should not meddle with things that are none of your business, and I hope you'll mind that."

" But she was such a helpless bit thing," said Jock.
" What else could we do? "

" She is a Romanist," said his aunt grimly. " You
could have left her to look after herself. Jock, Jock, I
fear you are no good churchman."

" I am what I was made," Jock said shortly, " by a
father and mother who were of different creeds."

" Aye," his Aunt Betsy said, shaking her head, " your
mother was of Covenanting stock."

" And I was hauled this way and that. A Covenanter
one Sabbath, an Episcopalian the next. And what am I
now? God kens! "

" The Covenanters—shame on them!—are to blame
for all the trouble the country is in now; the King fled
and all this rioting."

" Be not so sure of that, Aunt Janet. I would not lay
a' the blame at their door. God gave them memory and
they're using it. You've not forgotten already the Highland Host that treated the poor devils worse than vermin?
Whose wyte was that? Atholl's and Perth's. Scotland's
been cursed with a pack o' gentry that drove the country to
distraction, the worst of them all the turncoat Covenanter
Lauderdale. It's queer how men that turn their coats
are aye the hardest on their old friends. Mackenzie, the
King's Advocate, is another o' the same."

" Wheesht, Jock," his Aunt Janet said anxiously.

" Oh, I watch where I am when I speak out. This is
the first time I've said what was in my mind. But you're
maybe no' aware that Episcopalians are near as much
hated as Catholics in the town. That reminds me,
Alastair, your tartan's a danger. I should have been
fitting you out in Lowland homespun instead of dallying
here a' day. But it'll be dark by the time we're through
the port, and you'll maybe escape much notice."

" Come back soon, Jock," his aunts called after us, " and we'll never ask your errand."

" We'll be back soon, never fear," Jock answered, waving his bonnet.

But a crown had fallen, and Jock was a hunted man, before we saw Duddingston again.

CHAPTER XI

Revolution

GLOAMING was stealing the colours from the western sky when we left the loch-side, and by the time we drew near to the town a sombre blue was over it. I halted suddenly. Then, " Kettle-drums! " I cried.

" I have been thinking for some time I heard drumming," said Jock uneasily. " Listen! There's a most unholy row forbye the drums." He pointed excitedly. " See to yon. A big lowe! Somewhere about the Abbeyhill. Now what——" He gripped my arm and said tensely: " I believe that's the Chancellor's house. Aye, that's just where the Perth mansion stands."

We hurried on past Holyroodhouse and headed towards where a broad tongue of fire was licking at the gloom, glowing and growing with what it fed on.

" It's the Chancellor's place right enough," said Jock, smartening the pace. " The Duke of Gordon was feared for something like this and was keen for him to go into the Castle. But Perth's not one to take advice; he's the kind that aye kens best."

We found a large, excited crowd round the house, the front of which was now sheeted with flames. Hogsheads of ale and casks of wine, taken from the cellar, were piled on the grass. These were rapidly being broached and sampled by men who staggered back and forth, brawling round the spigots. Empty barrels were rolling about, and whiles these would be pounced on by a band of unruly bairns and trundled up the slope. Then, screaming with excitement, they would start one down the hill and yell with laughter as it swept the legs from the unwary.

Presently the cabars fell in with a crash, raining a shower of sparks over those who had ventured close. At this the crowd raised a great cheering, and it was a signal for a rush to the barrels to toast the fall of the ducal roof-tree.

" Every man and boy is armed," I said, " and did you ever see such a collection of weapons? "

We had halted some distance away and were observing the scene from the shadows.

" Aye, they're an ugly lot," Jock replied. " Muskets, pistols, cudgels, sickles—what have they no' got? See to that! Even the laddies have knives tied to the ends of staves. And the trouble is, that the malt's abune the meal already."

" I hear them saying the Chancellor has bolted for the north, taking the Treasury money with him."

" That's a lie, about the money, anyway. But very likely Perth's making across the Forth for his castle. I wonder what this blaze will kindle? Alastair, d'ye ken, I'm feared to see this lot so out of hand. You have no notion of the fury of an Edinburgh mob. They'll stick at nothing and will face a regiment with but sticks and stones in their hands. You'll maybe never have heard o' the Stoppit Stravaig? There, an unarmed crowd held up a whole troop o' horsemen fully armed, and the Duke of Montrose was the only one to win through." He shook his head gloomily.

The noise about us was deafening, but under and through it all, low and menacing, came the insistent summons of the kettle-drums.

" Here, you," said Jock, catching hold of a laddie who

was skirmishing with a knife on the edge of the crowd.
" What are the drums making all the ado about? "

" The Catholics have planned to fire the toun this
very night, and the drums are crying the burghers to
arm and defend their hames."

He was so worked on that the words poured from him
in one breath, and he was so eager to be off that he tore
himself free and dived down a lane of legs.

" A plot to fire the town! " I exclaimed, startled.
" Surely that cannot be true."

" Perfect havers! That's what it is. Hatred and fear
hatched the story, and that pair have aye an ugly brood."

A blaze farther east now told that the Niddrie mansion
was going up in flames, and soon the whole night sky was
shot with the glow of fires for seven miles round, even as
far as the chapel of Rosslyn, as the torch was set to the
houses of well-known Catholics. Then suddenly there
came the rattle of musketry and the bursting of hand-
grenades, and the fire-raisers, forsaking the ruin before
them, pushed and scrambled towards the sound of
fighting, sweeping us along with them.

When we came to the Water Gate we found a sullen
crowd retreating from the entrance to Holyroodhouse, a
crowd that, not to be cheated by the Provost and a locked
port, had been gathering since afternoon in the Cowgate,
and now had rushed up the Netherbow and stormed
down the Canongate. In front of the Palace was drawn
up a company of soldiers with smoking muskets, and on
the wide, open piazza in front a dozen still figures lay
a-sprawl, while three times that number writhed on the
ground or rose swaying to their feet. Then the crowd
was gone, with the same haste as it had come. But not
for long. Soon from over a thousand throats we heard
the roar, " To Holyrood! To Holyrood! " and it was

back swollen in numbers, stronger in purpose, headed this time by the magistrates and the soldiers of the train-bands—back with an order from the Privy Council to surrender the Palace.

Captain Wallace, who was in command of the small band that held the Palace, stepped forward and shouted defiantly when asked to lay down arms: " We take orders from none save the King. Withdraw, or I fire. Men, present arms! "

At that the bailies scurried away to safety, and breaking through them came the Militia and the Westland Whigs, loading and firing, closing in fiercely on the little group of King's men.

" The odds are terrible," Jock groaned. " I should be helping Wallace, if I could win through. What a mistake he made in not staying indoors and firing from the windows. He'll not stand much longer."

And now their backs were to the wall, and they were stabbing and parrying at close quarters, many down but the remnant still gallantly holding off the attack, so few against so many that the end could not be long delayed. It came quickly. Some of the City Guard slipped round to the rear, climbed the wall and attacked from the inner court, and the game was played. Muskets down and the stand for the last Stuart King was over. Then, with the mutter and threat of a thunderstorm, came the rabble, treading on the dying, thrusting at the prisoners, sweeping into the old home of Scotland's royal line, slashing pictures, smashing cabinets, tearing down tapestry; into the private garde-robe of the King, plundering and rending, nothing left unsoiled, unhandled. Then into the private chapel—vestments torn, images smashed, vessels fought over; into the Abbey Church and out again, leaving a toppled throne, an organ for ever silent, a fouled altar-cloth stamped to ribbons, even the marble floor torn up and carried off; ruin and destruction, where fury and force had passed.

But there still remained lust and brutality, so up the Canongate again to the houses of the Catholics, where terrified women crouched in corners, telling their beads, and Holyrood was left to the night and silence. And a pale moon looked through the great window on the rifled coffins of queens and kings, where all that was left of beauty and power lay pitifully exposed.

We watched it all in impotent rage. Again and again my sword arm flew to my haunch, but each time Jock gripped it, whispering: " Madness, man! We can do nothing."

But when we were left alone in the moonlight Jock cried bitterly: " Alastair, this is no riot. This is Revolution. The sun has gone down for the auld house o' Stuart, and, if you ask me, it's a gey bloody sunset. And to lose Scotland for a mass! My King, but a damned fool! That auld Abbey he took for the Papists, from the folk that had aye worshipped there. They've taken it back with blood and vengeance this night, and if I ken them they'll keep it. He had Edinburgh at his feet when he was Duke of York, cheered everywhere he went, crowds following him and watching him at his games o' tennis. Never did a king ascend a throne more loved and rejoiced over. One of the bravest men in battle, on land or on water, that ever lived, the hero of the great sea-fight off Lowestoft. What has come owre him? Now a fushionless, off-puttin', swithering auld wife, quaking in his shoes because his son-in-law's landed from Holland; his throne lost, everything lost. And all for a mass! But he's still King by right, and as long as there's a chance to bring him back, I'm his man."

"You make too much of it, Jock," I said. "This will not be the end for King James. His daughters would never grab the crown from their father."

"A pair of bitches!" said Jock angrily. "And these are no' my words, but the words of one of his Ministers. Mary's holding up her head for the crown already. The only thing that's keeping it off her brow is that Dutch William wants to be king and no' just the queen's husband. Aye, after what I've seen the night, I feel gey sure we've seen the last o' the Stuarts. But, when even his daughters have left him, he has the more need o' friends."

"Hear to that! Do you ken that song? I never thought to hear the Scots singing it."

A band of young men swept out of the White Horse Wynd, shouting the gay, mocking chorus: *Lillibulero-lero-lero, Lillibulero, bullin-a-la.*

"That's the song a' London was singing when I left —the song that helped to put King James off the throne. They sang it even under the very windows o' the Palace."

He broke off suddenly and started at a run towards Holyroodhouse.

"Ye lousy gnaff," he shouted furiously, as he leapt at a figure crouching in the doorway. "Would you fire the Palace?"

He struck the fellow—a little maggot of a man—a blow across the wrist, making him drop the torch he was carrying, and stamped out the heap of rubbish smouldering at the door. The man reeled drunkenly at Jock, who, with a disdainful push, sent him sprawling.

"Now, march," said Jock, waiting to see him stumble to his feet and lurch off unwillingly, scattering wild and uncouth oaths.

"I will wager that by to-morrow yon one will not

even be knowing what he tried to do," I said, watching him go. "He is needing all his head to keep his feet."

"It's as well I noticed him," Jock returned shortly. "I felt like murder when I got to him. I let him off owre easy. He has reason to be glad I'm done with him."

But the man was not done with us, for as we crossed the Girth we found him waiting, nursing his grievance, and he fell in behind. It was strangely quiet and deserted here, but screams and clamour told where the crowd was busy higher up the street. Suddenly our follower, stumbling along at our backs, gave tongue to his thoughts.

"Papists!" he bawled. Then, taking a few uncertain steps, he stood still and bawled again: "Papists! Romanists!"

"Listen to that cuddy's braying," Jock muttered uneasily. "I doubt I'll have to stop him staichering along behind us."

He had just spoken the last word when two men crossed the street and blocked the way. Where they came from we never knew.

"Stand, Romanists!" ordered the one who took the outside.

"Romanist yourself," Jock said indignantly. "Let me by."

He made to force a passage.

"I said 'Stand!'"

"I would like to ken by what law or authority you give the order to anybody to stand."

"There is no law in this town to-night——"

"You're right there," Jock cried bitterly; "neither law nor order."

"—but the law of the strong arm of vengeance." The stranger sternly completed his interrupted sentence.

"Very good, then," Jock observed jauntily. "We have a reason to be among the law-makers. Let me by. I have said we are no Romanists."

I took stock of our opponents. No drunken scum of the closes these. Both had an air of command and carried good swords. The one who, so far, had done all the talking, and who confronted me, was powerfully built, had singularly piercing eyes and spoke with a strong burr. The other, who faced Jock, was smaller, walked with a limp, and throughout the encounter seemed angrily impatient to come to blows. He fidged withte his sword-strap and fingered the hilt all the time his friend was speaking.

But the fuddled brain was working again. It had got hold of one idea and worked it hard.

"Papishts, I say. Came out of Holyrood," went on the thick voice.

"Do you hear that?" The man with the limp spoke for the first time. "Why do you wait to listen to them?"

"Would you take the word of that drunken hash before mine?" Jock demanded, with flashing eyes, his hand going to his side.

"Will you stand aside and let us pass?" I said very softly, but there was no mistaking my determination.

The man in my path swept me with a disdainful glance.

"Your cloth, of course, is always on the side of oppression."

"If by my cloth you mean my tartan, I will have you know it has never known an oppressor, and it will not be taking kindly to oppression now. Let me pass, or draw."

The hot words poured from me breathlessly and my hand leapt to my haunch.

"Draw," said my opponent.

" Papishts! " came the monotonous tale for the last time, for, in drawing my sword, the hilt caught our follower by accident in the teeth, knocking him senseless.

And the swords were out.

Jock was not long in finding he was more than a match for his man, and was unwilling to take advantage of one so inferior in foot-work, though he fought with the ferocity of hatred. But he tired quickly and Jock, making up his mind to finish the fight before supports arrived, quickly disarmed him.

I was better matched. The tall man was no mean sworder and fought with a bitter determination and boring strength that in the first rush took all my skill to combat. But he had seemingly not met a left-handed opponent before, and the passes of my big broadsword bewildered him. He fought doggedly, but I had no doubts about holding him. I lunged in what I meant to be the final stroke. My sword met empty air, and the big man, with a strangled cry, staggered backwards. He clutched at the air, vainly trying to keep his feet, then plumped down like a toddling bairn. He blinked up at me stupidly.

It was Dileas was the cause of it.

He had been off on errands of his own and I had not seen him since leaving the Palace. Seeing me being attacked he had taken part in the fight, and the part he took was the seat of a pair of breeches, which he still worried, growling savagely.

There came the sound of hurrying feet.

" Run," said Jock in my ear.

And we ran.

Into a close that connected with a wide, square court we pelted, and over to the door of a house in the far corner. Here Jock did not use the risp, but knocked on

the door with a curious tattoo, the knock being evidently
a signal. The door was instantly flung open.

"Shoot the bolt," Jock gasped. "Through the house
and out again is all I'm asking, Archie. Where's your
back door? And dinna speir what brings us, for I canna
bide to tell you."

Along a dark passage we were guided, a door was
opened and closed, and there again was the sky, with a
sparkle of stars. Without a pause or a word spoken we
were racing down a strip of garden towards a high wall.
I bent my back.

"Up, lad, and over," I commanded Dileas, who
obeyed with guilty haste. With a leap Jock and I were
clawing our way up the wall together. All was quiet as
we dropped on the grass.

Then, on the banks of the Cowgait Burn, we gave way
to a storm of silent laughter. We rolled on the turf,
holding our sides, choking in our throats the sounds we
were forced to hold in. I laid down my face, which was
wet with the tears that laughter brings, on my dog's neck
and gasped: "Oh, Dileas, Dileas, you are no gentleman.
That was no way to be ending a fight, and it was a bonny
fight. I had him, but now he will be saying that you
kept him from getting me. Och, boy! You will have to
learn to keep your teeth from a gentlemen's quarrel."

"See to him," said Jock, gulping. "He doesna care
a docken leaf."

And we lay back on the grass helpless once more,
aching with the pain of our mirth.

Jock was the first to recover. He sat up suddenly and
said: "Alastair, we'll have to be moving, and it's not
up the Canongate I'll walk again this night. We'd better
keep out of sight for a bit. I think yon pair are some
kind of leaders; they've been sodgers at any rate. Balfour

of Burleigh's in the town, back from Holland, and there must be a wheen of the old Bothwell Brig Cameronians with him. Yon lad o' mine was a fierce birkie, but I suspect it was revenge he was seeking for the limp. Poor devil, he maybe got it in Lauderdale's torture-chamber, if he didna bring it from Bothwell. Now you two are a kenspeckle pair, Mackenzie tartan and a hound the size o' a calf. So we'll e'en take a by-road."

We moved off along the base of a wall which served as a boundary to the gardens of the Canongate. The hard ground rang under our feet. The crisp knife-edges of the ruts crackled as we trod them down. We heard the ripple of the burn, that was a silver thread among the rushes. About us streamed the moonlight, its cold, calm gleam condemning the angry glare over the town, which lay like a huge tailed monster, black against the lurid sky, here and there a bright claw of flame cleaving the smoke pall. Whiles there came to us the crack of a musket, but the sounds of rioting were toned by distance to the buzz of a furious wasp.

" Where are we going? " I asked. " The ports will be closed."

" Dinna let that fash you," answered Jock. " I'll show you a way to speil the wall near the Potterrow. I've done it often afore."

CHAPTER XII

A Knock on the Door

IT was the old woman who answered our insistent knocking. We heard the feeble, dragging steps and the slow fumbling with the sneck. Then she opened to us.

"Mirren's no' in. Come ben; I want a word wi' ye," she said grimly, pointing the way into the kitchen.

She walked painfully, leaning heavily on her stick, and to help her I put an arm under her elbow, leading her to a chair. She looked at me distrustfully, but took my guidance.

"I want nae truck wi' your kind," was her gruff response, "and I'd liefer stand. I want to ken," she went on, with a warlike glint in her eye, "if you're a Papist."

"I am not. I am an Episcopalian."

I took a seat on the table, smiling at this dour old catechist.

"H'm, then ye drink from the same quaich. Ye belong to a persecuting Church, and you're not biding here longer. I'll hae nae enemies o' the Covenant under my roof."

I was so astonished at this sudden attack that I could find no words, but Jock, who had been carelessly spinning his bonnet on the tip of his forefinger, said warmly: "Come now, mistress, we took a room and we're paying for it. We're going soon, but we'll gang at our ain time. We have nothing to do with your persecutions."

She turned slowly towards him.

" Is that e'en sae? And will ye be good enough to tell me what Kirk ye belong till? "

Jock said, looking puzzled: " I dinna rightly ken, and that's the truth. There's no Kirk for one o' my upbringing."

Though bent nearly double over her stick on which she leaned, with two twisted, knuckled hands in front of her, she painfully straightened her old bent back and a flame of anger kindled in her eyes.

" You! " she flashed scornfully at him. " I ken your kind. You'll gang the grey gait yet. Neither ae thing nor the tother. Like the people of Laodicea, neither hot nor cold. And what says the Book of the Revelation about them? ' Because thou art lukewarm, and neither hot nor cold, I will spue thee out of my mouth.' "

" Och, haud on," said the outraged Jock, but she interrupted him:

" Little as I like this callant, better him than you, for I ken what he stands for."

There was a vigour in her speech that matched strangely the frailty of her body, but she could stand no longer, and sat down heavily in her chair.

" I do not understand your dislike to me or to my Church," I said, pitying the old woman, " but we will go as soon as possible. You would not have us go at once? The town is wild to-night."

" Aye, the toun's wild," she repeated; " but wild only for those and such as those, and they'll maybe learn the meaning o' persecution now."

" They are learning," I told her gravely. " Houses are in flames. Women are being shamefully abused; the

L

closes are ringing with their screams. And this is all being done in the name of God and the Covenant."

She eyed me steadily, then said quietly: "So you're he'rt-sair owre a wheen screeching Papist limmers, are you? And what do you feel when you think o' the hunder-and-odd men and women that they hanged in the Grassmercat for God and a broken Covenant? And what o' the eighteen thousand that from first to last, Episcopalians and Papists atween them, have slaughtered for their faith? Your name's Mackenzie. Are ye sib to Bluidy Mackenzie, the King's Advocate?"

"A kinsman of my chief. But I do not know the gentleman under that name."

"Dinna ca' him that! Mackenzie of Rosehaugh, Scotland kens, and will aye ken, as Bluidy Mackenzie. A bonnie crew you're in wi': Bluidy Dalziel, Bluidy Claverse and Bluidy Mackenzie. They've soaked the heather and stained the causey till their very names shout o' their crimes."

"I do not know about that, but I saw the very threshold of the Palace stained this night. Some of the guard were murdered."

"Never mourn for yon brats o' Belial," she said, with contempt. "And you'll be grieving because Perth's braw mansion's brunt and his duchess canna bide mair in Embro? Wha are they, you should lament for them? Her!—a strumpet that married him, and his wife a bare week i' the mools. Him!—one o' your ain persuasion that turned Catholic to keep his job and invented the thumbikins to torture the martyrs. I wad rejoice if I was sure an end had been put to him and his ill-doing."

She paused for breath, and went on: "Ye dinna ken. Ye havena heard! But I ken, and I ha'e seen—lots and

lots o' things in my long, unhappy life. I was glad,
glad "—she thumped on the floor with her stick twice—
" when I heard the rattle o' drums outby this nicht, for
I said to myself that a new day will have dawned for
Scotland. Often enough I've heard the drums beat to
close the ports and seen the sodgers burst in here as they
searched from house to house for some field preacher
they were seeking to find. And owre often they would
find their man. And next I would see him dragged before
Lauderdale. And the end was aye the same—his head
on a Tolbooth spike, his hands in mockery clasped in
prayer. I ken fine what ye think o' me. A dune auld
runt, bitter and hard, ye say. Weel, I'm what the times
ha'e made me, for we live in bitter, hard times, God help
us! Thirty years o' the boot and the wuddy ha'e I seen,
and a' for seekin' to worship our Maker as we saw fit.
I ha'e ae prayer now and ae prayer only: ' Lord! Lord!
Mak' we ready and tak' me awa', for I'm weel ser'ed o'
this world.' "

She bowed her head silently for a moment's space.

" And wait you till you young sprouts ha'e seen as
many storms and frosts as I ha'e seen, ha'e stood as
long, after watching your best and bonniest broken,
broken——"

There was no anger now in the old woman's voice,
only sorrow, and sorrow in the place of scorn in her dim
old eyes.

" I had twa sons," she said tensely, leaning forward in
her chair. " One went doon at Bothwell Brig, a sad loss,
but a clean death, a sodger's death. The other was taken
prisoner at the Brig and brought on here. Awa' back in
'66 I saw Dalziel, wi' his long black beard, ride in his
rusty armour at the head o' his prisoners from Rullion,
faithful men that he had loaded wi' weary chains. That

was bad, but no' like this. No, never as bad as after Bothwell. They put my bonny laddie in Greyfriars' Kirkyard among four hunder—men, women and bairns. For five months they kept them wi' scarcely a bit o' bield, in sun and rain, the frost in their hair in the morning, the dew on their faces at night, ill-clad and half-starved. Never a week passed but some o' them died. Ha'e ye been in Greyfriars?"

I had, and I had killed too, in Greyfriars, something brave and bonny, and had left in its place for Barbara nothing but dolour to keep. And for myself, what had I now but the ever-fresh pain of regret. At the bare mention of the word "Greyfriars" I saw again Barbara, with the tears in her eyes, and I heard again the catch in her voice. I nodded my head.

"Ye ha'e been? Then go again and stand, as many a time I ha'e stood, at the gate, and see it a' owre again for yourself, the quiet, driven folk dying like sheep in the snell winds; and if ye ha'e any sorrow to spare for a wheen screechin' limmers the nicht, I ha'e nane!"

Her voice had grown hard, but it broke as she continued:

"My laddie they shot in the nicht-time, shot him doon in an act o' mercy, and he died in his agonies, beggin' for a mouthfu' o' water."

I could not make her understand that Jock and I had as little to do with the persecutions as the fish in the sea. But I did not blame her, for her sufferings justified her anger.

I looked round the dark little kitchen, hearing the run and squeak of mice, myself half-stifled in the air, hot and heavy with fifty old smells. A great pity was on me for her, that here she must sit till the end of her days, without ever again the smell of the sea-wrack, the sound of the wind in the trees, or the light of the sun in her eyes.

" Very well," I told her. " We will be going now."

" And where may you be for? "

Jock flung me a warning glance, but too late, for I had spoken.

" To serve King James."

" Then God help you, for you'll ha'e the toun, and indeed the hale o' Scotland, against you."

" Not quite, mistress," said Jock. " The King has still a wheen friends. The Duke of Gordon has a good garrison and he'll have a better."

" The Duke of Gordon! " she said scornfully.

" The Duke of Gordon," Jock repeated angrily. " A very gallant soldier."

" I ken nought about him as a sodger. What I ken is, that he wouldna be where he is if he hadna been chief wi' the King and so wasna made to take the test."

She laughed a hard, croaking laugh.

" Oh, that test! It's made the hale country laugh when there was little enough to laugh at."

She turned in her chair to face me again.

" Even the bairns o' Heriot's Hospital made a fool o' it. They wrote it on a paper and offered it to the dog that runs about the yard, but the beast wouldna lip it. Then they rubbed it wi' butter, but he licked the butter off and turned tail on it. Syne they tried him and hanged him, the poor beastie. Oh, willawins! When even the bairns make a gowk o' the King, it's high time he was awa'."

She looked at Jock with a smile of malice.

" Aweel, if you're for the Castle, you'll be needing

your braw uniform, and you'll can play you're a sodger again, for a wee while."

A flush spread over Jock's face.

"You've been looking through my gear," he said angrily.

"Deed and I have. And I ryped your pooches when I was at it. I like to ken a' that is to be kent about them that sleeps under this roof."

She looked keenly at me.

"It's little enough I ken about you, but it was gey and queer the way you breenged in here, wi' nothing but that muckle beast and no' even a clean sark to put on your back."

A knock sounded through the house as she finished speaking, a loud, commanding knocking that echoed along the empty passage.

"That's no' Mirren's rap," she muttered, looking uneasily from Jock to me.

"Wha's there?" she called sharply.

"Is that you, Mistress Binnie?" a man's voice came back.

"Is't Mirren ye want? She's no' in. What do ye want wi' her?"

"Open the door. We have some questions to ask."

As quiet as a stalking cat Jock took his stand between her and the door. The pair measured glances. My eyes roved round the little room.

"I canna win to the door," she called back. "I'm auld and near a cripple. What is't ye want to ken?"

"Have ye two men lodging wi' you, enemies of the Covenant?"

"What's that ye say? I'm hard o' hearing," she grumbled.

And all the time her eyes were on me.

They repeated their question.

" We've been bedding twa callants, but this very day I telled them we could keep them no longer. But," she demanded tartly, " wha sent ye to me for enemies o' the Covenant? Is this a likely howff to find such in, that sent twa lads to Bothwell Brig? Awa' wi' ye and seek elsewhere and dinna waste my time and your ain."

There was a short dispute outside, then a gruff voice said: " You're right, mistress. We'll seek in a more likely howff."

The three of us stood still as posts, till we could no longer hear the retreating footsteps.

" Well! " said Jock awkwardly.

" Well? " the old woman questioned dryly. " You're mim for once. But if it hadna been for the ' auld limmer ' it might not have been well for you."

" You have our thanks," he said, flushing.

" Dinna cheat yoursel'," she returned quickly. " It wasna you I was for saving. When it came to the bit, I could not hand owre this laddie to God kens what end, even though he is a Mackenzie."

A further rap made her pause anxiously.

" That's Mirren," she said, with relief.

Mistress Binnie came in, so excited she could scarce speak.

" Sic a rowth o' folk. The toun's as thrang as if it were a fast day," she cried. " There's some gey wild work now. I'm thankful to get out of the stir."

She turned to me, looking troubled.

" There's a queer story going and I'm feared it has to do with you. First I got it that the ghaist o' a muckle hound, with bleezin' eyes, was roving the toun, grabbin' folk by the throat. Then some said it was nae ghaist but a livin' beast, and they thought they could lay hands on it. I ran home to tell you, for I'm feared for you and the dog."

" Thank you, Mistress Binnie. It is Dileas they mean, but he did not attack anyone who had not first attacked me, and the man did not wear his breeches round his throat. It is time we were away, and we will be going as soon as the street is quiet."

" You'd best not take a light into that room," she said anxiously.

Through the long disturbed night, Jock and I sat waiting, no light in the room, but often the gleam from passing torches travelling round the walls. The causey rang with the tread of many feet. The air was heavy with smoke and loud with the cheers of the revolutionaries, who were making a bonfire at the Cross of the organ, the throne, the stalls of the Knights of the Thistle, and other furnishings torn from the Abbey. There would be no safety for us, in going, till flames and rebels alike had glutted their hunger for destruction. Midnight passed and the street was still echoing with cries. Slowly the Watch drawled out the dragging hours.

" If only the King would raise an army," I wished. " I would be in its ranks to-night. There is nothing I hate like waiting, when trouble is afoot. It is marching and fighting I am wanting, not sitting still in a garrison. Would it not do if we were to seek other lodgings to-morrow, and hear if there is word of a stand for the King ? "

" It would not; it would be madness. You do not seem to have got it into your head that you are a marked man. Riven breeks will aye sit still, but no' the breeks ye rove some hours syne. Yon lad will scour the town till he gets you. He was a dour birkie. If you had beaten him in a fair fight he might have forgiven you, but you've made a gowk o' him, and that will rankle like a burr down his back. Na, we'll slink away up to the Castle, you and me, with as little ado as we can, and if you've any sense you'll be michty glad to see the far side o' the ditch."

CHAPTER XIII

The Castle on the Rock

IN a cold dawn we climbed the steps to the drawbridge and found it raised. A single plank spanned the ditch, and at the end of it we had to wait while a sentry went to seek someone in command. An officer appeared and took stock of us.

" It's you, Lieutenant Grant! " he said, very evidently surprised. " And not alone! "

" It's myself, Ensign Winchester, and a friend. Do we bide at this side of the ditch? "

" No, no. Of course not. Come across."

We ran lightly along the plank.

" We are expecting Gordon of Midstrath to-day, and some score of his clan. I thought, when I was summoned, that you were a messenger from him. Have you any news of him and his band? "

" None, except what you know already, that they are lying at the Port of Leith. But there are far more than a score; there is a whole garrison."

" I know that. But the Governor is for sending most of them back."

" Sending them back! I can assure you, from what I saw in the toun last night, the King is needing all his friends. It is folly to refuse any help at all."

" So we have said. But he does not want to rouse the burgh folk by bringing in the Highlanders. Midstrath refused point-blank to serve unless he was permitted to bring his own tail at least. I've no doubt he'll be here soon. Who is your friend, Lieutenant? You have not told me yet."

"Alastair Mackenzie; not an enlisted soldier, but a good sword for the King—Alastair, this is Ensign Winchester."

We bowed.

"Come, then, both of you, and see the Duke."

We had been standing in the gloom of the portcullis arch, and now advanced into a narrow defile, winding upwards round the shoulder of the rock, truly an amazing and well-planned approach. We passed through gate after gate, one of them a second portcullis, all of them of the stoutest wood and iron-studded. From the shores of the Nor' Loch I had thought the Castle impregnable. More than ever I thought so now. It was keep within keep, barrier behind barrier, and the storming of the outer drawbridge and towers by no means meant the capture of the fortress. Seven gates there were in all, and some of these must be assaulted in the narrow defile overlooked by tower and bastion in front and flank.

Over one of the gates was the crest of the Duke of Gordon, two hounds in support. His quarters were on a plateau close by the royal apartments, and we were ushered into a small chamber, where he sat writing at a table.

The Duke looked up quickly and rose to his feet, pushing back his chair, a tall, thin man, very neat in his dress, very soft of voice, not at all my notion of a soldier's leader.

"Lieutenant Grant and a friend to join us," said Winchester, saluting.

"The addition of any friend loyal to the King is welcome here," said the Duke. "But, Grant, I thought it was understood you should remain in the town and keep us posted with news."

" Quite impossible now, sir, with things as they are. Unfortunately, we are both marked men, and I doubt if we had not come here this morning we might never have come at all. We ran into a quarrel last night with two men, and they took the worst of it. And the serious bit of it is, that I think they are some kind of leaders."

" Damn it, man! That's a pity. You should have kept clear of quarrels."

" An accident, sir. They forced the fight. But I can still go out by the tunnel for news. The King's friends in the town will have to lie quiet for a bit, but I ken where they are to be found, and they'll keep us posted."

" Well, give me your account of the rioting and you can go to your quarters."

Jock told rapidly of the events of the past two days, the temper of the townsfolk, and the ten thousand crowns damage done in the royal palace.

" I have been expecting something like this, since the news of the landing came," the Duke said gravely. " I hope the magistrates will have it in hand soon. Any word of Midstrath, Mr Winchester? "

" Not yet, sir."

" I have sent word to my own tenants that they are to return to the north."

" But, sir," Winchester protested, " we cannot trust the garrison soldiery, the gunners least of all. The mutiny last night, which might have had very serious consequences, taught us that. And without gunners, where are we? We need every man we can get, and there we have a garrison lying at Leith."

" I can load, fire and train a gun," Jock put in,

" although I have no skill of marksmanship. With practice all could learn."

" Yes, Grant, with practice; which it is impossible to get," said the Duke. " We have no powder for practice. All the ammunition I ought to have had now lies in Stirling Castle, removed from here by the orders of the Duke of Hamilton. So, Mr Mackenzie, you see how we stand. It will be steel against cannon-ball and musket-shot at the finish. Are you willing to stay, knowing this? I shall deceive no one in this garrison how serious is the position of the King's cause. Only those who are willing may stay."

" It is quite willing I am to stay, sir," I said in answer.

" Very good."

And then he noticed Dileas standing at my knee.

" A hound! " he exclaimed. " Is he yours? We would be better without him, for food is like to be as scarce as powder. The magistrates have withheld part of the meal and bisket required for our numbers."

" I cannot very well leave him outside, sir, since he will stay with none but myself."

" Well, well, it would ill become a Gordon to refuse hospitality to a hound. Find your quarters and report to Midstrath when he comes."

We followed Ensign Winchester to a building on the Hawkshill, which must have been used at one time as an ordnance store, for remains of broken musket-stocks and an old burst leathern mortar were piled in one corner. There I found the gentlemen in whose company I was to spend the next seven months. There were some fifteen of them, seated at an early meal of oatcakes and ale. Jock seemed to be well known to most of them, for they greeted him pleasantly by name, and at once made room for us at the table.

At our entry they were discussing the events of the
night before, when a drunken Catholic had by accident
stabbed a Presbyterian, and the Duke had been called
from his bed at midnight to quell an ugly mutiny, which
he had done fearlessly.

When the meal was finished, one, a thin, girlish-looking
lad, with long, yellow hair, an Elliot from the Buccleuch
country, began to string together some good-humoured
verses about Jock, myself and my dog.

" Never mind that havering gomeril," said another.
" He thinks he's a poet."

" And I am," Elliot assured us, " but wasted in this
company."

Then, noticing the hilt at my right haunch: " Left-
handed! " he cried. " I must have a bout with you."

> " Honoured sir, come draw your blade,
>   We'll match our skill ere daylight fade."

" You daft deevil," said Jock, grinning. " That's a
rhyme without reason anyway, for daylight's but newly
begun."

" What does it matter! " Elliot said airily. " Surely
a poet may be permitted to shift the sun, if need be, to
make a rhyme, dull clod that you are! "

He drew his weapon, a rapier, thin of the thinnest,
scarcely a finger-breadth at the hilt, the point tapering
to a thread of steel.

" I never had the chance but once to pit myself against
a left-handed swordsman, and that was in Monsieur
Barossi's school in Paris. Will you honour me, sir? "

" I am no swordsman without the dirk," I said frankly.
" I have no skill of fence whatever. Also, our weapons
are not matched, and the fear is on me that I might smash
your blade with my heavy broadsword."

" Try it, sir," he laughed, bending the hilt round to the point in a beautiful curve, from which it returned with a twang. " Not so easily broken. But draw dirk and let us see your style."

Myself, I was reluctant to fence before so many strangers, some of them probably noted fencers, but, not wishing to appear a churl, I set myself *en garde*, with but the sword drawn. And in this I was foolish, for this lad Elliot, I saw before many passes, was master of weapon and fence. He played with me, as he might have done with a bairn, and there I was well served, in that I did not take my own style from the beginning. The rapier rippled like a living snake along my blade, while its owner danced in and out on lightest feet, quick-moving as a roebuck. Three times he touched, twice on my body, once on my arm, and, try as I might, I could not get a lock on that wand of steel. He had no strength of wrist whatever, but a suppleness in it that matched his foot-work.

One thrust I took on the basket-hilt, when the point ran through the openwork and seared my fingers. I had the chance there to snap the point, but drew back with a wince. But the prick roused the devil in me, and, throwing aside this pretence of fence, I drew my dirk and set myself to fight.

And here I may say that small-sword or rapier is no match for the Highland broadsword with targe or dirk. And the trick of sword-play which Finlay had taught me —and he had it from his father—was one which, when used by a left-handed sworder, none could withstand at the first meeting. It meant brisk foot-work, a parry with the sword holding off the opposing weapon, a quick slew of the body from the right, and the dirk-point was at the brisket. I had yet to find it fail, and it did not in that bout. I stopped the point barely short of Elliot's skin and straightened up.

" Ho, Elliot, you were done there. The dirk was playing on your backbone if carried through," called Winchester.

" Mr Elliot touched four times to my once," I said. " I am no match for him at all in pure fence."

I sheathed sword and glanced at my fingers, from which blood dribbled.

" Oh! " cried Elliot. " I did not know I had touched you."

" Your point was through the basket-work. It is a scratch only."

There was a sudden clamour outside the door and a voice shouted: " Midstrath's coming! " We all piled out of the building and went to watch the approach from the gun-platform of the Half Moon Battery. From that stance we could look right down the High Street almost to the Netherbow Port, though the Tolbooth, jutting out as it does close to the Kirk of St Giles, hindered a clear view down the causeway. It was not until they came to near the Weigh House that we saw them well, Midstrath's piper at their head, blasting like to blow the chanter off the stock.

And when they came under the drawbridge, and I heard the Gaelic, I could not contain myself longer. Strange how our tongue, which Lowlanders tell me sounds harsh to their ears, calls to the Gael with the soft murmur of burns and the breath of the wind from the bens. Och, the Gaelic! How I had missed the lilt of it since coming among the strange tongues of the Lowlands.

The cry of the chanter! The swing of the kilts! I was off in a run to meet them, those Gordons who spoke as I did, even though they were from the wrong side of the

Highland Line. I was on fire as I marched with them up to quarters.

Later I walked round the ramparts with Midstrath, admiring the ordnance, especially the great gun, " Mons Meg."

" She's a bonny lassie, is Muckle Meg," said Jock, who was our guide, laying his hand fondly on her iron muzzle, " and has dinged doon many a wall o' the auld enemy in her time. They fed her on ball the weight o' a cow and as solid as good Kirkcudbright granite can be. How think ye they trailed her and her fodder as far as Norham in the auld days? Over the Carter Bar, mind you! They had by-ordinar stout hearts to tackle a Cheviot pass wi' you, lassie. But she's dumb now for ever, is poor, proud Meg. She burst eight year syne, firing a salute to King James, when he came here as Duke o' York."

A bad omen that, I thought, that the gun which so often had roared defiance at the enemies of his fathers should have fallen silent when asked to roar in his honour.

Many a time after that I stood by the big gun and thought sadly that she and I had something in common, for it was not long before my fire was damped, and I too could no longer roar in honour of King James. The long hours of dreary garrison duty, the forced society of men who did not think my thoughts, the wind that everlastingly snarled in my ears, the haar that crept hostile from the sea and hung the valley with its dismal streamers —och! a few weeks of them and I had no heart at all for a barrack soldier.

It would be about a week after we joined the garrison that the Privy Council sent to the Duke, demanding the surrender of the Castle.

" I am bound to obey only my King," said he, and

M

thereafter they left us alone, only taking care to post a
guard at the Weigh House, to see that none joined us.
Only a little food was smuggled to us, through the sally
port, by friends, and as the months went on our supply
of provender fell perilously low. Jock went out regularly
by a secret tunnel, and as regularly returned with news
of the town, a duty he took a delight in, but one that
brought him often within grips of danger.

And so the weary months of investment went by.

Many a time I wondered what had brought me there.
It was as if, in the short time I had been in the town, an
eddy wind had caught me up and dropped me on the
Rock. But it was no wind that the fairies travel in, but
the eddy wind of politics, a whirling gale that had brought
down a crown, had tossed up some men, exalting them,
and had hurled others from their high stations, sweeping
them into dungeons, to lie with common malefactors.
And me, a free Highlander, it had seized on and let fall
in a beleaguered Lowland fortress.

The men among whom I found myself proved, for the
most part, good comrades, but we were of varying creeds
and habits, cooped up together in long weeks of siege,
when winter days were short, and rations were short, so
it was not strange that tempers went short likewise, and
we were apt to get at each other's throats.

Jock and Walter Elliot were the two who kept up our
spirits. They minded me of Tearlach and myself as we
used to be. They had always a laugh and a jest on the
darkest day, when despair would be in my heart.

There was the time when John Auchmouty deserted.
He was a lieutenant, a sulky, secretive fellow, ill to get
on with, and when on guard one night he went off, taking
with him some of the sentries. Worse than that, his wife,
who had refused to leave the garrison, discovered the

secret of the tunnel, and they took the key with them. We had had desertions before, but here was the first officer who had left us, and he had sworn an oath of allegiance on the Bible.

Jock and Walter Elliot found me sitting alone, with my shoulder against the carriage of " Mons Meg."

" For pulling a long face when anything goes wrong, did ye ever see Alastair Mackenzie beat? " Jock asked, taking a seat beside me.

" I never did," said Elliot, striking some wild notes from the viol he was carrying and smiling down at me. " Are the Mackenzies all dead? "

" How can you talk like that? " I asked, annoyed at them. " Here is Auchmouty away, and our secret with him! "

" Let him go," said Elliot carelessly. " What says the play? ' An aching tooth is better out than in. To lose a rotting member is a gain.' "

" Aye, Wat," said Jock dryly; " or, as we say in Scotland, ' Ae scabbit sheep can smit a hirsel,' if ye havena forgotten your ain tongue. He's better away."

He had a great store of verses and ballads, yon Elliot. He had lived much in England and in France, and, as well as being a master of fence, could play the viol very tunefully. Indeed, we had often to silence him, for he would sometimes play and sing in jest, over and over, a certain mournful ballad, till we were like to murder him.

He began singing it to me there at " Mons Meg ":

> " Oh, fare ye weel, young man, she says,
> Fareweel and I bid adieu——"

but Jock stopped him by stuffing my bonnet in his mouth.

" Now we are cut off from the town entirely," I said. " We can get no news after this."

" Havers ! We've found a safer passage already down to the Nor' Loch, at the side o' the sally port. And all we do is signal our good friend, Mistress Ann Smith, when we are going out, and fire a musket from the Half Moon to let her know we are safely back. What could be simpler ! And now, will you look less dowie ? "

CHAPTER XIV

A Summons

ON an afternoon early in April I had newly come from sentry-go, in a mood of fierce resentment against fate. I had heard a blackbird singing from a ragged thorn below the Half Moon, and had watched a lark soar joyous overhead, and they had seemed to mock the poor fool that I was, that for months on end had gloomed inside confining walls. I stood in one of the gun embrasures, avoiding company, surly as a badger dug from his winter den.

For the first time, in this eyrie of the winds, the airs of spring were soft on my cheek, and the sunshine was a gift from advancing summer. Beyond the Nor' Loch the whins were powdered with a dust of gold, and overnight the hawthorns had rushed into shimmering green. From Berwick Law to Stirling the land drowsed in the sun, and far beyond yon cloudy bens lay the land of my heart, where I was barred from going.

And towards it even now was marching the man I had waited to meet, through weary months of inaction, that had irked me as Jock had never understood. Aye, and there was reason enough for my resentment, for I had just heard that Mackay of Scourie had stayed a night in the town on his march north, and in command of a company was Mackay of Kyle-ron. Had I been freely ranging out yonder I would have striven to meet him, would have paid my father's debt and been ready to go home or to lie still for ever. I had not Jock's fire for the

King's service, that had not brought me what I had hoped for.

To me came Jock, newly back from a reconnaissance in the town. White he looked and tired and grim.

" I have permission from the Duke for you to go to Allan's Close, and you're to go at once. You had best change out of that rig and get into less kenspeckle duds."

I was surprised at his manner, no less than at the curtness of his speech, and I drew myself up haughtily. The mention of Allan's Close came at a bad moment.

" If you think you have won a favour for me from the Duke, it is a bad mistake you are making," I said coldly. " I have no intention whatever of going near Allan's Close, now or at any time."

His eyes narrowed and his voice was very hard as he replied:

" You're my friend, but you'll go if I have to make you. Mistress Stewart has been at death's door and keeps asking for you, and Mistress Barbara—but you'll learn soon enough for yourself."

Something in his eyes brought me a feeling of dread and I asked anxiously:

" Is anything wrong? '

" I'll tell you nothing more," he said more kindly. " You'll learn when you get there. But, Alastair, you must go."

Impatient now to be away, I went with Jock and changed hurriedly into a suit of rough homespun, and with him as guide went down the passage to the Nor' Loch. By the Duke's orders there had to be six of a guard with any going out. Jock commanded the boat and we hugged the south shore. I was landed safely and, on Jock opening a garden gate, I climbed the steep, passed through the house of a friend and walked unchallenged down the High Street. I was admitted to Mistress Stewart's by a serving-woman, hard-featured and of dismal countenance, who left me in the passage, where she gruffly told me to wait. She left the room door ajar, so that I heard her announce my arrival.

"Oh, my me!" said Mistress Stewart's voice, "and me no' buskit. I did not look for him so soon. Give me a sight of myself in that glass."

"You might be done wi' buskin' now, I'm sure," the woman chided grimly. "What does it matter to the Almighty whether ye're wearing ribbons and laces, and you on your last bed."

"Done wi' buskin'!" I heard Mistress Stewart say indignantly. "Na, na, Maggie, I'm no' done yet. It's hard for an auld mare to leave off flinging, and I'll busk myself as long as I'm able, and I'll leave the last buskin' to you. Would it please the Almighty any better, think you, if this lad should see me looking like a wally draggle? And wheesht wi' your talk o' my last bed. The Almighty will settle that and no' you. I'm better already, I tell you, at the thought o' seeing a man. I was aye fond o' the men and will be to the end. A house without a man in it is like a drink o' loowarm water, gey and wersh."

Surely, I thought, smiling, as I paced the floor, there could not be anything seriously wrong with Mistress Stewart or any of her household when she spoke like that. I felt relieved, but wondered the more what I was there for. I was quite unprepared for the change I saw in her when I was called to her bedside. She lay in a great walnut bed with green silk hangings, a bunch of ostrich feathers tied to each post, and she seemed small as a child. She lifted a thin hand in greeting.

"Come your ways, Alastair Mackenzie. You were to look in, in the by-going, but you've been long about it.

Oh, I ken you're in the Castle, but my friend Jock can manage to give us a cry-in. Did he tell you why I sent for you? "

I shook my head, disturbed at the change in her, so frail-looking was she, so white, so hollow-eyed.

" Stop glowering at me like that," she said impatiently. " You're as bad as Maggie Gibb. I ken I look like a ghost, but I'm no' one yet. I ken my eyes are far ben, but they'll come forrit again. I'll no' be shutting them yet for a wee."

They twinkled up at me with some of their old gaiety, then with a sudden change of manner she said sternly: " You've never speired for Barbara yet."

" Is she ill? " I asked, startled, and when she did not reply: " Mistress Stewart, has any ill come to Barbara? " I demanded. " Tell me, will you? Is she here or has she gone? Why do you not speak? "

" Because I was waiting to find out something and I've got it. Your eyes and your voice told me. You're still fond o' the lassie! Alastair, what came between you and Barbara? She'll not say anything. But I've watched and I ken how it's hurting her. I found her one night with a face all bluddered for greeting. The life went out of her yon Sabbath."

" What's happened to her? " I asked hoarsely. " Tell me, will you not? "

" Listen! "

I looked at a small door, on the other side of which a low muttering had begun, a sound unlike ordinary talk, a muttering that went on and on, filling me with a cold dread. I turned horror-filled eyes to the bed.

" Aye," she said sadly, " Barbara's in there. She took ill after nursing me, but the fever will not leave her, and the doctor and his physic can do no more. I am at the

end o' my wits and that's why I sent for you. Night and
day she has cried your name, and I thought you might
help me with her. Oh, she's no' worse than she's been,
but I'm beginning to fear she'll never more be better, if
she does not make a start soon. Alastair, what came
between you? You havena told me. Can it no' be
mended?"

I sat with my hands locked between my knees, every
muscle tense, my eyes not seeing anything.

"Never yet have I told anyone the story," I said low,
after a long silence, "but I am going to tell you now. It
cannot be mended, because I have sworn on my dirk to
kill her father."

"What's that you say?"

She had been lying propped up on pillows. Taking a
firm grip of the bedclothes she drew herself upright,
staring at me out of frightened eyes.

"What's that you say?" she repeated harshly.

"I have vowed to my father that I will kill hers," I
said miserably, talking quickly to shut out the sound of
that strange voice beyond the little door. "No, do not
judge until you have heard. Her father, twenty years
ago, wanted to marry my mother. So did my father, and
she could not make up her mind which one to take.
Then one day, riding home through the birch woods
near Loch Garve, my father was challenged to fight by
William Mackay. Well, my father is a fine swordsman,
one of the best in Ross, but he was left for dead among
the bracken. You see, the other man was wearing
chain armour under his doublet, and even the best
swordsman in Scotland could do very little against a
man of that breed. Well, my father swung between
life and death, and that helped my mother to make up
her mind.

" When this brave one of the Mackays was told of
her choice, he talked of my mother in Inverness and in
every change-house in the north in a way that could
not be forgiven, and that made my father swear a
black death to him, though himself could not lift head
from pillow."

" Stop!" Mistress Stewart commanded. " You mean
William Mackay, my niece's husband, lightlied your
mother? "

" That is what I am saying, but he was not married
then."

" I will not believe it. It does not sound like him.
Have you spoken with him? "

" I have so, but at the meeting I did not know the
kind he was."

" I'll never believe it," she said, slipping down on her
pillows.

" Mistress Stewart, you have more to hear. My Uncle
Alastair, my father's older brother, followed him to
Leith without loss of time, and so to Holland. They met
in a duel, but again the steel doublet saved the life of
a dirty fighter, and my Uncle Alastair lies buried in
Utrecht, while Kyle-ron is captain in the service of the
Prince of Orange. Then, seven months ago, my father,
finding Kyle-ron was alive, when he had long believed
him dead, tried again to settle his score. But I left him
in his bed, and I have taken up the quarrel, and this time
it will be finished. I am no great sworder, but I know
a trick from which not even two suits of armour will
protect him, and my mother, and my father, and my
Uncle Alastair will be avenged. But, oh! the pity it is,
that it should be Barbara's father I must kill."

" Poor laddie," said Mistress Stewart, and again, very
gently: " Poor laddie! "

I leaned my head on my hand and sat there thinking about it all.

" If you were to break your vow——" she said. " I'm no' saying this because he's my kinsman, but for your own sake."

" I have sworn on my dirk. It is the most binding oath, and I must keep it. I could never go home again if I broke it. But it is not only the oath that makes me want to find him. I hate him for what he has done to us all, Barbara and myself now too."

" I could warn him," she said.

" You could, and it would give him another advantage over me," I said coldly. " But it would make no difference in the end."

" I'll not warn him, never fear. He must suffer, if God wills it, for the ill he did. And to think he sat in that chair yesterday——"

I started violently.

" Yes, he did. He is far on his road now with Scourie's army, but there he sat, as kind seeming a man as you could meet."

" Fate has been kind to him, has she not now! I wish it had been to-day he was to visit you. *Dhe !* what has he done to be so favoured! "

Behind the closed door the muttering broke out afresh. I heard my own name cried. Then silence. I looked dumbly at Mistress Stewart, sweat on my brow, my nails biting hard into my palms.

" No, I don't think she heard your voice, if that is what you're thinking. I have listened to that for many a night, and wearied for Jock Grant to get a message sent to you. Now, hearken to me, Alastair. Gang your ways into that room and let her hear your voice. She'll no' ken you, but maybe it might quieten her. That's what

I'm hoping for. But stay beside her for a wee and speak to her. That can do no harm to your vow, and it might do her a pickle good."

I had to stoop to enter the little door, and I found Barbara lying in a room so small it scarce was bigger than a powdering closet. Maggie Gibb, the serving-woman, gave me a dark look as she turned from the bed.

" Would you be good enough to go away? " I said to her at once. " Go in there, and I will call you if you are needed."

She made her mouth into a straight, hard line, looked me up and down, and went out slowly, leaving the door open. I closed it. What I had to say to Barbara was not for that one's ears.

I sat on the edge of the bed and wondered where was the Barbara I knew. I saw with fear the bright flush, the glittering eyes that met mine without a sign of know-ing me, the dark hair lying in wet strands on her brow and in tangled masses on the white linen. Her head moved restlessly on the pillow, from side to side, and the hot little hands, that held my heart, lay limp on the counterpane. I took them both in mine and put them against my cheek. She was speaking now to Nancy, little broken sentences from her bairn-time.

" *A chiall mo chridhe*, my dearest heart, listen to me. Alastair is here. Forgive me for what I have done to you; that was no fault of mine. I love you, Barbara, and always will. Do you not know me? Barbara, it is Alastair. I'll not leave you again," I finished desperately.

It was a hard task her aunt had set me.

Dhe! but this den was hot. After the clean airs of the Castle of Kyle-ron this must seem like a coffin. I rose and forced open the wooden half of the small window. A little more light came in with the April airs. I laid my hand on Barbara's brow, and watched the tip of her tongue moisten the dry, cracked lips, that had been, not long ago, like crushed berries. I threw open the door.

" I want something for her to drink. Have you anything? "

Maggie Gibb said she had.

" Then fetch it," I said shortly.

I got Barbara to take the barley-water, sip by sip, as my mother had done to me as a bairn. How I wished for someone like her, with cool fingers and coaxing voice, to help to stay this fever. Fever? What if it were plague? It must not be plague, I told myself desperately. It must not. But Barbara had no one but Maggie Gibb, and it was not likely that a woman with so ungentle a face and voice could be a good nurse.

A man may not be the best of nurses, but a man with love in his heart is a better nurse by far than a woman with no heart at all. So I sat, sponging Barbara's brow, moistening her lips, holding her hand, and when she cried out, reassuring her with Gaelic endearments. Each time she called for me she plunged a knife in a wound, but gradually, as I repeated, " Alastair's here, *mo ghraidh*, my darling," the glittering eyes would search mine, as though she were trying to puzzle her way back from the tortured world of delirium to a saner world of peace and understanding. I stayed with her till near dawn, waving Maggie Gibb away each time she approached me, and at last I had my reward, for Barbara lay still, her breathing quieter, the eyelids down over the feverish, questing eyes. Her hand still held to mine. I kissed it and laid it gently on the counterpane.

I rose, stiff, aching, drenched with cold sweat, and went in to Mistress Stewart's room.

" She is sleeping," I told her cheerfully.

" God be praised, Alastair," she said brokenly, " for I do not know when she has slept this fortnight past."

I started, as there came a great bang at the door. Could this be someone who had discovered that one of the Castle garrison was in this house in Allan's Close? Mistress Stewart's eyes, meeting mine, showed she had the same thought.

But Maggie Gibb was already opening the door, and before it seemed she had time to swing it on its hinges I was nearly thrown to the ground. Dileas! Leaping upon me, licking my face, whimpering joyfully, there he was, while Maggie's frightened screech still hung in the air.

" How did you get here, boy? " I asked, bewildered, scratching his head and patting him, for, in truth, there was never a time I was not glad to see him. " I wonder he knew where to come."

I found later that he had first tried Mistress Binnie's house, and not finding me there had rushed to Mistress Stewart's.

" My, but he's a skeleton! " that lady said. " We'll give him a good feed now he's here."

" And that will be something he has not had for many a day."

While I was speaking, a thought leapt into my mind that showed me a way out of a difficulty. I resolved to speak of it.

I sat down on a clothes chest beside the bed.

" Mistress Stewart, it can be no secret in the town that food is scarce with us. The men are grumbling at what Dileas eats, and the Duke of Gordon has said that I will have to consider soon either turning him adrift, or shooting him. I cannot do either, and I cannot bear to see him starve. Would you—would it be asking too much for you to keep him? "

" Keep him! " she repeated.

She looked at him, a kind of dismayed smile on her face. Dileas sat down, put a paw on the bed, thumped the floor with his tail and returned her look. Yon one knew his life was being asked for!

" He's a bit on the big side for a sma' house," she said ruefully. " But you've done a lot for me, and I'se keep him for you."

Then she added, with her old playful look: " He'll maybe gar me believe there's a man about the house."

I warned her not to lay a hand on him or he might snap.

" But he took to Barbara," I said, " as to no stranger before, and you will find him obedient."

I led him into the small room.

" Stay here, Dileas," I commanded, " and watch."

I left him at Barbara's bedside, his nose on the counterpane, puzzlement and devotion in his eyes.

CHAPTER XV

Siege

BUT in telling of my visit to Barbara I have forgotten to write of something very important to us, and to Scotland, that happened some weeks earlier.

In March, things began to move, and John Graham of Claverhouse, recently given the title of Viscount Dundee, was the one who set the heather on fire for King James in Scotland.

A Convention of Scottish Estates met in the middle of March—an illegal assembly with no rights whatever—and decided to offer the crown to the Prince of Orange. Of all the nobles in Scotland who attended, two only took a stand for their King. The weary deliberations dragged on for days, and then these two, Viscount Dundee and Colin Lindsay, Earl of Balcarres, called by his friends " the gentle Colin," walked indignantly from the meeting. In the evening, entering the Castle by the secret passage, they had a talk with our leader. After they had gone he came to us, saying he had been urged to hold the Castle at all costs, and must ask for a renewed assurance of loyalty. Two of the gunners refused to give him any promise and they left us that very night. We were now left with only one gunner, and later, on our chaplain asking for an oath on the Bible, we lost many more men, and our little garrison was reduced to thirty, and one sergeant was already sick.

On the forenoon of the eighteenth of the month our sentries reported a stir before the House of Parliament.

We ran to the Half Moon Battery, looked down the High Street and saw a body of horsemen drawn up there, waiting. Out from the Convention strode Viscount Dundee, threw leg over saddle, wheeled his troop, then, to the roll of kettledrums, clattered down the High Street to the Netherbow Port. We lost them for a bit, found them again at the foot of the Leith Wynd, and watched them turn west. Along the Lang Dykes, under our eyes they came, making a brave show, the sun glinting on breastplates, the wind of March lifting their feathers. The Duke, pale and anxious, watched them through a spy-glass, sighing deeply as Ensign Winchester cried out: " There go sixty friends we can ill afford to lose."

The notes of trumpet and kettledrums came fitfully on the breeze to us, a small, forlorn and silent band, leaning elbows on the ramparts, hearts sinking under the feeling that we were being abandoned. And well might they sink, for alone of all strongholds in the two kingdoms the Castle of Edinburgh flew the Stuart standard. Alone in the two kingdoms our garrison remained loyal.

Suddenly the Duke spoke to Ensign Winchester, who ran for a flag and began signalling. Viscount Dundee waved his hat, wheeled his troop, galloped down the Kirk Brae and halted his men under the Rock, by the King's Stables. Dismounting, he threw his reins to a trooper, and without a pause began the stiff clamber up the rocks. Anxiously we awaited him, and the townsfolk, getting wind of it, ran in droves to watch. Yon was a fine, daring climb, for he was loaded with cuirass and heavy cavalry boots with spurs. When at last he stood safely under our walls, and the Duke went to speak with him at the postern gate, we gave him a great cheer.

What was said at that meeting no man ever learned,

N

though some say that Dundee tried to persuade Gordon to go with him. Myself, I do not believe that. The two did not talk for long, and soon Dundee turned away, to begin the clamber down.

"Where, then, are you going?" Gordon called after him.

Dundee faced about, raised his plumed hat and said sadly: "Wherever the shade of Montrose may direct me."

And he was gone.

This was the one they call "Bonnie Dundee," and truly, in all my life I never saw a bonnier man. He had long, heavy, curling, brown hair, threaded with grey, that fell about a face finely shaped as a woman's, and his eyes, large and brown, soft as a fawn's, were more beautiful than many a famous toast's. He was the idol of his men.

And yet, this was he whom many call "Bloody Claverse," the tale of whose cruelties, if they be all true, make him appear a monster.

Ah, well, are there not two men in all of us? Our friends see the good one, and our enemies the bad, and only God sees both.

A strange man he was, certainly, and a very unhappy one, as I learned later. But this I can say truly of both Viscount Dundee and the Duke of Gordon, that neither thought at all of himself or his ambitions, but only of his King. Merely for the asking, both could have had places and honours from the Prince of Orange, but they chose the place of duty and the honour of serving where their oath of fidelity had been given. And they found that way hard.

The excited crowd of townsfolk, that had watched the clamber up the Rock, hung about, wondering and dreading what it might mean for them. The bells clashed in the steeples and the drums rolled; the soldiers brought in by the Duke of Hamilton came out from the garrets and cellars where they had lain hid; thousands of Cameronians poured into the town, and the real siege of the Castle began.

We loaded and ran out the guns on the town side, throwing the burghers into a frenzy of terror lest Gordon open fire on the houses. To his credit, though it was to the injury of his cause, not one cannon-shot was fired by him on the town, not even on the trenches towards the head of the Lawnmercat, lest a ball ricochet and kill innocent folk. If he had chosen otherwise he could have made of it a rickle of rubble and lime, and driven every soul from their homes.

And now came days and nights under constant fire, until every building on the Rock was roofless, and we had to live in the dungeons below; when water could scarcely be had, because they drained the Nor' Loch to lower the level of the water at the Well House; when, latterly, we were reduced to one salt herring a day, and a handful of meal, and that raw, for no coal or timber was left for firing. Yet our small band tightened belts and held out for other three months against Prince William's best generals, and we surrendered with honour at the end.

Against us were batteries, placed, one on Mutrie's Hill, one at Heriot's School for orphan bairns, and another at the ruins of Castle Collop, at the High Riggs, and from there a line of trenches ran to the West Kirk.

If ever there was a more foolish placing of batteries and trenches I have yet to hear of it. Had not the Duke been merciful, and had we had the wadding and powder necessary, we could have blown them out of action in a

few minutes, but so desperate were we for material to
wad the guns that Midstrath and his Gordons made
a sally on the trenches on the Castlehill one night,
dirked the sentries and were back inside our walls,
with their bedding and straw, before ever the alarm was
raised.

But not only did shortage of powder keep us from
firing, but fear of shortage of water in the well beside the
Half Moon Battery, for the firing of the heavy guns
lowered the level, and in faith, it was low enough. On
the seventeenth of May it was only ten feet deep and the
other wells were dry. Never did men rejoice more when
rain fell in blinding sheets.

Sunday, the nineteenth of May, is a day I mind well,
after weeks when each day was like its six sisters. Jock
and I were to be on sentry duty all night. Of our small
number many were sick, and those who were fit must
stand to, on double duty, even the women taking their
turn whiles. We had no men now to spare for post at
the high guard-house. Our main strength had to be all
at the sally port and low guard. We were trying to get
some sleep in the afternoon, but a new mortar battery
on Mutrie's Hill opened fire for the first time, and, finding
it impossible to rest, on account of the noise, we went
outside to see what harm they were doing. We found
their efforts to shell us highly diverting. The first bombs
sailed over our heads and landed in the village of Portsburgh. Others followed, until the houses were like to be
demolished, we cheering on the gunners, though they
could not hear us.

"Well done, Mutrie's Hill," chuckled Jock. "Dod,
if they keep that up, the Portsburgh folk will up and
spike their guns for them, and we'll get peace to
sleep."

But at last their battery got our range, and when it did it harassed us sorely, night and day. At night we went on sentry-go. The wind drew devilish cold from the north-east, and moaned up the Rock face and through the gun ports like the wail of the bad one's bagpipe.

" Gad, it's cold," chittered Jock, through cracked, parched lips, " yet I'd give all I have for a big stoup o' cold water."

His eyes, sunk in hollows above the ridged cheek-bones, looked wearily at the sky.

" You will have your water before long, Jock. I am thinking we will have snow before morning."

" Snow? Havers, man! It's after the middle of May."

" And colder than it was in March. It will be snow before long. I know it."

And I was right.

In less than an hour a mist of flurries came down in a dry swirl that curled and twisted in rings like smoke from a heath fire. Hour after hour it drove in from the north-east, sheeting everything in a smother. We stamped up and down our platform, vainly trying to coax a little warmth into limbs dead below the knees, stumps with no feeling in them. We sucked the snow to deaden a thirst unquenchable.

" It's an ill wind that blaws naebody guid," quoted Jock. " This snow will raise the Nor' Loch again and our wells will fill."

Up and down, up and down I walked, through those dead hours when hearts beat slowest, and men's thoughts are dreariest. Just the very night for an attack, I thought, and shivered as I thought it, picturing myself lying out wounded in the drifts. Just the very night for witches to walk! How many score did Jock say had been burnt

on the Castlehill? Was that a footfall? What if it were
the ghostly drummer they had told me of! Och, but this
Castle was an eerie place, the home of ghosts! I said a
spell, and another to make it surer, and wondered how
long till morning. My bonnet was heavy as a stone on
my head. My fingers were so numb I could scarcely
have drawn trigger. The path I trod now lay between
snow walls a foot high. I peered through the storm. I
had indeed heard a footfall. A figure appeared sheeted
in white. With difficulty I found voice to challenge.

" Halt! Who comes? "

" Friend."

" The password."

" Dundee."

" Would to God it were," muttered Jock, who had
come up when I challenged.

" Amen to that, my friends."

It was the Duke going the rounds himself.

" If wishing could bring him, he would be here fast.
Anything to report? No? I think it highly probable that
Leven may choose to assault under cover of the storm.
I wish with all my heart I could send you relief at once
on a night like this. But it won't be very long now till
you are relieved."

We saluted and he passed on.

" That's a sick man," said Jock, " though he tries to
hide it. He has the courage o' ten men to go round the
walls to-night, with a fever like that on him. He could
have sent Winram or Midstrath."

Still the snow fell, the wind howling like a hungry wolf
that now prowled the bastions, now nosed among the
battered walls and cabars. Deeper gathered the drifts,
until parapet and gun platform were one. By dawn it
lay to a level of two feet, when Winchester appeared with

a relief. We stumbled off to quarters and stood in the doorway to shake off the snow.

> " Welcome, lads, to the festive board,
> And help diminish Gordon's hoard,"

cried Elliot, himself now a living rapier for thinness.

This sally was greeted with a cackle of laughter.

What a breed, I thought, and, turning to Jock, whispered: " How does that thin one keep going? He looks a living death, yet jokes and chants his couplets as if among his friends at ' The Ship.' "

" Guts, man! Guts! Elliot's first whimper will be his last."

Here Elliot, with a wary glance at Jock, and barricading himself in a corner behind a table, began to sing his favourite ballad. Jock paid no heed, giving all his mind to taking off his boots and stripping off his sodden coat.

> " Sin ye've provided a weed for me
> Amang the simmer flowers,
> I will provide anither for you
> Amang the winter showers.
>
> The new fall'n snaw to be your smock,
> It becomes your bodie best;
> Your head shall be wrapt wi' the eastern wind
> And the cauld rain on your breast."

Jock swung round on his stool as the song ended, and, diving under the barricade, drew the singer out by the feet.

" Now, my lad," he said to Elliot, taken by surprise and struggling hard to rise, " I'll provide you wi' a taste o' winter showers."

He caught up his three-cornered hat, on which the snow had melted, and to the last drop ran off the water on to Elliot's face.

"And your head's goin' to be wrapped in my wet coat to make sure there'll no' be another squeak out o' you this day."

And there the pair of them were, heaving and struggling in high good humour on the floor, till the coat was bound round Elliot's head, and he lay kicking and uttering muffled threats.

Where, I wondered, did they get the gaiety to wrestle like that. I was younger than they were, but beside them I felt old and sad.

All that day the white flakes drifted, and did not cease till near evening, and for two days more the wind held cold out of the north-east, so that the snow on the north side did not at once melt and fill the loch and springs as we expected. Such a storm, coming as it did in the middle of May, had not been known in living memory.

The soldiers toiled patiently at collecting and melting the snow, though sixteen bombs fell in twelve hours on the Castle, one blowing up the Chapel steps, the broken stones falling among the men as they worked. Poor souls, their uniforms were in rags as they, knee-deep in snow, stood bravely to the guns.

With us in the Castle were a few women who had refused to leave their husbands, and one of them, the wife of a sergeant, was taken in labour the third day after the storm. The Duke beat a parley and asked that a howdie or doctor be allowed to attend her. But no! Neither howdie nor doctor was permitted to give services. This inhuman refusal roused in us such a fury that, had we had a good supply of powder, the

Lawnmercat would have lain in ruins before sunset. As things were, it set fresh fire to our endurance and determination.

We had need of fresh resolve, for more than ever were we cut off from the rest of the world. Jock had been finding his way out for news, and always he brought back some little addition to our board. A woman who could not keep a secret—and may plague take all such!—who knew of our entry to the town by the Lawnmercat, now betrayed us. And Jock went out no more. Another source of information failed us, a house from which two gentlewomen, Grant by name, signalled us. The signals mysteriously stopped. So now—no news, no friends, for most of the King's best friends lay in the Tolbooth, among them " the gentle Colin." And all this time never a word from Dundee.

To crown all, the bombardment became worse, as many as twenty bombs falling upon us in a day. The sight of the crumbling buildings and heaps of broken masonry was saddening, and provoked the thought that our cause was similarly crumbling to ruins.

On the fourth day of June the bombardment became so fierce that the spirit of the men broke, and angry mutterings were heard that we ought to give up the Castle.

" For God's sake, sir," said Jock to Colonel Winram, the Lieutenant-Governor, " persuade the Duke to let us reply. This is more than flesh and blood should be asked to stand."

Winram shook his head.

" The Governor errs on the side of humanity," he said. " But what right had the devils to place a battery beside a children's school? Then, if we shell the Castlehill and Lawnmercat we shell the families of some good friends.

But I'll see him, for this cannot be allowed to go on."

" Tell him, sir," shouted Elliot after the departing Colonel, " that I'll lead out a sally and spike the guns if he'll let me."

" Myself as well," said Midstrath.

CHAPTER XVI

Jock makes his " Bit Splash "

IN no time Gordon was among us, swaying on his feet, a desperate sick man, the fires of fever burning him up. He passed his hand wearily over his eyes.

" What is this now, gentlemen? "

" Sir," said Midstrath, " something must be done soon, or the men will not remain loyal much longer. Let me try a sally."

" I dare not sanction a sally," the Duke replied. " Think of the casualties. Already with sickness and wounds we have only twenty-four available to hold this fortress."

" Only twenty-one, sir," said Colonel Winram, " by this morning's call."

" Worse and worse! Well, you may reply with the guns, but be careful of the powder. We must save some for a day when we may need it even more. Afterwards you will all come to me. There are matters that must be talked over."

We jostled out of our dungeon like callants from a schoolroom, eager to get at the guns. We whipped off their covers and ran them out.

" Stand by with the match," cried our sergeant, as he squinted along the sights. " Wedge her up."

The trunnions creaked as the muzzle went down.

Below us lay the West Kirk, which Argyll's Campbells were using as a billet.

" The match," cried the gunner.

"Boom!" went the gun. A flying cloud of stones and lime went up from the gable-end. Slowly the wall bulged outward and crumpled, while long after it was down came the thud of the ball and the crash of the masonry. Gun after gun belched, while Argyll's men scurried for shelter among the corn.

"They run like whitricks from an old stane biggin'," said Jock gleefully.

Midstrath's piper, with but the one drone going, and a bag as dry as a sun-bleached bauchle, strutted and blasted, *The King shall enjoy his Own again*.

Faith, but that little barking of the guns put new heart into us all.

Too soon for us Gordon ordered, "Cease fire," but by that time we had dismounted most of their ordnance.

"Gad!" jested Elliot, as we turned to our meeting with the Governor, "the West Kirk is a holey enough place now."

Gordon was lying in a dungeon below what remained of the royal apartments. I write lying, and lying he was. He sat up stiffly as we entered.

For all his illness he was still the gentleman in dress and manners, the lace at his wrist and neck worn but unstained. How he contrived to keep his person so orderly under the conditions of illness and siege I am not the one who can understand. If the Duke of Gordon had been condemned to the scaffold, he would have been particular about niceties of dress even on the morning of execution. He nodded approvingly when told the enemy battery was silenced.

Then: "Gentlemen," he said, "I need not remind you our case is desperate. Powder—practically finished! Provender—the quartermaster reports our last two barrels of salted meat rancid. Nothing is left now but a boll or two of meal. Frankly, we are at the end of our resources."

He smiled up at us wearily.

" I never thought I should have to speak those words, but there they are, spoken. I have no news of Dundee or how go the fortunes of the King in Ireland. As you know, ours is the only fortress that flies the King's flag. God forbid we should have to give it up. What do you counsel, my friends? "

" Cut our way out this very night," said Midstrath.

The Governor glanced kindly at his kinsman.

" 'Twas ever the Gordon way, my cousin, to go down fighting, with ' A Gordon ' on the lips, but what of the Castle? I am loth to give it up while a spark of hope remains."

" Anything is better than surrender," said Winchester stoutly. " Climb down the north side of the Rock; seize the boats on the Nor' Loch. Once on the Lang Dykes, then hey for the north and Dundee."

" Be damned to this talk of surrender," burst out Elliot, the flame in his face. " Time enough when every one of us is on his back. The Castle is the key to Scotland. Can we not get word of Dundee somehow? It may be he is on his way to relieve us. Dundee to come again, with an army of bonnets at his back, and find we have surrendered—not yet, sir, not yet! "

" But how to get news, Elliot? Short of flying, I see no way out of this cage."

The Duke's flush had faded; he looked grey and old.

" I can go out," said Jock quietly.

Every eye turned to him.

" You can? "

" Yes, sir. With the help of Alastair Mackenzie, who

is a bit of a cragsman, I'll make my way down the Rock, swim the loch and scour for news."

So it was planned that Jock should go that night, and, making his way to Stirling or Perth, find how went the fortunes of Dundee, and signal to us from the Lang Dykes his report.

" There is only one bit, a matter of thirty feet of bare rock near opposite the West Kirk, I dare not try in the dark," said Jock, as we left the meeting.

So that night, in an eerie silence, I let Jock over the slide on a rope, and climbed up the Rock again to the parapet, feeling as if a bit of myself had gone there in the dusk below. For close on seven months we had been little separate, and I had come to have a great liking for this harum-scarum Jock Grant, late lieutenant—or lieutenant, which? for Jock still swore he held the King's commission—of the Scots Royals.

Eagerly each day the Duke, with his spy-glass, and we as eagerly with straining eyes, scanned the ridge opposite for Jock, and on the fourth day he suddenly rose from a whin-bush, like a duck rising from a dive.

Out went his arms, extended three times. *No hope !*
A groan burst from us.

The musket of a sentry on the Kirk Brae cracked, and Jock disappeared among the furze.

" Keep a watch on the north rampart," the Duke advised me. " He will try to come in the same way he went out."

" Indeed, if I were he and out, I'd stay out," said Midstrath to me.

" No, Jock will have something to report, and he is the one will make his way back, if it is at all possible," I told him confidently.

" Then may God be with him ! And now hear this.

I am going to make a sally to-night on the trenches below
the Half Moon Battery. The mining there must be
stopped. But say nothing of this to anyone. I am not
telling the Governor, for he will not give me leave to go.
I am counting on you to help me. I am taking just the
men of my own tail."

For some days past we had seen the danger of this
undermining, but we could do nothing for want of
powder. So close were the enemy trenches that we could
near have thrown a ball among them, and now the sound
of picks underneath was becoming ominously loud. A
charge of powder, and our walls would go down, and our
outer defences be gone.

That night was cold and wet, for even in June we were
still paying for the fine days we had had in March, and
the wind stabbed us like a knife-blade as we stood waiting
for Midstrath's whispered command to go—six of us,
all Gordons but myself. When the word came we crept
forward, with never a sound, on the trenches where men
lay, as they fancied, secure.

Then it was sword and dirk in the dripping dark, with
the uncanny fear added of meeting the slash of friendly
steel. The sentries were caught dozing, their first dazed
awakening their last. Of the others, taken completely
by surprise, we made short work, all but the few who
took the back gait down the slope with the pith to run
till morning drum.

" The hammer and powder," called Midstrath.
" Quick, lads, before they counter-attack."

A burly Gordon swung up the hammer and smashed
each mortar on the muzzle. We tumbled them off their
carriages, and laid the keg of powder in the tunnel, quick
as hands and legs could move. Midstrath snapped his
pistol on the fuse. We ran, and before we had hauled

in the plank we had laid to bridge the ditch the muffled
boom of the blast shook the ground under our feet. The
tunnel was destroyed. Quick work and never a casualty!
A short respite, but the end inevitable!

We had shown them we still had claws, and in the
morning, to discover what terms we were likely to get
if we capitulated, the Duke beat a parley and raised the
white flag on the Half Moon Battery. We had a rest
from bombardment and the discussion of terms began.

Sir John Lanier, who had been left by Mackay of
Scourie to conduct the siege, sent one of his majors with
a message to our Governor.

"Sir John Lanier's compliments to the Duke of
Gordon," said he, "and he will be pleased to meet the
Duke half-way between the Castle and the city."

The Duke would have gone; but we were fearful of
treachery, and begged him to go no farther than the
portcullis.

"It is the Duke of Hamilton you have to reckon with,
not the soldiers," said Ensign Winchester, with a worried
frown, "and there you have one no man trusts, not even
his own friends. Let me tell the messenger you will meet
General Lanier here."

The messenger—he was Major Somerville—was
furious when he was asked to deliver the Duke's
reply:

"This is a reflection on the honour of Sir John Lanier,"
he said, nearly exploding with rage.

"Not at all," said our ensign, "but there are some
behind your General we would not trust save on the point
of a pike."

"Let me tell you," stuttered Somerville, "Sir John
would not break his word for six times the Castle of
Edinburgh."

Ensign Winchester gave him a long, straight look before speaking.

" Sir," he said sternly, " he has broken his word to a better man than any here among us—his King."

Out went Somerville's mouth like the snout of a pig, and his face flushed an angry red. The taunt stung him sorely, for he too, like his superior officer, had held King James's commission.

All this time we were lining the defences of the outer wall, when a diversion on our left drew our attention, and we saw a man running like a hare along the loch-side. The man was Jock!

He took the Rock face like a mountain goat, and we noticed at the same time one of the enemy sentries hurry away, evidently to report what had happened.

I went off light-footed to meet Jock, and was I not glad to see his freckles and his grin again, when he came in at a place where the wall had been breached. Going to join the others and find the Duke, we met him labouring up towards us.

" Grant, Grant," he cried, in great agitation, " this is serious, disastrous, I might say. By a foolish act you have placed in jeopardy the lives of all of us here. As a soldier you must have known the consequences of breaking in during negotiations while the white flag is up, contrary to all the rules of war."

Jock went white as though he had received his death-stroke.

" Sir," he said stiffly, " I kent nothing about the parley. From where I lay in a cellar below a land in the Lawnmercat I could not see the flag on the Battery. For two days and nights I have been waiting for a chance to win in to you to report."

" Unfortunately, our opponents yonder will not

o

believe that. They will certainly demand your surrender.
No, they will never take that story."

"Well, sir," said Jock, and I detected a shake in his
voice, "they will take it from myself, for I'll ram it
down their throats with an ell of steel. I can go out the
gait I came in."

There was a droop to his shoulders, and something
so forlorn about him, as he took his solitary road to make
amends for his unwitting fault, that I could not bear to
see him go like that. No, I could not.

"Wait, Jock," I called. "I will go with you."

He halted and looked at me, a new light in his
eye.

"Will you, Alastair? It is good to ken I have one
friend left in the Castle of Edinburgh."

"Stop, stop!" the Duke commanded irritably. "Let
us thrash this matter out."

I looked at him closely. There was no doubt whatever
the man was done. There were dark shadows under
eyes which held the dregs of many sleepless nights.
The skin of his face was like old parchment, with a spot
of scarlet burning on each cheek-bone. His hands
fumbled foolishly with his Order, and his breathing was
difficult.

"The matter is thrashed out, sir," said Jock quietly.
"I made a mistake—I swear it was an innocent one—
and as a soldier I'll accept the dirdum. But as for
surrendering me, I'll save you the trouble of that by
walking out with my sword in my hand—drawn."

"No!" cried Gordon. "No! Here, Midstrath.
Damned if we give Grant up. Do we?" His eyes
glittered with excitement. "Let us take Winchester's
plan. To-night we will go down the Rock, seize the boats
and cross the loch to escape, or die fighting in the open.

Better that than starve to death, like rats in a hole. What do you say? We cannot let Grant go. We——"

He paused for want of breath, and Midstrath put out an arm to support him.

"Certainly not," Winchester said soothingly. "We cannot think of any surrender of Grant. But what is to hinder him slipping out again to-night? He can enter and leave this place like a warlock. Then we can renew the parley with a clear conscience."

"Well thought on, Ensign. But is the parley suspended already?"

"It is, sir, until Grant is given up. Colonel Winram took the liberty of telling Sir John Lanier that it was not the custom of men of honour to betray their friends."

"A right reply," said the Duke. "I'm glad of that. Now will you two," nodding towards Jock and myself, "come with me? I am afraid you will have to help me, for I confess I am feeling damnably unwell."

It required all his breath to climb the slope to his quarters, and for some time he lay on a settle, panting like a sick dog.

"Water, Grant. A drink! No, I had better not. That turbid water only makes me feel worse. Now, what news have you of Dundee?"

"Only bits and scraps o' news, sir, not all of it to be depended on. According to some, Mackay is chasing Dundee over the Highlands and has him bottled in Lochaber, and for a while I believe he did just that. But I had it for certain that Dundee took Ruthven Castle at the end o' May, and then he was the one that did the chasing, for he forced Mackay across the Spey at Cromdale, and only missed by an hour wiping out his forces for him at Alvie. The last certain news I had was that Dundee was ill, had disbanded his army for the time

being, and retired to Lochaber, while Mackay was returning to Edinburgh for larger forces. There is no doubt
at all that Dundee's campaign is held up in the meantime,
and we can hope for no help from him."

Gordon lay for a long time with his eyes closed, then,
as if speaking to himself, he said: " What a blow this
is to me; I have been counting on Dundee. I have
looked for him to come riding back to take the town in
the name of the King. A vain dream now, for I must
capitulate to-night—or to-morrow at latest. I fear a
capitulation, for I have been minding the fate of Kirkaldy
of Grange, who held this same Castle before me, for his
Queen. He was promised a full pardon, yet they hanged
him ' in the face of the sun ' at the Tolbooth, and put
his head on a spike before the walls he had defended so
gallantly through years of siege. To be hanged in the
face of the sun like Kirkaldy—that is the fate I dread."

" But, sir," I exclaimed, as his eyes rested on me for
a moment, " you said you meant to make a sortie this
evening according to Winchester's plan."

" Did I ? " he said, bewildered. " I must have been
wandering in my mind. That plan is not feasible for a
small band like ours. No, I can only try to get the best
possible terms for us all. But, Grant, I think you might
try that plan and win to safety. You see, if we capitulate
with you here, I fear it will go ill with you."

" Have I permission, sir, to go with him? " I asked.
" Not because I am seeking safety, but because I want
to keep with my friend."

" Willingly. And now that is settled, may I offer you
a few guineas to assist you? I have some left which I
intend to share with the others."

" No need, sir," said Jock, thanking him for his fore-
thought. " If we win out safely, I can soon come by

enough for my needs. And Alastair here has his money-belt almost untouched. If we fail there will be the less for these corbies down by to quarrel over."

" Good-bye then, and God speed you both. Did ever the leader of a forlorn hope have more loyal friends than I have had to support me! I thank you, gentlemen."

He closed his eyes again wearily as we left him.

Since neither of us could speak, we walked across the Hawkshill in silence.

CHAPTER XVII

A Fight in the Nor' Loch

LIFE is a tale of good-byes, and the longer folk travel the friendly road together the harder come the partings.

I have often wondered what the world would be like if the word " Good-bye " had never to be spoken. There would be no partings from the good, but we would have to thole a lifetime of the bad.

There are farewells we say carelessly both to places and folk, not caring if we will never see them again. Some we say blithely, glad to be done with a bad bit of life. There are the farewells that sadden us, and the long last farewells that tear our hearts. Aye, and sometimes it is so hard to say that we cannot speak the word at all. Only a strong grip of the hand and a long look into the eyes—that is all we can manage. But the worst of them all is the bitter farewell where words are spoken in anger or scorn, for there poison is left in the wound that rankles on and on, without end to it.

What we cannot put in words we can sometimes put to the chanter; a lament will tell for us our yearning and regret. I have aye had an ambition to make a pibroch. *Leaving Ardmair* is the name I would give it. The notes are in me, but these same will never come right on the pipes. But I am thinking that maybe some day one of the great MacCrimmons will get the notes for it. The pibroch of all farewells has yet to be made.

I had been six months in that Castle on the Rock—

indeed, but it seemed like six years—and I had come to have a liking for all, and to-morrow these men would face the risk of the scaffold, while Jock and I were scurrying to safety. It was hard for me to say them good-bye.

" Where will you make for? " said Elliot.

" A safe hidie-hole until our belts are out an inch or two. The buckle o' mine is near rubbing my backbone. Afterwards, the north and Dundee," answered Jock.

" Fortune favour your venture, then," said Elliot, as we went over the wall.

One of Midstrath's Gordons, the burly lad who had swung the hammer in the sortie, was waiting under the wall with the rope by which we were to slip down over the buttress of rock below. Jock went first and made the descent safely. Then it was my turn and I went hand over hand, scraping the rock with my toes, until the belly of the buttress had me swinging in mid-air. The farther descent was only a matter of twenty feet, yet it seemed as if I should never touch ground. A shake of the rope signalled our landing, and it quickly wriggled out of sight like an adder.

" Will it be swimming? " I asked Jock, as we came to the water's edge.

" For a bit on the other side. With the sluices up it should not be above six feet. We could lift a boat, but we'd be both seen and heard. Safer to wade and swim."

I took my pistol and powder-horn from my belt and tucked them high up under the double folds of the belted plaid, and stealthily we set off, wading the loch. Now it was scarcely dark in the short June night. A saffron and green belt, left behind by the sun, had hung low in the north-west sky till eleven of the clock, and though it was now some time after midnight a faint glow still filled the lift. Whether the plash of our feet or the broken reflections cried our presence I cannot tell, but sound carries wondrous far over water, and there was the Rock behind to multiply its echoes. Whatever of it, some of the Campbell gentry along by the West Kirk were roused and bang went an Argyll musket. The ball ricochetted off the water and whined into the night. We threw off all further pretence of secrecy and splashed ahead.

"Duck at the flashes," cried Jock, "and then run like a water-hen."

Ducking was not for the moment, for, faith, we'd have been ducking till morning and making little forrarder, since the shots kept coming in singles and couples, lighting up the Rock and the ramparts, and a glisk I had of them showed me our friends above, watching our progress.

And now Argyll's men had launched a boat, and were pulling down the loch to head us back. The rattle of the thole-pins and the groan of them backing to the pull sounded loud in the night.

Services rendered unasked, by friends, have sometimes a doubtful utility, and so it was now. What did they do up above but open fire on the boat, and with the poor light a number of their balls spat into the water unhealthily near us. But worse, the flashes showed us plainly to the rowers.

Out of the night surged the boat, the bow lifting at every heave of the oars, bearing straight down on us. Now the pity of it was, that ten paces would have set us knee-deep, yet there was nothing for it but turn and fight.

Lucky the man who can choose time and stance in a bout of arms, and were the choice left to me, at any time,

then the last place of my choosing would be a boat to
fight from. The three—they were all Campbells—
learned that lesson, quicker than ever Tearlach and I
learned the first declension.

As the boat came down on us they ceased rowing. The
one in the bow, springing to his feet, seized an oar and
drove the blade like a pike at my chest. He overreached,
missed me by half-an-ell, and before he could recover,
or make even a move to draw dirk or broadsword, came
over the side on to my point. Down I went, with him
on top of me. I struggled up, to see the boat five paces
away, drifting stern first down the loch, Jock wading
alongside of it, worrying with his blade the other two, who
had as much to do to keep their balance in the swaying
boat as to ward off Jock's thrusts. I splashed through
the water towards it and gripped the bow, when one,
placing his foot on the gun'le, made a mighty leap shore-
wards. The other, rocked clean off balance, went head
first over the side, taking the water like a gannet. His
feet flailed the surface for a space, and when he righted
he came up with neither sword nor targe in his hands,
and blundered off along the shore, vomiting a cargo of
Nor' Loch slime. When I looked to his friend I found
Jock had him at the sword-point, disarmed.

"Into that boat," I ordered, giving him a prick to
hasten his going.

I swung the bow round and gave the boat a mighty
shove across the loch.

A faint cheer drifted down from above as we turned
and scrambled up the steep bank.

"After the rise," said Jock, "it's clear downhill.
Shake a run out of your shanks and ye'll near roll the
rest."

"Where to?"

" Royston. There's a crack in the crags I ken there'll suit us brawly till we get some provender under our doublets."

The road was easy, slanting steeply downhill, and already dawn was flushing the sea before us as we came down to the firth, and after a scramble over the rocks found the crack. It was no great cave, nothing like the great rocky halls of our west and north coasts, but offered ample shelter for two.

" I'll scour about for meal," said Jock. " It's got to be had somehow, and that without the word of suspicion trailing after us."

Away he went, to return shortly with a poke of meal and some dried fish.

" You are the quick one," I said.

" Not so quick neither," he grinned. " The man I spoke to was a suspicious auld deevil, and I doubt if the story I told him, of having missed the regiment through lingering owre long in the tavern last night, was swallowed. He looked hard at my uniform, which, ye'll admit, looks as if I'd been spending a month o' nights in the taverns."

Jock looked down at his stained and threadbare breeches and laughed.

" But I jinked him, for I made off for Leith and, as soon as I was out o' sight, doubled round the braes above. He'll talk, though, and we'll have to move the night. Get a fire going."

I withdrew the ball from my pistol, loosened the charge, snapped the lock and flashed the powder on a clump of dry moss. Jock blew on it gently, and we soon had a fire blazing merrily, glowing blue in the embers as only a fire of salted driftwood burns.

Folk speak of hunger and tell of it as a pain gnawing

at the vitals, which but shows they have never gone
hungry for months on end, for the slow starvation we
endured in the Castle was more than a pain. It was a
cruel torture of the mind, for, as the slow weeks went
by, the store grew less and less, and our bodies craving
more and more all the time. In time and out of time we
thought of food, and spoke of food, and in my fancy I
was aye seeing the loaded table at Ardmair.

That day at Royston we were like to go on eating till
the cows were at the milking, had prudence and a thought
for the next meal not stayed our hands. We lay down,
the lap of the tide on the shingle a pleasant sound to my
ears. I lay listening to it happily.

"Jock," I said sleepily, "the tide on the east coast
has a harsher sound in it than the tide on the west."

"Blethers!" Jock grunted. "Get to sleep."

But I knew I was right. Our western tide has a softer
sound, just as our winds are warmed and softer than on
the east coast, and a great longing came over me to see
Ardmair again, to run with Dileas on the point, to climb
the crags of Coigach and stand facing the Minch, with
the salt wind blowing through my hair, as I had done
before the days of that fateful foray. The happy days
of boyhood! How little we prize them, aye questing
ahead and snuffing the future like a hound following a
blind trail, for a blind trail it is, and a mercy on us that
we cannot see the road beyond the bend. I was sick for
home. Had I foreseen what soldiering was to be for me,
then, by the saints, I would have stayed at Ardmair. If
the taste I had gotten of it already was all that wars and
soldiering held out, then I had had enough of it. Weary
sentry duty, when a man learned to doze on his feet like
a horse, lacking daily provender for months on end,
battered at by bombs and balls, with never a chance of

swinging a blade and hitting back. " Never again for me," I swore, " the siege behind walls."

When I wakened I found Jock had blown up the embers. What little meal we had left was eaten, and we prepared for the road again.

" And where now, Jock? " I asked.

" Duddingston's the best place to make for," he said. " We are sorely in need of rest and feeding, and yonder we'll get it and no fear o' gossip. Yon aunties o' mine are the grandest talkers in the three shires, but after an hour—and, mind ye, ye'll swear ye never said a word— they have ye squeezed like a lemon; and what ye've got from them you could set down on your wee finger nail. But tell them a secret which touches the family o' Grant —and, mind ye, the Grants are big folk in their eyes— and they'll keep it close till ye can walk to the Bass. Gin we get yonder unseen we're safe."

We took the road as the shadows were lengthening, and made easy journeying south, to pass between the town of Edinburgh and the Port of Leith. We crossed the river by a bridge at a clachan of mills at Bonnington, and then turned farther south, to pass another clachan of the name of Restalrig. It was then we crossed the main road from the south, pausing to look along it.

" That road," said Jock, " could tell a story. Roman legions made it and tramped it; English bowmen, many a time to Scotland's peril, marched it. It saw the Scots broken and fleeing after the bloody battle o' Pinkie. I said yon night in December the Revolution looked like the end of the Stuarts, but now I am seeing the end further back. It was the night Carey galloped past Jock's Lodge there to Holyrood, three days out of London."

" London to Edinburgh in three days? No horseman could do it," I said.

"Three days to an hour! That was a ride! But Carey nor none then knew he brought the doom of the Stuart line, when he carried to James VI. the news of the death of his cousin Elizabeth. They've been a misguided family the Stuarts, from Mary on, and it's hard to ken which of them was worst guided. Folk blame the throne for bad government. No' me! I blame the men behind the throne, and the Stuarts aye chose badly. Scotland has little enough to thank some o' her nobility for, past and present," said Jock savagely. "She's had owre many traitors and self-seekers to serve her. Who's to blame for the past generation o' misery in Scotland? The Earl o' Lauderdale! And King Charles, away in London, never kent the half o' it. I'll not say James has been a good king, but he would have been better had he been better advised. I'm no' fighting for him so much as for the royal house o' Scotland, and now the Stuarts' last hope is Dundee and the Highlandmen."

"And if Dundee is likely to do no more for the Stuarts than we have done already, I tell you, Jock, I'm for the north and done with it," I said.

Jock halted and peered at me in the dim light.

"Do you mean that, Alastair?"

"This much I mean, that neither Stuarts nor Dundee will have me bottled up in a fortress again. Man, Jock," I said passionately, "have you any notion how I felt in that siege? I'll wager you could never understand what I suffered. Give me the heather under my feet and the pipes screaming *Tulachard*, and I'm a Stuart's man till summer's snows melt off Ben Dearg."

"You'll get what you want with Dundee," said Jock, with relief. "Dundee's a cavalryman, and a cavalry officer is aye for action. Let's on. Ye gliffed me there, Alastair."

Already dawn was lifting the bars of night as we climbed the tail of Arthur Seat and looked down on the village of Duddingston. Not a curl of smoke showed yet from the cottages below.

" I doubt it's soon enough to be tirling the pin doon by, early birds though they be. Let's sit." Jock laughed and went on: " Now in a whilie ye'll hear the back door skliff open and Aunt Janet will take a bit look at the morning. Syne she'll shut that door wi' a couple o' big slams, fit to rock the foundations o' every house in the village. That's Duddy's revally, and the auld regiment rolling *Dumbarton's Drums* was no' to compare wi' Aunt Janet's big bangs. Now wait ye and tell me if I'm wrong."

We sat among the whins.

CHAPTER XVIII

A Knot-Hole in the Floor

A WISP of smoke lifted suddenly from the Grant chimney, and soon a thin blue pillar, growing like a mighty pine-tree, was reaching for the sky.

" Annie's up and ganting her head off, I'll warrant. That's wood reek; she is piling on the thorn twigs to make a clear, red fire for the girdle. And that's good news for two hungry lads. Alastair, think of it—hot bannocks and butter again ! "

He thumped me joyfully on the back.

" And kail for dinner, and sowens for supper ! Man, it's worth while living through a siege to have an edge like mine on hunger, and food at hand.

" What did I tell you ? There's Aunt Janet out to give a look round to see that a' thing's right, and then at the clouds to tell the weather."

Jock was right. The door was somehow warped and did not close readily, so Aunt Janet tried and tried again, and the reverberations, though we were well up the slope above the house, minded me of a cannonade.

" I wonder the door stands up to it," said Jock, rising.

" And I am wondering how the house stands up to it," said I.

Jock laughed.

" Well, we'll away before the village is stirring."

We slipped down, entered the village unobserved, and caught Aunt Betsy mixing the barley meal for the

bannocks, and Annie finishing the sanding of the floor.
Aunt Janet was directing both at their tasks.

All three stopped what they were doing and looked
at us, startled as roe-deer surprised among the birches.

" Jock! " said Aunt Janet, who was first to find her
tongue. " It's you! What a fright you gave us. What
are you doing here? And Alastair Mackenzie with you!
Has the Castle fallen? "

" It has, damn it! "

" And what now? "

" God kens. Ourselves, we're beaten men, sair in
need o' rest. Will you keep us for a wee, till we can let
out our belts a bit, and are fit to take the road north, to
join my Lord Dundee? "

" We'll do that if you say so. Laddie, I hardly know
you. You're no' like yourself at all."

Aunt Betsy came forward, shaking her head over us.

" A pair o' skinny hoolets is what I see. Arms and
legs like porridge-sticks! What have you been feeding
on? "

" Air. And one salt herring a day."

" Oh, laddie, laddie! But you would go, so you've
nobody to blame but yourself."

" And I'm no' blaming myself. Wait till Annie has
thrawn the necks o' a wheen o' the best hens, and I've
put them under my doublet, and then I would not call
the King my cousin. But I'm warning you, you'll have
to hold your tongues about us being here. It's no' owre
safe for you to take us in."

" We'll not let you away, now you're here," she said
stoutly. " But do you mean you're in any danger? "

" Alastair's not. But I'm different. If they could lay
hands on me they would be glad to clap me in the
Tolbooth."

" That's bad," she said anxiously. " Well, then, you'll bide quietly upstairs and not show yourselves at all. We'll feed you up, and you can go out at nights to stretch your legs."

" Annie, can you hold your tongue? " asked Aunt Janet sharply. " Or will you set the news flying round the whole countryside? "

" Me clype on Mister Jock! " said Annie indignantly. " I'd sooner cut out my tongue."

" We'll not ask you to go that far," said Aunt Janet dryly, " though maybe Adam Robb will one day be sorry we did not."

" Adam Robb! " said Annie, tossing her head.

" Yes, Adam Robb! He's the only man I've seen that's daft enough to look twice at a hilty-skilty lassie like you. And now, up the stairs with you both, and stay still, and nobody need ever learn you're here."

We lay at Duddingston for a week, and in that time did little but eat and sleep. We lost the gaunt, starved, hollow-eyed look of the Castle days, and my doublet began to fit me better. Annie carried our meals up the steep stair, and, every chance he got, Jock teased her about Adam Robb.

" A decent man, Adam, but a wee thing old for you, Annie," he would say. " But you'll get no' a bad doon-sittin', and what's a few years this way or that? "

Or, another time: " Has he speired you yet, Annie? Tell him from me it's high time he did."

And " Him! " she would say, banging the dishes about, her cheeks aflame.

Our coom-ceiled chamber was over the kitchen, and Jock had found a knot in the floor that could be removed, and he would apply his eye to the small hole and watch

P

the activities below, when he wearied for a sight of other folk.

One evening he was restless. He wished supper would come, yawned and walked about for a bit, then lay down with his eye at the knot-hole.

" I'd give something for a sight o' Adam Robb's wooing," he said mischievously, " but I never get a glisk o' him. It's dooms hard on me, for he must be below here whiles. But the trouble is, my view's a bit circumscribed. I canna see the ingle and that's Adam's seat. Dod! but I would like fine to see him courting Annie."

He looked up at me with the wide, happy grin I had not seen so often of late. Life did not seem quite so gay to him now as it had done before the long months of siege and privation. From myself the wild exuberance of youth had gone the day I left Ardmair. Jock had kept it longer, but it had died on him in the Castle. We could both be happy enough at times, but never again would we hold out both hands to life and shout it a welcome. Never again for either of us the untroubled sleep of boyhood or its unshadowed eyes.

" What ails you at Adam Robb? " I questioned, noting with approval the grin, and the rested, less haggard look of him.

" Nothing. He's a decent, douce body."

" What is he like? "

" Have you never seen him? "

He laughed, rolled over on his back, clasped his hands behind his head and looked reflectively at the ceiling.

" You ken the way a cod looks at you? A cod wi' a beard—that's Adam Robb! But I wouldna say he has as much backbone."

He shook with silent laughter.

" But a decent soul, mind you."

He rolled over again and took a lively interest in the scene below. In a little he wagged a hand vigorously.

" Come here, quick, if you want to see him. He's just coming in. Quick! "

I took a sudden step forward. Jock made room for me. My feet became tangled with his. I stumbled, made a great effort to keep my balance, and failed. I fell to the floor with a crash that shook the house.

" You blundering deevil! " said Jock, sitting up and looking annoyed. " What made you do that? "

" The same thing as landed the cat in the sea in the storm," I said crossly, nursing my knees. " Because I could not help it."

" Well, Adam Robb now kens somebody's here, and that'll start him wondering, and soon it'll be the clash o' Duddingston."

My heart sank.

" Jock, what can we do? It was the bend in the ceiling that came in my way and made me stumble. Is the man to be trusted? "

" I'd trust him at most times. But if, like the lave, he's gone over to the Dutchman's side, there's no telling. A change o' politics can make a bitter enemy out o' a friend. I wish Annie would bring up our supper," he ended gloomily.

" What's kept you? " he asked impatiently, when at last she appeared.

" I've been hindered," she said, banging the pewter about in a great hurry to make up for lost time.

" What hindered you? "

" Adam Robb came in, and I could not bring up your supper till he went."

With downcast eyes she creased her apron in little

folds. It was a new apron of linsey-woolsey, and since our last meal-time she had changed to the red petticoat and red kerchief she wore on the Sabbath.

Jock looked at her keenly.

" Annie, did you hear a fall a wee while back? "

" Did I hear a fall! I thought the house would be down. I lookit for you to be coming through the roof."

" Did Adam hear it? " Jock asked anxiously.

" A body would need to be deaf indeed that did not hear yon."

" What did he say? Tell me, Annie. Come on, quick! Did he guess? "

" Aye, he guessed. He had just come in, when there came that michty dad on the ceiling. He lookit up and said: ' What'll that be? '

" I said: ' There's something doon. Mistress Betsy's aye lettin' things fa'.'

" I was feared he would notice I was shakin', and stirred the pot on the fire for dear life. Then he set himsel' doon in the ingle and lookit from me to the ceiling and back again.

" ' There's something doon, right enough,' he says slow, ' but let me tell you, that whatever it was, Mistress Betsy could not have carried it in her two hands. That was a heavy weight.'

" ' Then she'll ha'e coupit it,' I said.

" ' She might, if she'd been nearer it than the foot o' the yaird, where she's thrang about her herbs,' he says. ' Are you no' goin' up to see what it was? '

" ' It'll be Mistress Janet'll ha'e coupit something, then,' says I, careless like. ' I've nothing ado wi' it.'

" ' Aye,' says he, strokin' his beard, ' if Mistress Janet wasna ootby seein' to a clockin' hen, it might ha'e been her.'

" He sat quiet for a while, and when I lookit at him, here he has his eyes cockit at the ceiling.

" I kept stirrin' for dear life, and up he gets to his feet, and says he: ' What are you feared for, Annie? Do you think it's a ghaist? A ghaist would fa' softer than that. Would you like me to go up and see what is't?'

" ' Na,' says I. ' Ye'll no' go through the house when the mistresses are out.'

" ' Very weel," he says, sittin' down again and watchin' me at the fire; ' very weel.' Then, after a bittie: ' When did ye begin to tak' kail for supper,' he asked, ' you and the leddies?'

" ' Oh, we whiles ha'e it,' I telt him.

" ' Ye're a leear, my lassie,' he says. ' I've come about this house for years, and had mony a meal in this kitchen, and I never before saw kail on the fire at this time o' day. And what I want to ken is, why your face went the colour o' skim milk, and yet ye'll neither go to see for yoursel' what's wrang, nor let me go for ye.'

" ' Oh, I'll go,' says I, out o' a' patience wi' the man, ' if it'll pleasure you. But my kail'll stick to the pot if I do go.'

" ' Then bide here,' he says, and sits glowerin' at the ceiling, stroking his chin.

" I thought I'd get peace at last, but, as if speakin' to himsel', he began again: ' Aye, aye! I ken a lad that's wonderfu' fond o' kail; that I do. Let me see, noo. What day would it be the Castle fell? It was June the thirteenth —and this is June the eighteenth. Aye, aye! I wonder, noo, I wonder where a' the lads went that were in the garrison. There's ae man wantit, so I've heard tell, for he broke the rules, or something like that—ae man, and he was a Grant!'

" I stoppit my stirrin' and droppit my spoon.

" ' Your kail'll burn, lassie,' says he. ' Keep stirrin'! '

" ' Noo I wonder, if I was that laddie Grant, I wonder where would I go, if I was wantit. I think, lassie, I think I would go to my aunties at Duddingston. What do you think, Annie? '

" ' Oh, Adam,' I cried, ' you'll no' clype? You'll no' clype on Mister Jock and get him sent to the jail? '

" And there and then I grat like a bairn.

" He said naught for a bittie, and then, he out wi' it.

" ' I've been hingin' about ye for a while noo, Annie,' says he, ' and I'll say naught—if ye'll ha'e me.'

" So I said I'd ha'e him, and you needna fear, Mister Jock."

As Annie finished the tale of her wooing, Jock shook his head, as a dog does who has been under water, to clear his eyes.

" But, Annie," he protested, near breathless with surprise, " you don't mean to say you're going to marry Adam Robb just to make him keep his mouth shut? I'll not have it. I could soon find a way to tie his tongue. You'll not marry him if ye're sweir."

" Sweir? 'Deed no, I'm no' sweir. I've been wonderin' when in time he was ever goin' to speir me. He's come and he's gane, and he's come and he's sat, till I was sick tired seein' him there, for a' the world like a cloggit bumbee."

" Cloggit wi' your sweetness, Annie," said Jock, laughing. " That wasna his wyte."

" Weel, if it hadna been for you, I'd never have had him yet. I've you to thank, Mister Jock."

When Annie had gone, Jock put his arms about me, laid his head on my shoulder, and laughed till I had to hold him up.

" Fancy thanking me for giving her Adam Robb. Well, well, ye manna look a gift horse in the mouth, and Annie had better no' begin to look hers," he said, when he could speak. " This is something I never expected."

" But, Jock," I said, surprised, " you have always been teasing Annie about him. You must have suspected she was fond of him."

" I never did. If I had thought there was anything between them I'd never have said a word. I've told her fifty times he was owre old for her."

Aunt Janet was not slow to speak her mind about the match.

" The man must be blind," she said to Annie. " But try not to let him see how little sense you've got. If he knew you as well as I do——" She shook her head despairingly. " And try to talk less. A maid should be mim till she's married."

" And then she may burn kirks," Annie finished triumphantly.

And I will never know whether Adam would have given up Jock to the Privy Council if Annie had not promised to have him.

CHAPTER XIX

The Ferry at Cramond

THE hour of three in the morning of the longest day —and it not long enough for the journey ahead of us—saw us stepping out of the sleeping village under a silver sky.

We took the road by the Wells o' Wearie, the Grange and Corstorphine, keeping on the wide skirts of the town and passing by many towers and fortified mansions. It was a morning without wind, giving promise of a fine June day.

We swung along, I not speaking, being busy with my thoughts, Jock naming the seats and villages as we passed them.

" Why so dowie, Hielandman? " he said at length.

" I was thinking of the winter day when I first sat beneath the Castle. I thought then it was as solid a thing as a man might see. And look at the wreck of it now."

We halted and looked to where the roofless buildings huddled on the crag, dream-like in the early hour, as if not real at all.

" Solid as it was, even it is in ruins. Is it any wonder that the castles I built in the air are all down too? "

" Little wonder; for they're the easiest biggins to raise and the easiest ca'd doon. They cost least at the start, but they may cost a man his life at the end, if he tries to hold them."

" Or his happiness, if he gives them up. And easily

232

shattered they are, often in a minute of time. A word
may do it."

" Aye, or even a look."

" Did you ever build any, Jock? "

" Dozens. And they're all down. ' Colonel John
Grant of the Royals '—that was one. And what am I
now? Some folk say I'm no' even a lieutenant."

" No more of them for me! I have promised myself
that."

" Wheesht wi' you! Ye talk like an auld wife. You're
far owre young to stop building. Ye mind Elliot wi' his
screeds o' English poetry; there was a pickle sense in
some o' yon lad's havers. A bit came to my mind, the
now, he used to deave us with, about—

> ' castels buylt above in lofty skies,
> Which never yet had good foundations.'

I'm thinking we dinna fash enough about the foundations
whiles, we're that glamoured wi' the castles."

" I can put no foundations under mine. You are
happy if you can."

" I think a' body in Scotland's at the castle-building
the now, and they cannot all stand. There's William of
Orange, throne usurper, and James Stuart, rin-the-
country king, each building his castle. If the Dutch one
stands, the Stuart one comes down about its builder's
lugs. There's Hugh Mackay o' Scourie dreaming o' the
Scotland he'll help to make wi' his Lowland levies; and
John Graham o' Claverhouse hoping to do wonders at
the head o' the clansmen and bring the old Scotland
back—both o' them rearing towers in the clouds; but if
the one bides, the other goes. And Secretary Hamilton
sees his rising to the sky, and the Duke o' Atholl thinks
his should not be far behind. And what's to be the end?

Ruins for some o' them. But the man I'm sorriest for is the Duke o' Gordon, for he has seen both his castles go down."

We fell silent again, and it was not till we were passing through Corstorphine that I asked Jock how we would be crossing Forth.

" I'm making for Cramond," said he. " It's clear impossible to cross at the Queen's Ferry without a pass. The Council o' Queensferry have the watching o' the passage and have been advised by the Convention to put on the night watch again. I found that out when I tried winning north for news o' Dundee. Besides, Cromwell's old fort on Inchgarvie has been manned again, and, like enough, guns are mounted there. And Stirling Brig is guarded, and Mackay's troops are crossing by the Granton-Burntisland gait, so there's little choice left us but Cramond. God send they havena a guard there."

It would be about four in the morning we came down on a house standing at the bottom of the brae in Cramond village, a house not long built, for the harling was still fresh and clean. The tide was making in the Almond estuary.

" Give them a rap," said Jock, as we halted.

I knocked with my dirk-handle, which boomed hollowly on the door. Its echoes rolled within, and gradually died away. We waited a while and I hammered again.

" What kind of noise is that to be making at this time o' morning? " squeaked an angry voice above our heads.

Coming with a clap out of the air the voice made us start guiltily. Above us one half of a latticed shutter had been opened noiselessly, and half a head, surmounted by a woven nightcap, peered at us irritably.

" A queer hour o' day this to be hammering at decent folk's doors, wi' drawn dirks in your hands."

I hastily sheathed my dirk.

" We missed the road to the ferry," Jock lied boldly. " A bite and a sup, good man, is all we ask, and a boat across."

" It's but a step up the waterside to the Cramond Brig, and there ye'll get provender and the road to the Queen's Ferry. Ye'll walk it in an hour. This is no' a travellers' change-house."

" Good man," said Jock, " we'll tell you God's truth. We are a couple o' gentlemen in desperate need o' crossing Forth. We were both in the siege o' the Castle in Edinburgh, and all we want now is to get over without skaith. Here are a couple o' good bonnet-pieces for a sail in your boat."

I gasped. Here was Jock crying our secret to the winds!

" Bide a minute, then, and I'll let you in."

The head disappeared.

" Jock," I exclaimed, " what made you tell him? "

" Wait a bit. I ken my man, or I'm mistaken. Wait a bit."

In a minute the bars were drawn and we shown into a kitchen, where a fire of coal smouldered.

" Stir up the fire," said the man, drawing us a stoup of ale apiece from a butt that stood in the corner, " the while I get my clothes on."

" A moment," said Jock. " Have ye a nutmeg by chance? Cold ale sits ill on the stomach in the early morning."

" Ye're dooms particular," said the man, producing the nutmeg from a drawer, and setting oatcakes on the table.

We threw some wood on the fire, and when it blazed Jock heated the ale and rasped the nutmeg in it.

" Well," said our host, on his return, " ye're comfortable! What about your other wants? They're no' so easily seen to."

" Cramond must have changed a heap since last I kent it, if a boat is so hard to come by, or a lad to run a lugger out the channel to the back o' the island," answered Jock meaningly. " Yon sandy bits at low tide are fine and handy for landing stuff on."

" Ye seem to ken the place."

" Aye, and yourself better. Come on, what's your price for a boat across? "

" There's a haze on the water. I doubt my man wouldna risk the crossing while it hangs."

" The haar will lift in an hour," said Jock, " as fine ye ken."

" But it's risking my boat taking her out now and the tide will be on the turn in an hour. I doubt it canna be done under five guineas."

" Ye've mistaken me entirely," said Jock sarcastically. " We're not offering to buy the boat; just hiring it. Your boat has sailed out to Cramond Island many a night for less than that. I said two," and Jock laid the gold pieces on the table.

" No, no, it's no' possible. My man will want that for his share. What's to be for me ? "

" The whole o' it, if I ken you," said Jock sharply. " A plague on your dawdling! Come, man, is't a bargain? "

" And what's to hinder me keeping ye here and sending for the military? " says he, with a sudden show of valour that sat ill on the man.

" Just this," barked Jock, and clapped his hand on

the hilt. The steel snarled out and the point was at the man's middle before he could make a step. " I'll stretch it to three pieces. We're no' to be trifled with, as maybe now ye see. Three! Or we'll take your boat, willing or no'."

" Put up the steel," says the little man sullenly. " I'll get Dod."

" We'll come with ye," said Jock, putting up his sword and handing over a third bonnet-piece.

We walked down to the shore, and there at a small pier lay a lug-sailed coble, sail up and a man standing by.

" The mean auld deevil! " whispered Jock to me. " There he had the boat ready, and would have taken us for two."

We stepped into the boat and Dod prepared to cast off, when a horseman appeared, an officer in uniform, galloping madly down the brae.

" Guid sakes! " cried Dod, pausing at the untying of the painter, " the man's wud. The beast'll carry him into the tide."

He dropped the rope and cowered below the sea-wall, while we stood by, expecting the horse and man on top of us.

But the rider jerked his beast to the gravel ledge west of the jetty, and pulled him to a stop. With fores splayed out, and hind feet tucked under his lathered belly, he slithered to the withers into the water. Before he came to a stop, the horseman—and, faith, he was all that— threw his right leg over the pommel, and left the saddle with a vaulting leap. His heels ploughed the gravel, and the sparks flew from his spurs.

The horse, gathering his quaking legs under him, stood with head drooping, flanks heaving, and muzzle trailing in the splash of the wavelets.

I jumped ashore and led him from the water, a burning anger in me, for I hated to see a beast overridden. I turned, to see the officer leap into the bow. The shock loosened the painter and the boat shot out from the jetty. A puff of wind caught the sail, and with no guidance of helm she steered across the river, ground for a moment on the other bank, bumped off and, the sail swinging over, set straight down the estuary.

" Swing the tiller, Jock! " I called, and raced along the gravel, as far as the tide would allow, which was not more than half-a-bowshot.

Jock jumped to the tiller, when the officer suddenly drew sword, and had him at the point of it.

" Bring in that boat or I'll blaw daylicht through ye! " a voice yelled, and I turned, to see our late host with a wicked-looking blunderbuss levelled at Jock and officer alike.

" Shove the tiller hard over from you! " I cried to Jock.

He obeyed. The boat luffed, bobbed the tide for a moment, and then, the wind catching the sail on the other side, she came ashore with a grand sweep and dunted on the gravel.

" What rights had ye to lift my boat? " screamed the little man, near dancing mad with rage and excitement, and flagging the air, to the danger of all of us, with the muzzle of the murderous-looking bell-mouth. With a quick snatch I took it from him. He turned on me with a snarl, but I held him off with my sword, the while backing into the water, and reaching the gun to Jock.

" Step ashore," said Jock to the officer.

" I'll be damned if I do."

" You'll be damned if you don't," said Jock

menacingly. " If I touch this trigger you'll flee ashore in bits."

" I command this boat in the King's name," said the officer.

" So do we," retorted Jock; "and as our King happens to have the upper hand this morning ye'd be wiser to jump."

" Lieutenant Grant, you'll hear more of this," the officer said savagely, stepping ashore.

" Into the boat, and out with her! " cried Jock. Dod and I jumped together, and the boat swept into the estuary, till, clearing the bluff of headland, a puff of wind filled the sail, and she raced down the channel. The last I saw of the little man he was buzzing like an angry wasp about the officer, who stood looking grimly after us.

" I wonder if I could have taken her out myself," I asked Dod.

" Ye might, and ye might not. There's a twist in the channel just here ahead."

He spoke in a slow, singing voice, and, taking a quick glance to port, swung the boat in an arc, then straightened her head.

" Then," he continued, " ye might have held too much west and run her on the Drum Sands. The channel runs close to the island on the west side. But wouldn't ye think it should be on the east? "

" Indeed I would," I said, " by the lie of the island and the run of the tides."

" Well, it's no'. It's the west ye keep, until ye clear the Binks, and then it's deep water."

" There's never two of them the same," I said. " The Kanaird, at my home, comes out on a horseshoe swing round three points and as many rocks, hidden at high tide."

"Could you take us up the firth and land us beyond St Margaret's?" Jock broke in.

"I might."

"For something extra, you mean?" said Jock.

"I might."

"A plague on your doots," laughed Jock. "What orders did ye get?"

"To take ye across. He never said where or how to land ye, but I was aiming to put ye ashore about St David's."

"I'll make it worth your while to land us at St Margaret's," said Jock.

"As ye say. I'll take her past the Buchans and try for the passage by Inchgarvie."

He swung the tiller and we headed up the firth.

"What do you think, now, yon officer would be wanting the boat for?" I asked. "He knew you, Jock."

"He did, and I ken him. He's captain now, but he was Lieutenant Menzies when I last saw him. I met him at Portsmouth, when the Royals were there in '86, just after Sedgemoor. I'll wager he is bearing dispatches. But why he made for Cramond beats me to ken."

"He'd be wanting to land at Donibristle, unnoticed like," suggested Dod.

"Like enough," Jock agreed.

"Your master will get into trouble now," I said to Dod.

"No' him," he drawled, shaking his head. "Wullie Erskine's been dodging trouble a' his life, waiters and sic-like folk. He'll swear ye disarmed him and lifted the boat—as ye did."

The tide was turning against us, and it would be perhaps two hours later before we had cleared the point near to the Queen's Ferry and were running between Inchgarvie and the shore.

" I'll make to take her into the harbour beyond the ferry pier, and then swing her sharp across. Wi' the help o' the tide we should be over quick, before any o' the guard on Inchgarvie have noticed us," said Dod.

A little beyond the Queensferry Town House, and not far from the spot where I had anchored in the *Cromarty Lass* some six months before, Dod changed the course, and the lugger turned clear across wind and tide. A jabble of waves hit her, and although no great sea was making, she plunged heavily at times, drenching us with flying spray.

" She sails heavy," I said to Jock.

" She does not," Dod countered quickly, for the first time with any show of spirit. " It's the run o' the tide here, and the wind against it. There's a whirlpool there behind the island can spin a far heavier boat than this."

It is safer to cry down a man's wife than to speak lightly of the sailing of his boat, and I should have minded that same. Try as I might, I could not win him back. He gloomed at me the rest of the passage, and when we stepped ashore returned my farewell with a surly nod.

Q

CHAPTER XX

Over the Ochils to join Dundee

ALL of that morning we travelled hard west by the
north side of Forth. By mid-afternoon we were
over the Devon, a sluggish river, here winding and link-
ing on itself over a flat of marshy land. We had left the
sea road and were making for the high range of the
Ochil Hills, rising from the carse before us.

" I'll be glad to see us over the Ochils," said Jock,
pointing ahead. " If Captain Menzies means mischief,
he may be in the way of dealing out plenty for us."

" He is well behind, Jock."

" Be not so sure. He's in Dunfermline toun by this,
and if perchance any o' Claverse's old troop are quartered
there, and set on our hunting, it's hunting ye'll get. Yon
devils can quarter a bog or brae face like a hen-harrier,
or a hoodie hawking for peeweets' eggs."

" Once on the hills and it is no horseman would hunt
me down," I said confidently.

" It's little ye ken, Alastair, o' Claverse's dragoons,
or old Tom Dalziel's before him. They had their
training in the Rhinns o' Galloway and among the Kells,
and these slopes ahead are moudie-hills for steepness
compared wi' them. Forbye, the folk about here
get the name o' being a sleekit lot, wi' little love for
the Stuarts and less for the tartan and the house o'
Graham."

" It is little chance I have of forgetting that," I said,
offended. " Since ever I came south I have had that

sermon well dinned into me. The men of the north are only welcome when the Lowlands want soldiers to fight their battles for them. We were welcome enough at Bannockburn and Flodden."

" Tuts, man," retorted Jock. " Folk have short memories for favours and kindnesses, but remember an unfriendly act for generations. There was the Highland Host that rabbled the west; and Montrose, wi' a wild pack o' Macdonalds, slaughtered the Fife and Clackmannan men at Kilsyth. If ye——"

" Stop," I said sharp. " I would have you remember I am Highland, and though I hold no great regardance for a rabble of broken clansmen, whom your Lowland lordships hired to do their murdering for them in the west, I would remind you the Macdonalds are as good Gael as myself."

" And what better than I? " barked Jock. " The Grants are of the true line from Alpin, King of Scots, High Sheriffs of Inverness since Alexander, and we fought at Dunbar and Halidon Hill. If your clan can prove a longer descent I'd like to hear it."

" We received our charter to Kintail from David II.," I replied haughtily, " and before that held our lands under the Lords of the Isles."

" Which but proves my point," said Jock. " The Grants were an independent clan when the Mackenzies were vassals of the Macdonalds."

" You are Lowland in everything but name," I said scornfully. " You have not a word of the Gaelic, and for your forbears, from what I've learned, they were merchants for two generations back."

" Alastair," says he, going white about the gills, and his hand slipping across to his hilt, " I'll allow no man to cry down my folk."

" I never said a word against your people," I retorted, in my turn laying a grip on the hilt of my dirk.

" You did. It was you, said we Grants were not Highland."

" Not at all. It was yourself started it by crying down the Highlanders and the Mackenzies."

" For one that I took to be a reasoning being," said Jock, " ye have a queer way o' twisting another's sayings. I never said a word against the Highlanders."

" Indeed, and I swear to heaven you did. But as this looks like lasting till the crack of doom, we would better be moving."

I turned about haughtily, and caught the glint of the afternoon sun on a breastplate.

" Dragoons, Jock! " I cried, in alarm.

A quick turn of the head and he was off for the shelter of a scraggy wood of alder and hazel, lining the banks of a burn which wandered through the flats here.

" Into the burn," I advised, and we took to its bed, and splashed our way along its course, bent double under the shelter of its banks, until we came in the shadow of the trees.

" If only we can win to the hillfoots and keep clear till dark sets in," said Jock, " we can make our way into the mosses beyond Ben Cleugh, and give these lads the slip."

" There is not much chance of that," I said. " It is open ground for half-a-mile between us and the hills."

He raised his head over the burn bank.

" They've seen us. It's fox and hounds for us now."

We ran to the northmost end of the wood and crouched waiting there, while the Dragoons beat through the undergrowth. Nearer and nearer they came, and I could see no escape for us whatever. I looked desperately round, and spied a pool, with the roots of an alder spreading through the water, leaving a hollowed overhang of bank behind.

" Jock," I whispered, " crawl in behind the roots. It's our only chance."

We wriggled our way behind the screen, and, like a couple of otters in a holt, sat crouching there, three parts submerged in water and mud. A Dragoon rode along the bank, not ten paces from us, and halted to scan the pool. I could see every button and buckle of his accoutrements, and only hoped he was not observant enough to trace us by the flow of mud in the water. No Highlander would have missed that tell-tale trace of our nearness, since the burn was muddied all the way we had travelled. But our lad on the horse seemingly hunted to gaze.

Although the Dragoons were out of earshot, we feared to crawl out, and when at last I did, I had no sooner peered over the bank than there they were, approaching again in line.

" I told you it was hunting ye'd get," whispered Jock. " These lads will not leave off till they have us out of the holt or darkness stops their searching."

" That's like to be never, then," I whispered back, " for it will not be dark at all to-night. How many are there? "

The question was quickly answered. A cornet, a lad of about fourteen I should judge him, blew a whistle, and the troopers gathered round. As far as we could see, there were three, and a sergeant, the latter a grisly veteran of some fifty years.

" Where do you think they have got to, Sergeant? " asked the cornet.

" In the wood still, sir."

" Maybe they went down the burn, under cover of its banks," a voice spoke.

" Your advice was not asked," rapped the cornet to the speaker, whom we could not see.

After this rebuff there was a heavy silence for a minute, during which we heard but the champ of a bit, and the jingle of a chain.

" The advice is worth acting on, sir," growled the veteran.

" Very good, then," said the cornet snappishly. " Spread out again and beat down. And look here, men, if these two are not taken, it's the whipping-post for every one of you."

" Young cub," Jock fumed, as they rode off. " I'd whipping-post him. If he had not as many troopers with him in his hunt, I'd out and take a hand at hunter myself."

" Now, keep to the burn-bed," I whispered, " and make for the whins on the hillside yonder. We can be safe there until nightfall."

The troopers were barely departed when we set off up the burn, then, breaking away for the slopes, we were soon in the heart of a clump of whins, where the bees were lingering late among the honey-sweet blooms.

" If we could only win along to the silver glen there above the village"—Jock pointed west—" we could make certain o' a hiding-place. No trooper could take a horse up that gully, and we could work our way right into the heart o' the hills before showing a rag."

" If! There is half-a-mile of bare hillside between us and your ' if.' Let us spy our hunters."

We raised our heads and watched the troopers riding out from the southern end of the wood. They continued down the burn for some distance, then on an order wheeled in line, pivoting on the cornet, and, sweeping in a great circle a tract of moorland fringed with rushes, moved up and circled again.

" *Dhe !* but they're thorough," I said.

" I told you. That cornet's a puling bairn, but the sergeant there is one of Claverse's old troopers, and what he hasna learned about hunting down fleeing Covenanters is no' worth learning."

The troopers lined out again and trotted up through the wood, then, to our amazement, came straight towards the clumps of furze where we lay concealed.

" We're worse off than ever," gasped Jock.

The Dragoons dismounted, and, leaving one trooper in charge of the horses, began to beat up through the whins. I did some rapid thinking.

" Jock, is your tinder dry ? "

" I doubt it."

" Well, stand by to blow."

I quickly gathered a handful of dried grass and, piling if before me, drew the ball from my pistol and flashed the powder.

It took, and in an instant a blaze of flame shot up, and bitter, blinding smoke rolled in volumes as the wind fed the fire and rushed it through the undergrowth.

" Run under cover of the smoke and scatter the horses! " I shouted.

Coughing, and near blinded, we broke before the flames, to see the young trooper vainly trying to hold the beasts, already half-maddened with the smoke. At a yell from us he let go his charges, all but one, which he attempted to mount, but it reared and threw him heavily. He lay still. The horses went galloping madly west.

Still keeping in the smoke we ran along the slope, and burst, panting, into the gorge. Scrambling among the

boulders, splashing through the deeper pools, we came
at last to the entrance to some silver workings and threw
ourselves down, spent.

" It's no' safe to linger," panted Jock, " but until we
get our wind back after that burst we can risk it. These
lads will be owre busy chasing their runaways to meddle
with us for a bit. Man, Alastair, that was a great ploy.
How did you come to think of it? "

" An old trick in Highland warfare, Jock, either for
offence or defence. Set the heather on fire and charge
under its smoke, or escape, whatever you will."

" Damn it! It was Captain Menzies put these troopers
after us. The sooner we have the Ochils between us and
them the better."

Rising, we followed the gorge, until coming to a water-
fall. There we scrambled up the steep and made north
over the hills in the gloaming. It was never really dark,
and we travelled hard, save for a short halt of an hour
on the high flats, where we were forced to wait until
dawn broke before we could make the safe traverse of
a stretch of bog.

There is always to me an eerie feeling about that hour
before the dawn, yet suddenly, as we sat there, shivering
a little in our wet clothes, a lark rose from the grass, and
trilled its way into the heavens. Only the two of us
there, in that great silent waste, and a little bird soaring
to meet the sun, but no more did I feel lonely, and the
eeriness was gone.

By the time we were on our way the peeweets and
whaups were calling around us, and it not full light
yet.

CHAPTER XXI

The Cuckoo calls

I

THE day following, about ten of the morning, we came by Crieff, and there we learned that Dundee was still in Lochaber; but it puzzled us sorely to know the safe road to take for him; for no knowledge could we get of Mackay's cavalry, which was last heard of riding north from Angus. And neither of us knew the country between Crieff and the lands of Lochiel, which added to our difficulty.

Advices given us of the tracks to follow were as confusing as the old wife's tale about the cow. Some said that we should travel by Loch Tay and Rannoch Moor, while others strongly advised against that and urged the road by Blair and Lagganside. We made no secret of where we were going, and, indeed, there were plenty of pretty lads there eager for the chance to join Dundee, should he come south their way. But being on the Highland Line, between the wind and tide of Highland and Lowland strife, the older folk of Crieff had learned, like an old saugh by a burn side cleaving both to land and water, to keep their roots on land, though they might dabble their fingers in the ripples, when the wind of politics blew by.

The town was ringing with talk on the fortunes of Dundee, and Rumour was busy at her trade of gossip in every change-house. For the best part of the forenoon Jock and I sat in the corner of a tavern, hearkening to the harvest of talk, trying to blow the chaff from the grain and thereby learn of the best road north. Much of the talk was in the Gaelic, to my ears a poor Gaelic indeed, the speech of the borderline.

" I had it from Donald McGregor, who came down this week with a drove from Dunkeld," said one, " that Dundee had burned Ruthven Castle and defeated Mackay at Alvie."

" It is not the truth Donald McGregor is telling," said another, a McLaren by the tartan. " Donald was never past Trochrie. My good-brother, Angus here, was at Blair in Atholl, and Ramsay has joined Mackay and is chasing Dundee into Lochaber. Is it not so, Angus? "

" Donald was right and he was not right," said Angus slowly. " As I had it, Dundee has taken Ruthven and missed surprising Mackay only by an hour near Dalraddy by Alvie, and followed him close to Cromdale. But Mackay, getting a reinforcement of cavalry there, turned and chased Dundee back up the Spey. So now you see how it was? It is each other they have been chasing."

" And where is Dundee now? " I asked Angus.

" I did hear that he is ill, and lying in Lochaber."

" But the road by Atholl is clear of Berkeley's and Livingstone's Dragoons? " I asked, at Jock's prompting.

" They will be over the Highlands and north at Inverness or Elgin. Of that I am sure."

" Well, then," I said, turning to Jock, " the road by Atholl is open to us."

" Ask him how to make for Lochiel, then, that gait," said Jock. " Damn it! I'm fair lost here without the Gaelic."

" And like to be more so, my man, the farther north you go from here," broke in Angus in the English.

" Without your friend you would be wandering in Atholl or Badenoch till the hoodies pick your bones."

At which the company laughed.

" Well, well," said Jock cheerfully, " I'll cleave close to him."

" You will follow the road through the Sma' Glen and on to Drumouchdar, then at Dalwhinnie take the drove road west to come down on Lagganside and Spean. But you must first pass through the lands of Keppoch, and if Col's Macdonalds are about the braes you will go on in your hide and nothing more."

We followed the track without difficulty and without any happening till we came to Glen Spean.

There we were walking along the riverside, through birches and hazel, and I one minute wondering to Jock at the number of cuckoos calling, when out of the bracken and ling a score of clansmen in the Cameron tartan rose and barred our way, front and rear.

" There's your cuckoos," said Jock. " I thought they were unco rife the last mile."

" *Stad*," said their leader.

We halted.

Outnumbered by nearly ten to one, and with a fusil or two pointing at us, we could do nothing but stand.

" What will be your business in the lands of Lochiel? " said the spokesman in Gaelic.

" Gentlemen volunteers to join my lord Dundee," I said, " and carrying a letter to him from the Duke of Gordon."

Though the news of the surrender of the Castle of Edinburgh must have been through to Dundee long before us, I thought it better to add that to gain an importance in the eyes of Lochiel's clansmen.

" Your names? "

" Alastair Mackenzie, of Ardmair, in Ross, and Lieutenant Grant of King James's army."

" Grant," he grunted, and gloomed at Jock.

" A Grant of the Glenmoriston family," I added, at which the scowl disappeared, and very civilly he detailed guide and guard to take us before Dundee.

" Dark John, the Warrior, is at Strone, near to my chief's house," said he. " These men will guide you."

And there we were, walking down Glen Spean, with an escort of six clansmen behind us.

" We're arriving in style," said Jock blithely, " with a tail o' cuckoos."

" Keep your tongue still, Jock," I warned him in a whisper. " Some of these men may have the English."

" Dinna fash yourself, Alastair; I would as soon sit on a bees' bike as meddle wi' these lads! "

Near to Strone we came on the camp, where our escort handed us over to the guard. It was on a flat close by the Falls of Spean, and Dundee had no more round him than a single company of some four hundred McLeans, under Sir Alexander, and three troops of horse. A kinsman of Sir Alexander arrived to take us before Dundee.

" Has Dark John disbanded his army? " asked Jock, looking round the small camp we threaded.

" Oh no," said our escort.

" Well, where the deil are they? "

" There are a thousand Camerons and five hundred Macdonalds within a day's march."

" Where? "

" At their homes, of course. My lord Dundee has neither money nor food to hold an army together long. But a blast of *Cogadh na Sith* on the pipes would bring five hundred within an hour, and a fiery cross four times that number before morning."

" My lord Dundee is not well? " asked Jock.

" You heard that? And we trying to keep that news quiet! "

And then we were ushered before Dundee.

His quarters in camp stood a little apart from the other tents. In front were two McLean sentries, while three saddled horses were being walked up and down, with orderlies in attendance.

Jock saluted smartly as we entered, and I touched my bonnet. The brown eyes, for all their softness, gave us an observant stare, and his manner had a touch of arrogance.

" Two volunteers to join us," said our escort. " Lieutenant Grant, late of the Scots Royals, and Mackenzie of Ardmair. Both were in the siege of Edinburgh Castle and carry a letter of recommendation from the Duke of Gordon."

Dundee took the letter and read it carefully through twice, without lifting his eyes. He folded it thoughtfully and laid it before him.

" Where have you been since escaping from the Castle? " he demanded, with a swift survey of the pair of us.

" We lay quietly at Duddingston, sir, for over a week, until we won back strength to fit us to journey," said Jock.

" It was impossible to hold out longer? "

" Quite impossible, sir. We had no food, no powder, and only seventeen men fit for duty."

" I see! "

He pushed back his chair, rose and called for an orderly.

" Show these gentlemen to their quarters in camp."
We were dismissed.

II

Three weeks passed while we lay at Strone, and during
that time I saw little of our leader. Day after day he sat
writing in his tent, letters to the King in Ireland, letters
to every chieftain in the Highlands. Couriers came and
went, and rumours, varying with each turn of the sun,
ran among the clansmen and the troopers, and at the
end of it nothing for certain could we gather how went
the cause of the King beyond the borders of our camp.
And how these rumours spread to us, and where they
came from, is now a wonder I puzzle over often. Like
Jonah's gourd, they sprang up in a night, and were
round the camp and far beyond it before the sun was
strong.

For a day we had it that the usurper had been defeated
and had fled the country, and King James was back in
London, at the head of thirty thousand Irishry; and,
again, we had it that King James had been defeated
before Londonderry. But one thing I do know, these
rumours kept our minds active on the cause. Jock
fumed at the delay, but more at the absence of an
army.

He burst out irritably one day, on coming into the
tent: " What hope do you think we will have, if Lochiel
continues to advise against gathering the clans and
drilling them now? Dundee is set on it."

" Dundee knows nothing about the Highlanders," I
said, " and he would be better to take the advice of those
who do, and act on it. He will never make barrack-square
puppets out of fighting Gaels."

" But they'll never face Mackay's drilled battalions."

Jock strode up and down restlessly, shaking his head in despair.

" I wonder, will you say that when you have seen? The chief will charge, and nothing but death will stop his followers. Lochiel is right. Leave us to fight in our own way, and persuade the other officers to stop talking about drilling."

" Well, we'll see, Alastair, but dinna forget you were well warned, if you find the clansmen break at the first volley."

" Clansmen that have no order to begin with, can hardly break," I returned, " so I cannot follow that reasoning. I have never been much glamoured with your drilled soldiers since I saw yon feeble attacks on the Castle, the officers driving them on at the point of the sword. Men with as little heart for fighting as yon will never face a charge of Highlanders."

" Well, we'll see," said Jock again gloomily. " I hear we are leaving in two days to fight Mackay."

" And if that is not another rumour, it is the best news I have heard for a month."

No rumour it proved to be. That evening my heart lifted to the sound of the Camerons' March on the pipes, and Lochiel marched proudly into camp at the head of near a thousand Camerons. The Macdonalds from the Isles followed close, and before two days were gone Dundee had an army of near two thousand.

CHAPTER XXII

Leaving Lochaber

I

IF there is anything in warfare more stirring to the
blood than a good road underfoot, a marching song
with a fine swinging chorus and good company rubbing
shoulders, I have yet to find it.

Ho-ro! Leaving Lochaber was no lament with us.
With Lochiel's pipers crying on the Camerons, and
Macdonald pipes screaming *Glengarry's March* to the
braes of Glen Roy, and startling the ravens at the back
of Nevis Ben, we lifted foot blithely hour after hour.
And when the pipers had blown themselves out, the
marching songs were raised, with a "*Ho-ro, hi-ri-o, Ho-ro,
hi-ri-o*" in the chorus; and at the opening "*Ho*," clash
went the hilts on the bosses of the targes, till the road
ran under our feet like the Spey in spate.

Ho-ro! It was marching we went, and we left the
cavalry behind us, long before ever we were through
Glen Spean and in sight of Laggan's waters.

Dundee himself, at the head of the Macdonalds, set
us a brave pace, and each chieftain marched at the head
of his men. McNeil of Barra was lilting along with a
battle-axe near as heavy as himself, and the head of big
MacIan of Glencoe, with the beard blowing on each
side of it like the spray of a linn, towered above the
line.

"Hech!" said Jock, "I ken now how you Hieland-
men can cover fifty miles in a day. I'm trotting like a

water-waggy. Marching with the Royals was never like this."

" Step out, man, and lift to the lilt. Saw you ever marching like this in your disciplined regiments? " I taunted.

" I never did. Marching with the Royals was a snail's pace to this. They'll never keep it up."

But keep it up we did, and by night were past Drum-gask and over the hill road to Dalwhinnie. For two days we lingered there, while Dundee talked Cluny over into bringing out the MacPhersons. And on the morning of the third day, the corries of Badenoch echoed to the tramp of our feet and the skirl of Lochiel's pipes, to such good purpose that we made Struan in Atholl by afternoon, and halted there to await the arrival of a number of out-clans—Stewarts from Appin, MacDougals from Cowal,. black Lamonts from Glendaruel, and Robertsons from Tummelside, who were speeding east to join us at that rendezvous. Like the Garry itself, there charging down the glen, gathering in the waters of a burn here, taking in another yonder, our army swelled.

Having assurance that Mackay had left Perth for Dunkeld, and like to be in Atholl on the morrow, Dundee and the advance guard went on by Bruar, and evening saw our camp-fires twinkling on the Blair in Atholl.

II

We sat alone in the mid room of the upper storey of the inn of Blair, a small chamber where we shared quarters with two others, a Sergeant Gow, a coarse rough fellow I had no liking for, and a young lad, Warren, of good family, just new come from college. Little did either Jock or myself think that humble room was to

R

see two deaths, and swift eclipse to the hopes of King
James, within a round of the clock.

The small latticed window stood open, and the air of
the summer evening, with a touch of moisture in it,
came heavy with the breath of the bell-heath, and a
drift of wood smoke from the camp-fires below; and
softly, like a low croon, the Falls of Fender murmured.
The crest of Tulach Hill glowed golden in the rays of
the sun, that was sinking behind the moor above the
Milton of Invervack. Suddenly the door opened.

Dundee stood in the doorway.

" I was looking for Lochiel," he said.

" He has not been here, sir," I answered. " He is
perhaps over by the Castle."

" I have come from there," said Dundee, and stepped
into the room.

If he could have foreseen that, twenty-four hours
later, he would be lying, dying or dead, in that chamber,
how would he, I wonder, have acted?

Or had he fore-knowledge? Certainly his mood was
heavy that night.

He strode to the window and lingered there, looking
long towards the moor that holds Loch Vack. Was he
thinking of the fate of that other Graham taken on its
shores—the traitor Graham who killed his King and
disgraced his name? I cannot tell, for no man ever
showed less what he was thinking than John Graham,
Viscount Dundee.

He turned at length and saw us standing, awkward
and uncertain, for, whatever Jock's feelings, I felt ill at
ease in this strange man's presence.

" Sit down," he commanded.

He drew a chair towards him, swung it between his legs
and sat it like a cavalryman, arms resting on its back.

" What service did you see with the Scots Royals, Lieutenant Grant ? "

" I was with them at Sedgemoor, sir."

" Four companies were there not, under my old friend Douglas ? "

" Yes, sir. We were on the right of the line, behind the Bussex Rhine."

" Except those posted forward to support the horse, and few of them came back," added Dundee.

" But how——? Sir——? You were not there ? "

" No." A smile, so faint as to be hardly a smile at all, passed over the Viscount's face.

" I was in charge of that party after the first volley," said Jock modestly. " We carried the old matchlock, and when our drums beat the alarm we blew matches. Their flare showed our position, and we took the whole con-centration of Monmouth's fire, then the charge, and that saved King James's army."

" And those of you left, worked Feversham's battery of artillery," added Dundee.

I sat marvelling how this man knew so much about that other campaign. He seemed to have an exact know-ledge of the movements, even of companies and batteries.

" Dumbarton's regiment ! " he said broodingly, " the only regiment that stood by my King to the last." A tinge of sadness was in his words.

Dundee might mask his features at all times, but that night at least his voice betrayed him.

His eyes met mine.

" What service have you seen, Mackenzie ? "

" None, sir, apart from the Castle siege."

" Never a foray into Assynt or Lochaber ? "

I smiled.

" It was a raid into Reay turned my feet from home."

" And the consequences such, it were discretion to come south? "

I let it go at that.

He looked at me so long that I grew hot with anger, and gave him stare for stare.

" It is a pity, Mackenzie," he said arrogantly, " that you Highlanders cannot forget your petty grievances when you fight in a common cause. But no! It is Camerons at feud with Macdonalds, Macdonalds hating Mackenzies, Mackenzies at the throats of McLeods; in fact, not one clan but has some animosity towards another—a difficult crew to hold together."

He rose abruptly.

" But I must find Lochiel. Good night to you."

When the door had closed: " Jock," I said, " if that one had been Governor of the Castle, it is down the Rock I would have been in a week. I do not like your Bonnie Dundee."

" I did not expect ye would. I kent it would gall ye when he spoke o' the clans."

" He should not speak ill of the men he has at his back."

" I would not say he spoke ill, Alastair. I would say he spoke truth."

" Indeed he did not. The clans will unite when they see the need."

" That'll be when the Deil's blind, and he's no' bleare'ed yet."

Then, seeing my angry flush, he hurried on: " But they look grand fighters, Alastair, be they Macleans or Camerons or Mackenzies! "

" They *are* grand fighters," I said stiffly, " and they will be showing you, soon, both how they can unite and how they can fight."

" I hope to God they do," said Jock fervently, " for we're needing them sore. But they'll have a good leader in Dundee. That's a brave man! He'll fight at the head o' the army."

" It is little respect the Highlanders would have for him if he did not," I said shortly. " Our chiefs do not lead from the rear."

" Well, but, seeing he's the only real leader left to the King, they're all at him not to expose himself. But he'll not hear to them."

" It is just as well. He must show himself a brave man who commands the clans."

" Well, a brave man he is, but he's far from being a happy one this night. He is on a rack, torn between love and loyalty to his King, and love and distrust of his wife. And there you have the only two folk in the world Dundee loves. In his eyes his King can do no wrong, but now, he's no' so sure o' his wife. Suspicion has poisoned his love and he's wondering a' the time what's going on at Dudhope."

I said nothing, wondering what sort of woman she was, who had joined herself to this cold, haughty man.

" That was a queer marriage," Jock began again. " Him to take a wife from Covenanting stock! And it's Livingstone, his old friend and now bitter enemy, that her name is joined with. It's the common talk o' his troopers. He's a proud man and ye can guess how that must be eating into him. I ken nothing o' the truth o' the story, but there's aye a pickle water where the stirkie droons. I believe he would give his viscounty this night for a little kindness and understanding. But even his King, for whom he would give his life, has shown him little of either, and that little, late in the day. He has not one friend in this camp he can open his heart to, and forbye, there are some things no man can speak o' even to his nearest friend. He carries a burden under his buff coat there is no ease for here."

"If all stories of him are true, I am thinking there must be a heavy burden on his conscience."

"Remorse, ye mean? Ye're wrong! John Graham will suffer no remorse o' conscience. He'll go to heaven or hell wi' a smile on his lips. The Grahams are no' made o' soft clay and never cried 'Parley' yet at the gates o' eternity. He will take his judgment with no belly-aching repentance or twelfth-hour whimper o' remorse. And why? Because he believes he did the right thing. His conscience is tuned to but one note, and that's duty, and he'll commit any crime for its sake. If I had been an older man, and joined the Life Guards instead o' the Royals, I might have been in his troop and called on to hound fleein' Covenanters, however ill I liked the job. I would have been under orders; so was he. And mind ye, there's aye two sides to a story. Hear his side. His troopers were shot down singly from behind dykes, and he's kent throughout the army for his care o' his troopers and the stand he takes for their rights."

"It is easy to see you are his man, Jock."

"I'm a King's man and so is he, and when King James's ship was scuttled, and the Scots nobles a' forsook it like rats, I liked the way he stood by, with Gordon, Balcarres and very few more."

"You are forgetting the chieftains."

"I am not. But I'll remind you we near quarrelled on this question before. Ye're dooms touchy if another says a word against a clan, yet I've heard ye cry down the Macdonalds. Yourself may say what you will, but ye'll allow no other a word."

He threw out his hands with an air of such hopelessness that it disarmed me, and banished the ill-humours I felt after Dundee's visit.

III

War sends a man strange bedfellows. The caprice of a quartermaster in arranging billets may change the whole future of a life. It was none of our seeking that the two men, Gow and Warren, were quartered together and with us. Gow I despised for an overbearing bully. He was a sergeant of dragoons lately promoted to cornet, for what reason I could not fathom, seeing he was only an indifferent sworder and could scarcely have been a great horseman, for he lost his horse in the bogs, when Dundee made his lightning march across the Moor of Rannoch. He sneered at Warren and baited him whenever occasion would offer.

Warren I liked, though many a time he had me smiling at his ways. Poor boy—for he was little else—I often wondered how he found himself in that army. Apart from the knowledge that he had been a student in the college of St Andrews, and was something of a favourite with Dundee, we knew little of him, for he was not one to talk much of his own affairs. Since leaving Lochaber the four of us had been together, and a boy less suited by training than Warren for the trade of war, one would travel a long road to meet. He was of gentle birth, but what told heavily against him was that he was of gentle upbringing.

I was in no mood for sleep. There was on me a foreboding I could not throw off. There would be battle on the morrow. Of that we were certain, but of its outcome for myself and for others I had the strangest fancies.

There was one man I must seek out, and, having found

him, I must ram down his throat a twenty-year-old lie.
Sometimes I would see Barbara weeping over him;
sometimes with Dileas she would be searching the battle-
field for me, and myself the one that would never move
more. I wondered if I would ever see Dileas again, or
Ardmair and the kind folk there. I wished I could have
had a gentler good-bye from Barbara and left her with
less bitter thoughts of me.

I turned to the window. Below, on the Blair, watch-
fires glowed. A soft darkness was over the strath. My
eyes followed the officer of the watch going the round of
the sentries, coming into the light of each fire, outlined
blackly for a moment as he passed it, then growing dim
in the half-light until he reached the next. Though I
could not see him clearly between the fires, I heard each
sentry challenge his approach. Down by Tilt he went,
along the banks of the Garry, then up the side of the
Banvie burn, where the horse-lines were, and back to
quarters at the Castle.

So lost was I in my strange thoughts and fancies
that I scarcely heard Warren and Gow come in. When
I turned all were sleeping. Sleeping! I looked at
them. Where would we four be sleeping the following
night? I shivered as I lay down, and wound my plaid
about me.

IV

Drum or trumpet or pipes, I had hearkened to the
Rouse on them so often these last few months that they
had little immediate effect on my wakening. From far
distant the sound would come to me, and sleepily my
eyes would drag open and I lie staring at tent roof or
billet rafters, till gradually the sounds without would tell
me the camp was stirring.

But that morning of July 27th it was somehow different. A trumpet blared, and I was on my feet before the last notes had died away. Our door burst open; a trumpeter thrust in his head. " Surprise attack! " he shouted, and was gone in an instant.

On the breeze with the last notes of the trumpet came the scream of the pipes, and I looked from the window, to see the clans swinging into battle formation on the Blair below. Jock was thrusting his arms into the sleeves of his long coat, while Gow was fumbling with his sword-belt and cursing roundly.

I looked at Warren. The boy, deathly sick, was leaning with one hand against the wall, the other clutching his stomach.

Gow turned and caught sight of him.

" Sick already, before a shot is fired," he jeered. " What will the bairn be like later on? It's a nurse he's needing."

Warren heard him. His toy sword was out and he was into Gow almost before the long broadsword was drawn. A quicker rencontre I never saw. The swords clashed, quivering. Warren's blade slithered under Gow's guard, and before either Jock or I could move a step the reddened point played dunt on the wainscot behind Gow. He went travelling quick. As he slipped to the floor he released his sword, which hung, transfixing the boy's arm. Warren stood dully staring at the corpse, and not a wince came from him as we withdrew the dangling blade. Even yet, it surprises me to know how he still thrust after receiving Gow's point.

Jock and I exchanged scared glances.

" God! " said Jock, with a catch in his voice, " this is a bauchle o' a business. What are we to do about it? Here's a job for the Provost-Marshal."

"Please do not report it yet," Warren pleaded with us. "Bandage my arm and let me come with you. I will report myself later."

It was the word of a gentleman, and with the enemy at the camp skirts, for all we knew, it little behoved us to quarrel or waste time over a principle of military law. We quickly bandaged his arm and were running for posts, Warren with the blooded sword in his left hand.

CHAPTER XXIII

Garryside

I

IF Dundee had any doubts about the spirit of his small army of clansmen, that morning muster should have banished them.

It was no surprise attack, but the advance of the army on the march to Garryside. Clan followed clan, while Dundee sat his horse on a rise, and watched them swing into position. For some time I stood looking at him closely.

" What are you glowering at? " asked Jock.

" Dundee."

" Well, did you ever see a finer figure on a horse? You never did, for there's none in King James's army can sit a horse like him."

" It was not his seat I was admiring. The man draws me strangely and yet he repels me."

" And I'll wager before the day is finished you're his man like me. Just see to the clansmen there. He has won them already."

The main body, mostly various regiments of Clan Donald, followed by a brave array of Camerons, were footing it past Dundee, and took a stance on the banks of Tilt, facing the road from Dunkeld.

Those Macdonalds! As duddy and savage-looking a crew as ever gathered under the ling. A few of their chiefs and *duinewassals* looked well enough, dressed in trews and buff coat, some with a helm or a chain cuirass, but for the most part their men were as near nature as the rigours of the campaign would allow. Hardly a belted plaid was among them, a rag of blood-red tartan —ill-woven in many cases and not of the best dyeing— round the loins; and the chests and arms of them bare as they came into the world. No; not all, for some were hairy as badgers, and them yelping like wolves in a pack to be loosed at Mackay.

For arms, most of the chiefs carried the claymore with hilt near a dirk in length, and blade fully an ell and a half. Young Clanranald, or Captain of Clanranald as he styled himself, had a claymore fully longer than himself. Old MacIan of Glencoe, near seven feet in height, and dressed in a fine buff coat never made in Glencoe, bristling like a hedgehog with arms, had gun, pistols, targe, broadsword, two dirks and *sgian dhu*. Glencoe could grow more arms than corn.

Their rags may have been scanty enough, but, faith, the weapons of the clansmen Macdonald made up for the lack of covering. Fully half had the broadsword with the basket hilt, and those who had not, carried Lochaber axes, some fashioned rudely from scythe-blades tied to a hazel staff, others beautifully made pikes with rein-cutting blades on the point. Near every man carried a targe with a spike on the navel. As for *sgians* and *biodags*, their waist-belts lay thick with them.

Pipers were strutting up and down before the muster blasting *Come, Dogs, and get Flesh*, the rallying rant of the Camerons; all but Col of Barisdale's, who vied to blow out their neighbours with *Macdonald put the Brae on Them*. And across from the centre, a few of the Macintosh clan stood, girning behind their beards, and asking but a nod to throw themselves on Col's lean wolves.

The Scottish Horse, under Wallace, a sorry remnant, in all barely seventy, the ribs of their cattle near piercing the hide on their flanks at every breath, stood behind us. Their beasts had not seen corn for three months, nothing but bog hay and lickings of Lochaber ling. It is little help we could expect from them.

Dundee, a trumpeter in his wake, rode up and surveyed the parade and seemed well pleased with it. He rode slowly along the ranks, passing a salute with each chief, and calling the name of a clansman here and there, and the chosen one bursting with pride to hear his name called.

Then Dundee's trumpeter sounded " Officers " and the heart of me went cold. Chiefs away, and I saw Camerons, Macdonalds and McLeods at each other's throats, Highland blood flying like spindrift in a gale, and little enough of an army left to Dundee at the end. But at a word the pipers were silenced; and that stirring battle-call hushed, the clansmen stood leaning on musket or qroadsword, scowling down the strath before them.

In a few minutes the chiefs returned, and reported to their men in Gaelic that Mackay was advancing up the defile of the Garry, and that they would march to meet him in an hour's time.

Up went the bonnets in the air and from the clansmen broke a great cheer, ringing among the rocks of Fenderside and rolling to the heights of Ben y Ghloe. The clans swung off in files of three, the pipes roaring *Bundle and Go*. But Col's pipers, sly dogs, put on the chanter *Onward we go, with the Cattle before*, a foray tune these same could march better to the lilt of than any there, except maybe the Glencoe men.

We retraced our steps to the inn of Blair, and as soon

as we entered the room Jock threw Gow's cavalry cloak over the body. After hastily breaking our fast we left the room to join the ranks.

II

In less than an hour the trumpets sounded, and we were drawn up in marching order. Only a few days before, we had been joined by General Cannon, from King James's army in Ireland, with three hundred Irishry, the spear-head of a larger force of three thousand promised to follow, but which, I may say here, never did come. These Irishry, raw kerns and gallowglasses from the north-west hill counties of Donegal and Tyrone, with their lank, black locks and scowling looks, slouched along with no lift to their feet. But though they slouched as they marched, yet they were wonderfully nimble on their feet when, of nights round the camp-fire, they broke into song and dance. And this I must add, when it came to the long march and the hard march these same gallow-glasses were as fit at the end of it as any of us. They favoured the battle-axe, not of our Lochaber type, but shorter in the haft and heavier, a murderous weapon, murderously handled.

Dundee had given the order to march with the Scottish Horse in front, Cannon and his Irishry to follow, when Lochiel hurried to his side, saying: " Stay, my lord Dundee."

The Viscount wheeled his horse to Lochiel, and we, who stood near, heard what followed.

" For God's sake, General, put the Irish in the rear. If the Irish take the van, some will resent it."

Fine we knew which clan he was hinting at. Since ever the days of Bannockburn, Macdonalds had claimed the post of honour in every Scots army.

Dundee's eyes hardened as his glance swept over the Irish and rested on the red-tartaned crew behind. He called over General Cannon and whispered a word in his ear. Then, giving the order to march, the trumpets sounded a flourish, the kettledrums of the horse rolled, and we swung off, the Irish standing aside. We dismounted gentlemen marched in rear of the horse, the drums throbbing in front of us, the pipes shrilling behind. 'Twas a gallant beginning!

" Alastair," said Jock, " give me the drums or the pipes for the march every time. Yon wooden whistles o' the English regiments I could never march a mile to."

The road we took after the ford of Tilt had all of us amazed at our General's manœuvre. Instead of taking the road direct to Dunkeld and the south, up which Mackay's forces had no choice but to advance, we swung up the left bank of Tilt, passed the clachan and took the steep road up Fenderside. It was but a peat road, worn smooth by the carns used for dragging down peats from the moss above, and had it been wet I am thinking Dundee would have lost some more of his cattle in the gorge of Fender. As it was, the half-starved beasts were sweating and heaving in flank long before the top was gained. The steep soon silenced the pipers, and it was a grunting, gasping army that reached the flats of Loch Moraig. Dundee dismounted, and, walking by his horse, set a cruel pace.

" What is he meaning by it? " grumbled a Macdonald officer in my ear. " Is it advance or retreat? Look you, yonder will come Mackay." He swung his arm half back. " We are marching north."

" No," I said, " we are to swing east," and I pointed to a small troop of Glengarry's scouts, who, mostly mounted on garrons, were outriding and flanking the army.

Skirting the lands of Lude and still holding east until coming to the high lands between the gorges of the Clune and Glen Girnaig burns, we turned sharply south. Guessing no longer, the long line of clansmen squirmed down the steep side of Urrard Hill. It was plain now— we were to take Mackay in flank or rear as he came out from the Pass below. Dundee could have burst on him as he came through the Pass and hurled his army into the Garry, but that to our General's mind was not war.

We halted, and rested behind the slope of Rin Ruari, a hill whose southern face sloped gently down to the Garry. Jock and I, with a few of the officers, crawled forward and lay looking on the strath, where the Fingalian track from Dunkeld led out from the Pass below. Mackay, if he were to reach Atholl, must march through the gorge.

" I wonder does he mean to let Mackay through the Pass before attacking ? " I said low to Jock.

" It looks like that."

" No reason in it whatever," said a Cameron. " We could attack them in the Pass and hurl them into the river."

" Maybe," said Jock slowly. " But if a victory over Mackay is to count for anything south of the Highland Line, he has to be beaten fairly and in the open. That, I see it, is Dundee's plan. Forbye he could not use the cavalry in the Pass."

" We will not be needing his horse soldiers at all, whether he attacks in the open or not," said the Cameron confidently. " They are no use here whatever. But see you, see you ! " he said, pointing excitedly up the Atholl road.

And then I saw that which made me wonder again at our leader's tactics. Down from the road by Atholl came a small body of Camerons, not above a hundred, and took stations behind some crofters' dykes.

" I've got it," said Jock joyfully. " The Camerons are a ruse to draw Mackay. He'll take it they are the main body and choose his battle position to face the Atholl road. Claverse has got him."

Viewed from above the stratagem was plain, but I could believe that, seen by the enemy from the Pass below, the Camerons would give the appearance of being the advance guard of a full army.

" Here they come," whispered an officer.

Long before they appeared, Mackay's drummers were beating a tattoo through the Pass, and we craned necks among the ling and bracken to get the first sight of them. Not to this day can I fathom the mind of Mackay in advancing through that Pass. Either his intelligence served him badly, or he trusted to superior numbers and the trained troops of his regulars to overcome the Highlanders. And that latter I cannot understand, for Hugh Mackay was Highland himself and should have known the clansmen's fashion of fighting well enough not to despise it. It is never wise to underestimate an enemy, and I believe he thought light of Dundee; but Claverhouse outwitted and outgeneralled Scourie that day, and left me with nothing but admiration for him at the end of it. As Jock had foretold, before the charge was sounded I was his man.

As soon as Mackay's scouts, at the head of the Dutch Scots, issued from the gorge they came in touch with the Camerons blocking the road, and, after exchanging a few shots to no purpose, fell back on the main body.

General Mackay rode up, surveyed the ground,

s

deployed the Scots Brigade to face the road from Atholl, and as regiment after regiment appeared each swung with a rigid discipline into place.

Mackay had a strong position. With a slight decline on his right front, a marsh on his left, he might well have felt himself secure. Meanwhile the baggage-horses, to the number of some hundreds, came trudging heavily from the Pass. Some short leathern culverins were hastily mounted and began to fire on the Camerons. They threw a small ball with little effect, and, indeed, made more noise than casualties. The first discharges the clansmen heard with fear, but, noticing how little harm they did, were soon eagerly trying to trace the flight of the ball.

But action was swift to follow. Dundee gave the order to advance, and our whole army swung down the slopes of Rin Ruari, to the astonished gaze of Mackay and his soldiers below. Dismay was in their ranks. Aide-de-camps spurred furiously about; the cannon ceased their throaty bellow; battalions, at the excited command of officers, pivoted on a new front, and the whole army was swung round facing north, and in that manœuvre, gaps, never intended, appeared between battalions, and the whole front had to be extended. Scourie lost the advantage of the slope, and the marsh and Garry were now at his rear.

"He's bottled," cried Jock jubilantly, as we halted little more than a musket-shot above his troops. "The cavalry have his retreat to the Pass cut off." Jock pointed east where the Scottish Horse were deploying on the banks of the Girnaig. "If your Highlanders can break them, there will be a michty slaughter."

"No fear, Jock," I said. "They will break them or die trying."

Many have wondered how a general, however skilled, with but fifteen hundred undisciplined Highlanders, vanquished and put to shameful rout an army of veteran soldiers near three times their number. Garryside was won before steel met steel. While in Dutch service with William of Orange, Dundee had watched Mackay closely, and knew every weakness in his superior officer. The then Colonel Mackay had never given a thought to the ambitious underling, Captain Graham, and he paid for it that day, a lesson to all of us to look back on those climbing the ladder.

But Dundee was not done with him yet. The afternoon wore on as we stood facing each other on the slopes of Rin Ruari. Mackay's culverins continued to fire, with better effect, and sharpshooters from among the battalions steadily dropped bullets among us. Although a few clansmen dropped here and there, Dundee still held us chafing in leash.

Mackay could not charge. Dundee would not charge.

In time, what with " standing to " in stiff, disciplined ranks, Mackay's men were on the verge of desperation, ready to charge or run, but ill-fitted by now to stand still. Not a man among them, I will wager, but was bursting for action. Excess of discipline was riving the spirit of those men to tatters.

" Jock," I said, " your disciplined troops are already broken. They will run like roe-bucks at the first charge, and I only hope the one man I am watching now, will stand till I come up with him."

" Have you seen him ? "

" I have. He is on the right flank of Mackay's Scots yonder."

If the opposing troops were worn with waiting, it was not so with ours. We were drawn up in no stiff military fashion. Some lay on the heather, others, screened behind boulders, talked in groups of threes or fours, and not until late evening did Dundee give the order to form ranks.

We sprang from the heather.

Dundee swung his hat over his head. The lines of clansmen stiffened. Lochiel's Camerons, yelling as they went, firing muskets and pistols, burst down on Mackay's Scots with the rush and fury of a mountain torrent. At the war cry, while we were yet a hundred paces from them, I saw Mackay's cavalry turn and gallop madly for the Pass. Lord Leven, my old enemy from the Castle days, whom I had seen in front of his regiment, wheeled horse and galloped through the ranks. Mackay's own regiment, the Camerons hacked and hewed to pieces, and, in less than two minutes, Mackay found himself without an army. His trained regiments stood not a minute against our fury. Our clansmen caught pike or bayonet on the targe, cut the heads from off the pikes, and left our opponents weaponless, at our mercy.

The Macleans swept the left wing in their stride; Macdonalds broke the regiment of Balfour from end to end; and red-coats, pursued by blood-maddened Highlanders, were everywhere fleeing. No, not everywhere; for by one of the queer chances of battle some companies of the regiments of Leven and Hastings were left standing amazed, like a lone island of rock in the path of a Highland spate. These alone retreated in order. Past them swept the Highlanders in a pursuit that ended for some near Dunkeld. The field was strewn with dead and wounded, a sight of awesome carnage.

Down to the Pass of Killiecrankie and over by the banks of Garry the broken remnants were fleeing in terror. Blocked by the baggage-horses the mouth of the

Pass was a turbid boil of men and horses, wounded horses screaming and rearing, madly trampling down the frenzied foot, and on their rear, hacking at head or horse alike, were the infuriated Macdonalds. Soon the reddened pools of Garry were choked with mounds of dead.

Halted, disappointed at not coming up with Kyle-ron, I stood on a slight rise, watching the wave of men and horses blocking the Pass, when I saw a happening which made me laugh heartily.

A big dismounted dragoon, the skirts of his coat flapping like the wings of a running hen, was scouring for the river, pursued by a stripling Macdonald of not more than fourteen. The dragoon still carried his broadsword drawn, and as he ran, aye the quick glance he gave over his shoulder at the mite behind. Now the lad had but a *biodag* in his armoury, and every time the dragoon looked back he yelled and flourished the dirk, and put a harder burst on his running, until he would be no more than five paces behind.

Straight for the river gorge, where the banks narrowed over a boil of white water, went the dragoon, a place where there was no escape whatever. But with never a halt he lifted from the rocky ledge, and still clutching his sword, a droll figure of wildly waving arms and legs, sailed out for the opposite bank. He landed with less than an inch to spare, and clawing madly at the ling drew himself to safety. The lad in his eagerness near shot into the torrent below, and, balked, hurled his dirk in disgust at his quarry.

This serves to show how terror-stricken those soldiers of Mackay's had become in a matter of minutes. As for the leap, I measured it with my eye some days later, and made it out a good seven ells, a jump few men in ordinary senses would have ventured.

Though I went through the charge in the second line I never crossed swords with an opponent, for I looked for one man, and my blade was as clear at night as on the morning of battle. Five men, huddled in a group under a hazel bank, stark fear staring from their eyes, surrendered to me, and instead of taking them prisoner I pointed to the hillside above and told them to run for it. Faith, they ran. I had no time for such as they. I had an eye sharp only for the yellow facings of the Dutch Scots, and at last I found the man I sought.

He was lying with his head on a small grassy mound, his feet among the bracken—my enemy! He looked up at me out of dull eyes.

"Quarter," he said thickly.

"You would be the one to cry for quarter," I said scornfully. "Can you stand to your feet? What quarter did you give to Alastair Mackenzie in Utrecht, when you had him beat by a coward's trick? Or to Ardmair at Garve, when you left him for dead?"

A light came into the dull eyes.

"Ho," he said, his lips curving slightly, "it is the young cub."

"Ardmair's son; the young cub if you like. And he has found the old snake at last. Man, but we have waited long for this. Can you stand to your feet?"

"It is not possible. I have got my death-stroke."

Already his voice seemed to be weaker. I hastily parted the bracken and found his right leg was near severed from the body. After all my waiting he had not long to live.

"Tell me," he said, with an effort, "is Ardmair dead?"

"No, thank God, he is not."

"I do not thank God for that. I always hated Ardmair."

" And he you, but with better reason. Do you know that I could spit you where you lie? It is not only once you have done just that to a wounded man. But we fight fair," I said bitterly. " A plague on the claymore that did not leave that blow to me! What I meant to do to you for that blackest lie against my mother! And now I can do nothing."

I was near sobbing with baffled rage.

" I might have known a snake like you would wriggle out of paying for his dark deeds. But you are going, Kyle-ron, where you must still answer for them. You cannot wriggle out of that judgment."

" The young cub can scratch," he said, jeering with almost his last breath. " Tell Ardmair how I cheated him in the end." Then, very faintly: " You have your mother's eyes."

In a few minutes he had ceased to breathe. I turned away to find Jock and Warren.

In the heat of the charge I had lost touch with them, and now turned where Mackay's Scots lay mown down in great swathes. Back where the line had stood I found Jock, and at the sight of him my breath came fast. There he was, head and shoulders over the dead body of Brigadier Balfour, and clutching with his hand the cruel gash from a pike. And every time he breathed the blood welled up and oozed between his fingers. It was heartening at least to find him still alive. He opened his eyes and looked into mine, as I cut open his shirt and set about bandaging the gash.

" Look to Warren," he whispered. " He saved my life."

I was too busy at the moment stanching the wound to give heed to his words. Although the wound was wide, it was not deep, and loss of blood more than vital stroke had sapped his strength.

I quickly had a pad of the soft moss clapped on his side, and bandaging it on tightly with his sword-belt looked around for Warren.

The light was failing. A few clansmen and some robbers of the dead from the neighbouring clachans slunk about the field at their dark trade. Occasional flashes of musketry fire still came from the direction of the Garry. I must haste if I were to find Warren before full night fell.

The sun, which already had dipped behind Tulach, again for a brief moment reappeared, sending a shaft of light down the Strath, and throwing a beam on the blaze of bell-heath on Urrard Hill. The whole hillside changed to a sea of blood-red. To me it looked a bad omen!

But that same glint of late sunshine lighted on the jewelled hilt of Warren's sword. It was through the throat of one of Mackay's Scots. Warren was lying on his face a few paces distant, a bayonet thrust between his shoulders. I rolled him over, and the boyish, brown curls fell about his white face. There would be no call before the Provost-Marshal for him now.

To get Jock safely back to the inn was my next thought, and I looked about for help.

Near at hand a band of Macdonalds were quarrelling over the ownership of some plunder. I stood in hesitation, wondering whether I dare approach and ask their aid, when I seemed to recognize the ring in the voice of their leader, ordering them to fall-in and march. If not mistaken, it was Seumas, the tall one of Braemore.

"Seumas Macdonald of Braemore?" I questioned, peering into the bearded face, blackened with powder smoke.

"That same," he returned, scowling down on me,

and then, his lips breaking to a smile: " Alastair the left-handed! "

I told him my need for help was great, to save the life of a friend.

" You shall have it. Macdonalds never forgive; but they never forget a kindness."

He gave orders to four of his kinsmen and they, very unwillingly handing over their spoil to their comrades, quickly had Jock slung in a plaid, and with slow, even step paced back to the inn.

I fell in behind. In front of us, also making for the inn, was a similar company. Little did I think at the moment that the man in that other plaid was our General, Dundee. Whether dead or still alive during that passage was one of those dark secrets connected with his fate none of us ever learned.

As we approached the door, Cannon, Dunfermline, and the French surgeon who followed the army, gave way to allow the bearers to carry their burden upstairs. I followed hard on their heels. The door of the room, that middle bedroom upstairs where Dundee had spoken with us the night before, was guarded by an officer, who forbade me entrance.

" Take Lieutenant Grant to the next room," he ordered. " We have an officer here badly wounded, who must have quiet and attention."

I had Jock conveyed to another bedroom, and laying him on a pallet, with the help of a man from the tail of Seumas More, sponged and re-bandaged his wounds.

Some time during the night, while I was snatching a minute of sleep, the mid room was emptied, and the body of the great Dundee, with no roll of drum nor lament of the pipes, was buried in the churchyard of Blair, over behind the Castle.

There was good reason for the secrecy. At that moment it would have been fatal to the continuance of the army to spread abroad the news of our leader's death. Flushed with victory, eager to carry back news of it to the glens, and laden with spoils of war, many of the clansmen would have taken the road home that very night.

And so died John Graham of Claverhouse, Bonnie Dundee, after receiving a mortal wound in the van of the charge, while waving on his cavalry and Highlanders to victory, a gallant and fearless gentleman, as not even his worst enemies can deny. And with him died the blaze he had kindled in the heather, and perished the hopes of King James.

CHAPTER XXIV

Doom at Dunkeld

ILL news travels fast. Though the news of our victory was north of Brae Lochaber in a round of the clock, the news of the death of Dark John the Warrior went scurrying on the heels of victory, and won up on it before the isles were reached.

But still the clans came in, and, two days later, fully five thousand were in arms for the Stuart King. But there was no Dundee. General Cannon was now the leader, but he had no understanding whatever of the Highlanders. Had the victory been followed by a falcon-like swoop on Stirling and the Lowlands—and that, I am certain, is what Dundee would have done had he lived—then Scotland was held for King James. Dundee, that very night, would have put the cavalry and what clansmen he could have gathered hot on the heels of Mackay, who, having succeeded in crossing the Garry, was scurrying south with the battered remnants of Leven's and Hastings' regiments, arriving finally at Stirling with a bare four hundred of his men.

It was little of our army I saw in the days that followed the battle, for Jock claimed most of my time. There were days when I thought he would die, and it was to be a slow recovery for him.

One evening, near a fortnight after Garryside, as I sat with Jock, Captain Johnstone, who now shared the room with us, burst in.

"Here are tidings of importance," he said joyfully.

" Angus's regiment, the Cameronians, is lying at
Dunkeld in a state of mutiny! The Atholl men captured
a sergeant and took a paper from him. This is a copy
of it."

" Let me see it," said Jock weakly, stretching out a
thin arm.

" I'll read it to you."

He unfolded the paper and read: " Complaints against
Lieutenant-Colonel Cleland in command of my Lord
Angus's regiment." Then followed a long list of complaints: That he had brought into the regiment profane
officers, who were not soldiers of the Covenant; that
he had dismissed others at the point of the sword, men
of the true faith, and driven them from the regiment;
that he had disobeyed the orders of my Lord Argyll to
march on a Friday, and thereby forced the regiment to
march on the Sabbath; that he had marched them from
Stirling without sufficient ammunition, to the danger of
them all.

A further list of grievances followed.

" So," he said, finishing, " we are marching on them
to-morrow."

" And me lying here tied by the heels," said Jock,
with a sigh. " My fighting days are done for a bit, I
fear."

" Mine were finished at Garryside," I told him, when
Captain Johnstone had gone. " Had it not been for you
I should have been north days ago. Will you come home
with me, when you can travel, Jock? "

" If you can get permission to leave the army."

" Easily got, for I need not be asking it. I will take
it. After this march on Dunkeld we will see to it."

Two days later we breasted the heights above Dunkeld,
and looked down on a huddle of houses, with the Tay

winding in a half-circle about them. When a troop of
cavalry sighted us, at once they took the river for it, and
made off for Perth, leaving the Cameronians to defend
the post alone, and, as the village lay in a hollow surrounded by hills, and our artillery could fire down on it,
we thought the day already won for us.

But, my sorrow! when the guns captured at Killiecrankie—and that was every gun Mackay's force had—
were brought up and mounted, not a barrel of powder
was among the baggage. Through some blunder it had
been left behind. And here we were with guns and ball
a-plenty, but not a handful of powder to serve them with.
No reserve of powder was there even, for those of the
clansmen who carried muskets, so that after their powder-
horns were empty their weapons were useless. The
taking of Dunkeld in the face of twelve hundred desperate
men was now like to prove a much more difficult task.

But nevertheless we advanced, confident that claymore
and dirk would overcome bullet and bayonet. Before
ever we reached the barricades our confidence was rudely
shaken.

In the square tower of the Cathedral, Colonel Cleland
had packed as many picked marksmen as it would hold,
and as the tower commanded every front of our advance
the bullets took deadly toll, long before our first charge
swept up to the entrenchments. Then, such a blaze of
fire came from the outposts in the houses, that scarce a
man reached the barricades. Near three hundred were
mown down in that first volley, and only a footing was
gained among the houses on the flanks.

I had stood with the second line watching that first
charge, and now we were called on. Yelling our war
cries we swept down on the village. From every cottage
window, from behind dykes and barricaded doors, came

a belch of fire and the hiss of lead. How our line got through unscathed I always marvel, but through we got, and the claymore came to his own again. Gradually we hacked and hewed our way between the houses.

Colonel Cleland, on horseback, directing his Cameronians, fell shot. Another officer took his place, to fall almost immediately. Still another sprang to the front, to meet the same fate, and yet another. Five of their senior officers fell in the streets, yet still the regiment fought doggedly on, losing a bit of ground here and there, gradually retreating on the Cathedral, but never breaking, contesting every wynd and dyke.

" Mother of God! but these psalm-singing devils can fight," grunted a huge Irish kern at my elbow, as he hacked a way through the last close, his battle-axe ringing on the last barricade before the Cathedral.

" Up to the doorway and hold it! " I yelled, and we burst across the sward, driving them before us for the entrance, and packed through it in a swaying, scuffling, stabbing surge.

My sword was useless in that tulzie. An officer was forced up against me, the face of him so close I felt the breath hissing between his clenched teeth, as he tried to fling his sword arm above his head. My dirk was at his stomach when I looked into his face, down which the blood was trickling. Black eyebrows met heavily above his nose. It was the face of Kyle-ron, whom I had seen die on Garryside.

My dirk arm dropped. Dread swept over me, striking me limp.

A clansman, with a clubbed musket, smashed at his head. Staring affrighted, and scarce knowing what I was about, I threw up my broadsword and caught the musket-stock on the basket hilt. It glanced off and thudded on my arm. The feet slipped from me, and I fell violently against this other Kyle-ron. The next moment we were rolling together on the flags inside the doorway, his hands at my throat.

The door clanged shut. I was a prisoner.

This was no spirit, but flesh and blood. He kneeled over me, staring into my face.

" Will you give me your parole? " he said.

" What else can I do? "

" Then stay over by the pillars there, until I come for you."

He left me and ran to see about the defences. I rose and walked over to a pillar and seated myself there, out of the way. I was the only prisoner taken. Many wounded Cameronians lay on the flags.

It was indeed a stubborn defence this Covenanting regiment put up. Ringed on every side now by our men, they resisted with shot and bayonet to the last breath. Again and again our Highlanders charged the doorway, blazing faggots stuck on the points of their swords, to be repulsed by well-directed shots from the windows above. At each charge the sharpshooters at the windows were picked off as they opened fire, but, faith, they never lacked volunteers for the post. No sooner had one man dropped than another took his place. These men knew how to die, as well as fight. The longer I watched them in the defence, the worthier of admiration I found them to be; and still more so when, their bullets giving out, a party clambered to the roof, and began to strip off the lead, throwing it to their comrades below. Exposed to the full fire of our men, in a perfect storm of bullets, they worked like demons. One after another they went to their doom in that venture. First the thud of the bullet striking flesh—surely the ugliest sound in all the world

—the quick twist and fling of the body, the loosening of the limbs, then the wounded one rolling down the roof, and landing with the dull thud of death on the flags outside. *Dhe!* it was brave work yon.

The air reeked with the fumes of powder smoke; the walls rang to the crackle of shots and the texts of the defenders, who rammed home powder and ball with a text and pulled trigger with another. Fanatics? Maybe they were, but fine fighting fanatics.

A surgeon going the rounds of the wounded came and looked down on me.

" How come ye here? " he asked.

" I was taken prisoner, and have given my parole."

" To whom? "

" The captain directing fire over by the window."

" Hm! Captain Mackay. Wounded? "

" Broken," I answered, and looked to my arm, which hung useless, aching dully.

" To-morrow, if God spares us, I will see to it. There are many others more worthy awaiting my services."

He passed on.

The fire from without slackened, from which it seemed clear that my friends were withdrawing, for what reason I had no means of knowing, and I had no liking to ask any of those in the defence. From the looks many of them cast at me in passing I knew I had small chance of receiving a gracious reply. Evidently this Captain Mackay had passed the word I was his prisoner and not to be molested. Otherwise, I have no doubt a bayonet-thrust would have been my portion long before.

The slant of the sun told me it was well over noon. The firing ceased entirely, and I wondered why, for the Cameronian regiment was now separated and surrounded

in the two buildings, Dunkeld House, the residence of
the Duke of Atholl, and the Cathedral. What remained
of the village was held by our forces, but little remained
of it, for the Cameronians before retiring had put fire
to the thatch. Dunkeld was a smoking ruin.

The garrison set about repairing the defences, and for
a time were too busy to take notice of me. An hour later
I could have escaped, and I regretted I had given my
parole to Captain Mackay, for every one of the garrison
able to walk trooped out and gazed at the heights above.
I walked to the door under the tower, and winding over
the hills north was our army in full retreat. Cannon
may have named it a withdrawal, but if truth be told
it was nothing less than a retreat, for he left most of his
wounded lying in the streets of Dunkeld. The sight
saddened and infuriated me. Victory was almost ours.
The garrison, as I know, had barely a half-dozen shots
left in their pouches. Powder in plenty for our army was
only sixteen miles distant, and could have been had
before morning. Yet Cannon withdrew. An army of
five thousand clansmen to be beaten by a regiment of
one thousand—it galled me. Oh, for the arm of Dundee!

At first I thought that General Cannon must have had
word of a strong force advancing to the help of the
garrison in Dunkeld, but that was not so. No forces
were nearer than Perth or Stirling, and these of little
account. At the moment a black depression swept
down on me. All afternoon I had been hoping that when
the Cameronians were forced to surrender I would be
released, and now that hope was gone.

Captain Mackay came forward, accompanied by the
officer I saw taking command in the streets after the
others had fallen. His arm, broken by a musket ball,
hung in a bloody sling.

T

"Your friends have retreated," said Captain Mackay, casting a glance at the heights above.

I nodded.

"Have you seen the surgeon? Captain Caldwell here is needing his attention."

"He had a word with me, then went over by the chapter-house." I pointed to the north side of the Cathedral.

"Captain Caldwell wishes to speak with you later. We will send a guard for you."

I went back to my place by the pillar. The defenders now re-entered, grave, stern-faced men. Faith, but it seemed to me they took their victory sadly.

Forming up under the charge of an officer every man went to his knapsack, and brought forth a Bible. After a prayer of thanksgiving, followed by the singing of a psalm, came a long sermon, of which I heard little, for I was exercised in my mind about Captain Mackay.

The preaching over, a sergeant, with two of a guard, bayonets fixed, marched over to where I sat.

"Fall in," he ordered, motioning me between the soldiers, and, taking a place in the rear, gave the order "March," and off we went for the entrance. The main body of Cameronians fell aside, making a lane for us, and a very uneasy feeling it begets to be marched thus through hostile forces. I felt hundreds of eyes on me, and the looks they cast were north of friendly, but I may say I kept a calm bearing. We were marched straight to the House of Dunkeld, and I was led into a room where Captain Caldwell and Captain Mackay sat at a table, the latter with ink, quill and paper before him. The face of Caldwell was drawn and white, and he seemed to be suffering sorely. I have little wonder at that. Ache my arm did, but it was a clean break, while the bone of his was shattered.

" You speak English? " he asked.

" I do."

" Your name? "

" Alastair Mackenzie."

" Where from? "

" Ardmair, in Ross."

" Regiment? "

" Reserve of gentlemen officers."

He turned to Captain Mackay, who was writing my replies.

" Reserve! No such thing. Put it down unattached."

" When did you join Claverhouse's forces? "

" Six weeks ago."

" And before that? "

" I was in the siege of the Castle of Edinburgh, under the Duke of Gordon."

Here I noticed Captain Mackay pause in his writing and look up sharply at me.

" You have broken your promise, then, at the surrender."

A jubilant note came into Caldwell's voice.

" I did not surrender with the garrison."

" How was that? "

" I left the Castle before the surrender."

" Ah! In company with a John Grant? "

I made no reply.

" Speak, man! "

" I see no reason for answering that."

" You were at Killiecrankie? "

" I was."

" How many clansmen had Claverse under him there? "

" Fifteen hundred only."

And it was now my turn to put a jubilant note in my speech.

" Don't take more," he said to Captain Mackay, who stopped writing, sat back in his chair and scanned me closely.

" How many has Cannon under him now? "

" I refuse to answer that."

" It would be in your interest to commit yourself fully."

" A prisoner of war is not called on to give information useful to the enemy, nor is it the custom of gentlemen of honour to betray their friends."

" Prisoner of war! " He rapped the table angrily. " We can soon find a way to open your lips. You are a rebel and can claim no privileges. You are unattached, with an army of rebels who had no commission to be in arms."

" We had the warrant of King James to be in arms for the defence of his realms," I replied coldly.

" There is now no King James. I serve my master, King William."

" And I still serve King James."

" You'll whistle that to a different tune before long. Take him away, Sergeant."

My parole was ended.

" Prisoner and escort, right wheel," bellowed the sergeant, and we tramped out of the room, and through the hall, down a flight of steps, and I was thrust into a cellar, lit from above through a grating far above my head.

When my eyes became used to the gloom I looked around my prison. It had served as a store for firing, for a litter of broken peats strewed the floor. My only

hope of escape was by the grating, and it was little chance
I saw of reaching it. I was sure of bending or breaking
the bars, which were rusted and old, if only I could win
to it. I set about picking the mortar from between the
stones to make holds for my hands and feet. My finger-
nails were soon broken and bleeding, but though I
crawled on my hands and knees seeking something to
aid me in my task, nothing whatever could I find.

It was on the second day of my imprisonment that,
in the darkest corner, I came on a small door, which I
forced open. When I groped behind it there was my
means of escape—piles of peat.

That evening, after the visit of the guard, I set about
piling a platform of peats under the grating. I worked
feverishly, and it was not long before I had enough
carried to reach the grating. I eased it gently. It lifted
from its socket in the flags, and all I had to do was to
raise my platform higher and clamber through. Piling
up more peats I lifted the grating again and spied the
courtyard. All was quiet. I could hear the rush of the
Tay beyond the walls. A watery moon cast the deep
shadow of the house over half the courtyard. I had but
to reach the wall, or a gate, and I was free. With difficulty
I raised myself up, and softly replaced the grating.

Stealing quietly over to the outer wall I searched for
an easy place to climb. But here I was in full moonlight,
and the fear was on me that someone would spy me
from the house, or a sentry would appear. I could find
no place to climb. Back I came into the shadow and
worked my way softly round the house. At one side
outhouses or stables blocked a way; at the other a
passage led to a small doorway, but a sentry paced before
it. I stood in the shadow of the trees watching him.

It seemed that he had no thought that the night officer

might suddenly visit him, for he leaned his musket against the doorpost and blew on his fingers to warm them. His back was to me. I stepped quietly up to him, threw an arm round his shoulder, and gripped his throat. Not even a gurgle came from him. He gripped my hand, but my fingers were into his gullet like the claws of a fish-hawk. And then he kicked out. Down came the musket with a clatter, enough to waken a regiment. I let go my hold on his throat, grabbed the musket, and scoured round a corner of the wall—into the path of the guard.

The sergeant met the barrel full on his front, and went down like a felled stot. A bayonet thrust passed my ear, and I drove my musket butt into the bearded face of the corporal. Swaying back he lashed out with his musket, striking me on the side of the head. I staggered, and they were round me like bees, hurting my arm cruelly in their grips. I was marched back and thrust into the guardroom.

Not many minutes passed before Captain Mackay arrived.

" What is this? Breaking prison and wounding three of our men! "

And then he glanced at my arm in its sling, and looking amazed said to the corporal: " But how did he get out? And how did he fight off three men? "

" He strangled Private Goodson at the garden gate, took his musket, and fought like a wild cat when we surrounded him, sir."

" But how did he get out? "

" He piled up some peats under the grating and forced it."

" What fool put the peats there? " Captain Mackay muttered, and again looked me over. " It seems you can do more with one arm than many could do with two. It's a mercy all Cannon's men were not such fighters as you."

I did not answer, for the floor was rocking like a boat in a gale, and my knees were shaking under me.

" Look here, you gave me your parole before; will you give it me again? "

" I will," I said grudgingly, and my voice sounded far away.

The floor heaved again, and, after lurching against Captain Mackay, I remember no more.

CHAPTER XXV

The Opening of a Door

I WAKENED in a large room in Dunkeld House. I was lying under the window, and the wall opposite was spattered with bullet marks. Along the floor stretched rows of rough pallets, each with its broken or dying man. Some tossed restlessly. One or two lay so cold and still that I knew they were done with war and life. A veteran with a rusty bandage round his head uttered now and then an anguished moan. A white-faced boy on my right babbled endlessly. Of them all I seemed to show fewest scars, but I had to set my teeth to check the groan that came to my throat when I tried to move my arm. It had been badly mauled in my struggle for escape, having been twisted till it needed resetting, and tortured by fragments of bone piercing the flesh.

It was scarcely a cheerful place. Within half-an-hour of my awakening three were carried out for burial, and never a day passed, of the week I spent there, but one or more pallets were emptied, to be needed no more.

The surgeon visited me each day and examined my arm and the bruise on my head, but said little. Captain Mackay saw me once to remind me of my parole. I smiled wryly at that, for thoughts of escape were far from me now. My right arm was helpless; my head swam when I stood up. At times my mind was clear enough, but at others, and these mostly in the night hours, disordered visions went galloping through it, and I could not force myself to think at all. Jock at Garryside;

296

Barbara in Greyfriars; Kyle-ron with his life-blood spilling among the bracken; Ardmair, with my mother at the churning; Midstrath running after the firing of the tunnel; Dundee in the mid room—all pictures speeding by without end, each one vanishing as I tried to dwell on it, and another taking its place. Maddening it was! And sometimes I would wake at nights with the sound in my ears of the screaming of stricken horses, a sound I shall never forget.

And so confused was I between the two black-browed Mackays, that I came near losing my wits.

The portrait of a man in a buff coat faced me. It was gashed by a bullet and hung awry. The first day I thought him a fine, upstanding fellow, full of sense and spirit. Soon I had him mean and crafty, with eyes that spied and mocked. I hated him and did my best to keep from looking at him; and all the time his eyes on me. I began to have a horror of the room where I lay.

Those of the wounded who were able to speak had no words for me, nothing but black looks; I wore the hated tartan. And yet it was not all tartans they hated, for they welcomed the Mackay Highlanders and Argyll's Campbells. It was the Covenant that was the barrier, and it as big as the Grampians between them and me.

When a week had gone by an officer of the Cameronians came to me one morning, and stood looking down at me.

" Ready to move? " he asked. " You are going to be taken to Stirling Castle."

Along with a chieftain of the Macdonalds, who was so badly wounded he could scarce sit his horse, I rode in the centre of a troop down through the birches, and across the river, on the road to another prison. Under his breath the Macdonald cursed in Gaelic our escort,

Mackay of Scourie, the Dutchman and all that belonged to him.

"What do you think they mean to do with us?" I asked low.

"Och! who can tell what the Dutchman will order? Prison for life, or the gallows, it may be."

I caught my breath and repeated: "Prison for life, or the gallows!" in a stupid fashion.

I was startled, for I had never thought of that. My mind had run on a wall, and I set up against it before a firing party, a last look at the sun, and a quick death. But to grow old between walls, or to dangle at the end of a rope—a horror like that did not bear thinking about.

Thereafter I rode with chin sunk on my chest, heedless of the grey rain that turned the road into a burn-bed, through which our horses splashed noisily.

No, I had not thought of that ending for Alastair Mackenzie, and I hoped my mother and my father would never hear of it, if it had to be so. What had I done for myself and them when I had flung out of the house in my haste to take my own road? Nothing at all!

If I had waited till my father was well, as they had wanted me to do, I could still have joined Dundee and struck my blow for the Stuarts, and I would have missed the dragging months of the Castle siege. It had not been my sword that had killed Kyle-ron; he would have died yonder just as surely, though I had never left Ardmair. I had hurt Barbara more by going to Edinburgh than if I had never left home, and I had made it harder for myself to forget her. I had been a young fool; that was certain, and my folly was like to cost me dear. I had won the friendship of Jock Grant; that was my only gain, and it a big one. But what had I done for him? It was Dileas who had forced us both into the Castle, at a time not of Jock's choosing. Had it not been for me he might not now be lying at Blair, badly wounded. Who can tell what Fortune would have done for Jock had I never stood at his shoulder yon night in the High Street?

I know nothing of the road to Stirling, for I saw nothing all day but my horse's fores rise and fall, rise and fall, sending the water spraying at each step, and I heard only their steady splash, splash the whole of the way.

When at last the troop wheeled at a sharp order I raised my head, to see in the half-light first of all the gallows on the Heiding Hill, and then the Castle of Stirling, another castle in the air, that was like to be the last I would ever know.

I was not put beside the Macdonald, but in a dungeon by myself, a small, dank hole, where a small splash of light on the floor, from a beam that fought its way through a shot-hole, was all I saw of the August sun for two days. I found myself thinking often of the little chamber at Kyle-ron, where I could hear the waves and see the harvest fields, and from which I was let out to walk by the sea. I was not to be let out of here, it seemed, till the last letting out.

The Duke of Perth, the late Chancellor, was held here too, I knew, and he had been a prisoner for months. And in the magazine was the store of powder removed from Edinburgh Castle by the orders of the Duke of Hamilton, and placed here to fall into the hands, as he had intended it should, of the Dutchman's troops. *Dhe!* what we would have done with that powder, and how differently would have gone the siege if we had had it.

It was of that I was thinking on the third morning at

Stirling, when the door opened. Along with my jailer was an orderly of the Dutch Scots, who requested me, courteously enough, to go with him.

Where now? I thought. Is this the end?

I wished earnestly I had not given my parole, for I would have made a last bid for escape as I followed him, with fast-beating heart, along a passage.

It was not to judgment and the gallows he led me, but to a room where a man stood in the window with his back turned to me, his hands clasped behind. He did not turn his head as we entered, but said: "That you, Gunn?"

"Yes, sir," said the orderly, saluting.

"Very good. You may go now."

When the orderly had gone, closing the door, the man at the window wheeled round and walked slowly to the table, where he seated himself.

He was Captain Mackay.

He picked up a quill and began playing with it, twisting it in his fingers and smoothing the grey goose feather.

"Mr Mackenzie," he said, "you were brought here from Dunkeld in my absence, and I did not know how you were lodged till this morning. I am sorry you were not put into better quarters."

"A prisoner of war looks for little else," I said evenly.

"True, but you were my prisoner and in rather a different class, for you saved my life, and had your arm broken for your pains. Tell me, why did you save my life?"

I hesitated, then said: "I want no credit for warding off the blow. I threw up my arm, not meaning that at all, and with no more thought of what I was doing than when I draw breath."

" I see."

He held the quill still for a moment, looking at it thoughtfully, then began rolling it between his fingers.

" If I ever saw fear in a man's eyes I saw it in yours when they met mine. Yet you showed no lack of courage before or afterwards. I should like very much to know what made you look at me like that."

" I mistook you for a man I had seen die, a man so like you I thought he had returned," I said harshly.

" You saw him die? " he said swiftly, flashing a keen look out of eyes that, I saw now, were different from yon other's. Then, slowly: " Did you kill him? " he asked me.

" I am sorry the good work was done by another. I am wishing it had been left to me. But I saw him die."

" Had he wronged you? "

" He had wronged foully those whom I hold dear."

" What was his name? "

" The same as your own. Mackay."

" There are scores of Mackays in King William's service. Who was he? "

" William Mackay of Kyle-ron."

" I am William Mackay of Kyle-ron! " he said sharply.

He had the breath taken from me there for a moment, but I went on doggedly:

" The man I am speaking of was named William Mackay, and he came from Kyle-ron."

" He may have, and, indeed, I know one who did at times take my name when it suited him. But I am Kyle-ron. I see you doubt me, but I can soon prove to you that I am speaking truth. Your name is Alastair Mackenzie? "

" It is."

" You were held prisoner in Kyle-ron Castle, after a raid you made into Reay last year? "

" I was so, and if you are Kyle-ron, then this is not the first time you have held me."

" It was in my house you were kept, though you were not my prisoner. You made an unprovoked attack at night——"

" Indeed, it was not that," I interrupted angrily. " For half the provocation my father had, the torch would have been at his thatch years ago."

" Or so I was told," he went on calmly, " and as Kyle-ron Castle is not easy either to assault or to escape from, it seemed the right place to keep a man so young and daring as you were known to be. But for the disloyalty of one of my family, you would not have freed yourself from it."

My jaw dropped as I gazed at him, not at first understanding him. This, then, was Barbara's father!

With the dry quill he began to scratch the parchment before him, as if writing.

" And who," I asked thickly, " was the man we were after? "

" My cousin, William Mackay of Kyle-ron House. It lies half-a-mile west of the Castle. He is dead, so we need not say more of him than that he leaves none to regret him. He told me a tale of unprovoked raid and fury and asked for my protection. He also explained how much need there was that you should be kept securely, so that you could not attack again in our absence. He thought at first your father was killed and that you would return in force. I am sorry now I did not inquire into the truth of his statements, but I was leaving in haste the following morning. I do not like your father's methods of settling his quarrel by raiding among my crofts, but I will admit he had some justification for doing so. Then, if my daughter had not interfered with my plans for you, it is doubtful if you would have found yourself in this unfortunate rebellion. So I owe you something, as you see. I have some influence with those who stand near the throne of King William, and he is disposed to show mercy to some of his late enemies. Young man, you are free to go."

He pointed to the door on his right.

When I found my voice I said: "I thank you, Kyle-ron, though I do not like to take a favour from the Dutch Prince."

"The King of England, you mean," he said sternly.

"But not of Scotland yet, sir."

"The King of both kingdoms, and soon of Ireland too, as you will see. I do not like your politics, Alastair Mackenzie, though I cannot but like your spirit. I wish the King who commands your loyalty were a worthier man. And now that you are free, where will you go?"

"Home."

And I loved the word as I said it.

"The best place for you, and for all of us. I see far too little of mine; I hope I may see more in the days to come. Go now, and God speed you."

I took a few steps to the door, then returned to face him.

"It is very grateful I am to you, sir. I will never be able to speak my thanks."

"I do not like thanks for doing what I ought," he said testily. "I am only repairing a wrong done to you, and the balance of favours is still on your side. There was something you did in Edinburgh—— But, go now, go now."

He waved me towards the door.

"Would you tell me," I said boldly, "if your daughter——"

"Young man, I have two."

"If your daughter Barbara——"

"I refuse to speak of my daughter here. Go now, will you?" he ordered.

I went, and though my knees seemed weak, and I fumbled unseeing with the handle of the door, my heart was singing, for it was not the gallows that lay before me, but Ardmair, and who knew what else?

Then I opened the door wide and stepped, not into a passage, as I had expected, but into another room. The door softly closed behind me.

I had not a minute to think what to do, for Dileas was leaping towards me, and Barbara, whose fingers were clutching the hair on his neck, was forced too to come forward at a run.

She halted uncertainly, while Dileas was upon me joyfully, near knocking me down, licking my face, barking furiously and showing in his own way how glad he was to see me. And was I not glad to see him too!

"Down, Dileas! Down, boy!" I commanded him, as well as I was able, for there was a lump in my throat I was not born with.

Over his head I looked at Barbara. She was very pale, and there was a little tremor about her lips and a mistiness in the eyes, that were the bonniest eyes that ever looked into mine. They had the look in them that I had never hoped to see again, and it told me what my heart danced to know.

Thrusting Dileas aside, I threw up my bonnet to the ceiling and held out my one useful arm. It was my left one, which, as I have said before, is my best one, and it was long enough to go round Barbara.

" *Mo chridhe, mo chridhe*, this is the beautiful thing for us! " I said, after you might have counted to a score, " and have you forgiven me for yon cruel time in Edinburgh? "

" It is a foolish question you are asking, Alastair, for I would not be here if I had not forgiven you. And now I will be forgetting all about it."

" But your father, Barbara? I do not think he will give you to me willingly."

" Do you not think so? " she said, mocking me. " You should have heard what auntie said to him. Och, you should have heard what she said of the Mackays; she has a very poor opinion indeed of them."

Her eyes fell to the brooch of my belted plaid, which she fingered as she went on softly: " She told him how you risked coming out of the Castle to sit with me till I slept. I heard often about that, Alastair, and I will never be tired of hearing it."

She rubbed her cheek gently against my plaid and I tightened my grip.

" Then she told him that no Mackay was worth doing so much for, but, as there was a good deal of the Erskine blood in me, I was worth saving."

I saw the look of Nancy in her eyes as she laughingly flashed a glance at me.

" But your arm, Alastair! "

" It is nothing at all; just nothing at all now."

" And Jock? "

" He is lying at Blair in Atholl, badly wounded. I will be going home that way, and I will take him to Ardmair with me. And Barbara Mackay will be riding home that way too, I hope. How think you, Mistress Barbara, you will like Ardmair? "

U

" I think I will like it very well indeed, because it will be my home."

There is nothing more for me to tell except that the folk at Ardmair were well pleased with the wife I took from the Reay country. And that there was mourning among the crofts, as well as in the big house of Ardmair, when the news came that Colonel John Grant of the Scots Guards had fallen at Steinkirk, in Flanders, along with his leader, Hugh Mackay of Scourie.

GLOSSARY

Ae, one

aince errand, for a special purpose

Auld Hornie, the Devil

bauchle, old shoe, botch

bield, shelter

biggins, buildings

bluddered, disfigured with weeping

boukit, spaced

breenged, banged

broo, favourable opinion

brosie, chubby

buskit, decked, adorned

caird, travelling tinker

carnaptious, ill-tempered, quarrelsome

clash, gossip

cloggit bumbee, bumble bee overcome with nectar

clout, cloth

clype, report

coupit, upset

crouse, boldly, confidently

dad, knock

deave, deafen

dirdum, blame, disagreeable consequences

doit, small coin, a twelfth of an English penny

douce, sober, sedate

dowie, sad, downhearted

duds, clothing

fash, trouble

fushionless, pithless

ganting, yawning

gleg, smart

gliff, alarm

glisk, glance

glower, stare

gnaff, small, stunted object

good-mother, mother-in-law

gomeril, stupid person

gowk, fool

grat, wept

gyte, demented

haver, talk nonsense

hirple, limp

hirsel, flock

hoolet, owl

hotching, teeming

hotter, boil

howdie, midwife

howff, retreat

hunkers, haunches, to squat in crouching position

ingle, fireside

jink, dodge

jo, sweetheart

jougs, instrument of punishment for scolds

kail, soup

keek, peer

kenspeckle, conspicuous

lang-hefted, long-hafted

liefer, rather

lightly, to undervalue, talk ill of

limmer, abandoned female

ling, heather

lowe, flame, blaze

mim, quiet

mools, earth

moudie, mole

muckle, great, much

oxter, armpit

307

peely-wally, poor-looking

plack, small coin, one-third of English penny

ploy, diversion, game

quaich, two-eared drinking-cup

ramstougerous, boisterous, inclined to be riotous

rowth, plenty

runt, withered hag

rype, rifle

sark, shirt

shanks' naigie, legs

sharg, petulant, unnecessary expostulation

siller, money

skail, disperse

skirl, scream

skliff, scrape

sleekit, sly

smit, infect

snell, keen

sowens, food prepared from husks of oats

spaining, weaning

speil, climb

speir, ask

staicher, stagger

stook, rick

stoup, drinking vessel

stramash, disturbance

stravaig, excursion, wandering

sweir, unwilling

swither, hesitate

syne, later, ago

taigle, bother

thole, endure

thrang, busy

thrapple, throat

thrawn, obstinate

toom, empty

troke, familiar intercourse, business dealings

tulzie, brawl

unco rife, very plentiful

waiters, excise officers

wally draggle, slovenly female

wame, stomach

wersh, tasteless, insipid

wheen, number, quantity

whitricks, weasels

willawins, welladay!

wyte, blame

yattering, incessant talking

NEW FICTION 7/6 EACH

DARK ACRES
By J. H. McCULLOCH
Crown 8vo.

A Canadian novel dealing with the hardships encountered by an English settler and his family. The farm taken by the Englishman lies in the Hail Belt of Alberta, and against his neighbours' advice he attempts to grow wheat, with disastrous results. The book contains a vivid description of the Wheat Pool, and through the story runs a human and touching romance.

MARJOLAINE
By HILDA S. PRIMROSE
Crown 8vo.

This is a story of the drama of life affecting the various members of a scattered family. It centres round the old family home of Marjolaine, located in the Lothians, and the author portrays with vivid touch the intrigues, tragedies and loves of her characters. (*May*)

FISHERMEN, LET DOWN THE NETS
By ISBEL BENNETT
Crown 8vo.

A novel dealing with the Moray Firth fishermen and their post-War difficulties. The plot moves from Aberdeenshire to Yarmouth, and is a strong story written with vigour and life. (*June*)

TELL THE BEES
By MATILDA BRINKLEY
Crown 8vo.

A Warwickshire romance. The story is laid in a wide radius round about Warwick in the year 1522, and is based on documents lent to the author by the owner of Pinley Priory and on ancient books and records. Superstitions and customs of the time are dealt with, and the theme of the story is the hero's passionate love for a reputed witch, who meets her fate at Aston Cantlow. (*June*)

CLOAKED IN SCARLET
By MARION C. LOCHHEAD
Crown 8vo.

A charming story by the author of *Anne Dalrymple*. It deals with the lives of two girls—one musical, the other literary—and is laid partly in London and partly in Scotland, at an old country house which has been inherited by the heroine. Miss Lochhead's descriptions of village life are beautifully done and her characters are true and convincing.

THE MORAY PRESS: EDINBURGH & LONDON

RECENT FICTION

ANNE DALRYMPLE. By Marion C. Lochhead. Crown 8vo. 7s. 6d.
A novel dealing with the Oxford Movement of 1833. Keble, Newman and the others who led the Movement are all brought in, and the novel handles with skill a question of very wide interest.

GO BACK. By H. Mortimer Batten. Crown 8vo. 3s. 6d.
This is the story of an Alsatian Wolf Hound.

AN IDLE DIARY. By Louis R. Boyd. Crown 8vo. 5s.

WILSON'S TALES OF THE BORDERS. Illustrated with Pencil Drawings by J. Thomson. Demy 8vo. Cloth. 8s. 6d.
A selection of twenty-two of the best stories taken from *Wilson's Tales*, with an Introduction by Thomas Henderson.

A RAGGED RENOWN. By Oswald Dallas. Crown 8vo. Cloth. 7s. 6d.
An historical novel dealing with the Thirty Years War.

THE BANDIT TRUST. By Milligan Warrick. Crown 8vo. Cloth. 7s. 6d.
A mystery thriller by the author of *The Yawning Lion*. The scene is laid in Dumfriesshire.

BID FOR FORTUNE. By J. S. Flett. Crown 8vo. Cloth. 7s. 6d.
This book presents the story concerning the adventures of four young men left high and dry after the Great War.

KINMONT WILLIE. By Halbert J. Boyd. Crown 8vo. Cloth. 7s. 6d.
A romance of the Scottish Borders.

HAMISH. By J. J. Bell. Crown 8vo. Cloth. 3s. 6d.
A new character study by the author of *Wee Macgreegor*, and it deals with the life of a porter on the West Highland Railway.

BUNDLE AND GO. By G. and J. Cuthbertson. Crown 8vo. 7s. 6d. net.
A romantic tale of the Jacobites, dealing with the Rising of 1715.

THE CALL OF THE ISLAND : and Other Tales. By Charles L. Warr. Crown 8vo. 7s. 6d. net.
"Anyone who contemplates a holiday in the Western Highlands and wishes to abandon himself to the incomprehensible might do worse than take this book with him."
Times Literary Supplement.

THE UNSEEN HOST: Stories of the Great War. By Charles L. Warr. Crown 8vo. 5s. net.
"The tales reflect spiritual experiences and aspirations of soldiers fighting in the trenches and in the open during the European War, and, with all their insistence on the unseen and the imaginary, are obviously drawn from actual observation of the conditions described."
Scotsman.

THE MORAY PRESS: EDINBURGH & LONDON